Miss
Fontenot

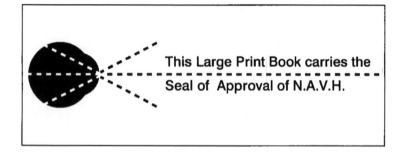

This Large Print Book carries the
Seal of Approval of N.A.V.H.

Heroines of the Golden West

BOOK THREE

Miss Fontenot

Stephen Bly

G.K. Hall & Co. • Thorndike, Maine

Published in 1999 by arrangement with Crossway Books,
a division of Good News Publishers.

G.K. Hall Large Print Western Series.

The text of this Large Print edition is unabridged.
Other aspects of the book may vary from the original edition.

Set in 16 pt. Plantin by Juanita Macdonald.

Printed in the United States on permanent paper.

Library of Congress Cataloging-in-Publication Data

Bly, Stephen A., 1944–
    Miss Fontenot / Stephen Bly.
      p. cm. — (Heroines of the golden West ; bk. 3)
    ISBN 0-7838-8729-9 (lg. print : hc : alk. paper)
    1. Women photographers — Montana Fiction. 2. Large type
books. I. Title. II. Series: Bly, Stephen A., 1944– Heroines of the
golden West; bk. 3.
    [PS3552.L93M57 1999b]
    813′.54—dc21   99-33512

for
Kay Olsen

"And as we have borne the image of the earthy, we shall also bear the image of the heavenly."

1 CORINTHIANS 15:49 (KJV)

One

Oliole Fontenot slumped against a large granite boulder and waited for the sun to move.

It was Montana-August hot.

Humid.

The morning's brief thunderstorm had settled the red dust, washed the cottonwood leaves, and refreshed the buildings. But it had left a sticky feeling in the air.

Her long blonde hair was braided and wrapped at the back of Oliole's head, but as always a few strands rebelled across her smooth, pale forehead. Round jade earrings held the heat of the sun against her already warm earlobes. The high collar of her long-sleeved white cotton blouse was drenched with perspiration. She repeatedly wiped her damp palms on the pansy-embroidered tea towel that stretched across her long, straight dark green denim skirt. Her tall brown leather riding boots radiated with heat like a woodstove in winter.

Oliole shaded her eyes with her hand to study the panorama below her. *The shadow from the cupola will distort the roofline of the hotel. . . . Besides I want the stagecoach in front of the hotel, the flag unfurled at the post office . . . and a slight reflection off the Yellowstone River in the background. Lord, out-*

door photography is very difficult when I'm not allowed to rearrange the subjects.

Oliole stepped up to the 17-X-19-inch wet-collodion-plate black bellows camera that faced the town of Cantrell stretching across the mountainside. She stuck her head under the black canvas curtain, swung the camera on its heavy hickory tripod a little to the west, then pulled out, and meandered back to the boulder.

And waited for the sun to move.

William H. Jackson told me he could unpack, take a panorama photo, make the print, and repack in fifteen minutes. I suppose he didn't have to wait for the sun to be in the right position. Perhaps all photographs should be taken on cloudy days.

She walked back up the hill fifty feet to the front porch of her studio/home. The green-lettered sign on the roof declared: THE IMAGE SHOP: Miss Oliole Fontenot, Photographer.

You are a long way from New York City, Miss Fontenot! It is amazing the galleries can survive without you. Survive? They wouldn't show my work when I was there, and they certainly couldn't care if I'm gone.

She glanced up at the rugged, empty mountains behind her shop.

And I'm certainly gone!

The glass and wood top half of the Dutch front door was already open. She swung the bottom half open and entered the 15-X-30-foot wood-frame building with covered front porch. The window-filled front room was a combination office, gallery, and sitting room. A thick black canvas was draped across the doorway that led to the back half of the building, which served as darkroom, bedroom, and kitchen.

For the fourth time in the last half hour, she examined the glass plates — the syrupy concoction of guncotton, alcohol, and ether — and the silver nitrate. Stashing them all in a tight oak box, she left the front door open and packed the supplies down to the camera.

She plunked them down in front of her so that her shadow would provide shade. Then she reached over and snatched the towel from the boulder and wiped her forehead, her neck, and her hands.

After I get this photograph, I should go for a swim in the river. But I won't. It's not proper. Oliole is proper. Mama and Daddy saw to that. Of course, Daddy always thought I should be a schoolteacher. He still thinks so. Mama wanted me to be a seamstress — like her. The only thing they ever agreed on about my future was that I should not become a photographer.

So, Mama and Daddy, how did I get way out here?

The Lord only knows.

Oliole stuck her head under the canvas curtain draped at the rear of the heavy, bulky camera. She soon popped back out.

The sun's moved! The cupola looks perfect. The river is starting to glisten. . . . Where is the stage? It's about time.

She glanced down at the gold watch that dangled from an intricate chain around her neck.

This is the picture I've been waiting for. If not now, when? By tomorrow the dust will hang in the air again like a cheap lens filter. The contrasts will be lost. And in black and white, contrast is everything. Stagecoach or not, this is it.

With the adeptness of years of practice, Oliole dipped the big glass plate into the collodion solution. Then while it was still wet and in the darkness of her black canvas-covered box, she dipped it into the silver nitrate. Out of the corner of her eye, she spied the Billings stagecoach rolling up Main Street far below her. She ducked under the canvas, shoved the plate into the camera, flipped open the shutter, and began to count, "One . . . two . . . three . . ."

But instead of "Boomtown at Noon," four horsemen romped into the foreground. She jerked her head out from the canvas and screamed, "No!"

The gray horse reared. The black one backed down the hill. The brown one pranced. The pinto snorted. And the four men stared up at her.

"Oh, were you takin' a photograph?" spouted the man with the drooping red mustache.

"Was I taking a photograph? No, I was knitting mittens for morons!" she hollered, shaking a clenched fist. "Do you have any idea how long I've been waiting for that shot?"

"But there weren't nobody in the picture. We figured you were just waitin' for someone to ride up," the one wearing the narrow-brimmed bowler replied.

Oliole stormed straight at the men. "A person can take an image without having anyone in the scene!"

The largest of the four chewed on an unlit cigar and tilted his head. "Why on earth would you want to do that?"

"For artistic value!" she fumed.

"I reckon that there Art can buy whatever he wants. So we'll just back out of your way, sweet darlin', and wait our turn," the black-haired one suggested.

All four rode their horses over to the big boulder, halted, and continued to stare at her.

She put her hands on her hips and sighed. *Photography would be a wonderful profession if I didn't have to make a living!*

The stagecoach rolled away from The Marquesa Hotel, the reflection on the Yellowstone River dimmed, and once again the edges of the cupola began to look fuzzy at a distance.

"It's too late for that." She folded her arms across her thin chest. "I presume you are cash customers?"

"You take gold, don't you?" The heavy one sprayed tobacco juice with each word.

"Yes, but you'll have to wait right there. I've got to take care of this negative you so carelessly ruined before the plate dries." She started up toward the shop, then spun back. "And I do mean wait right there," she demanded. "Don't get off those horses, and don't touch any of my equipment. Do you understand?"

"Yes, ma'am."

"Good."

The oversized negative revealed four startled horsemen in the foreground center of the frame on blurred horses with the outskirts of Cantrell around the edges in the background.

I don't believe this. I've waited all summer for the air to be clear, the sun in the right position, the buildings clean. . . . This is like a horrible joke.

I am not amused.

She left the negative in the darkroom and traipsed back down the hill where all the men waited, still mounted on their horses.

"What are you toting that shotgun for?" the one with unkempt black hair curling out from a floppy wide-brimmed hat asked her.

"Because I thought about killing all of you for ruining my portrait of the town."

"You're joking, right?" Red Mustache piped up. "I mean, a town's a town. Ain't nobody who really wants to pay a cash dollar for a photograph of a town."

"Yeah, and besides the town won't change," Bowler Hat added. "You can take its picture any old time. It ain't ever' day that you get to photograph four handsome and famous men like us."

Oliole took a good look at the men. All wore gray wool suits, black vests, white shirts, dark ties, and overcoats of red road dust. Slinging the shotgun over her shoulder, she shaded her eyes with her other hand. "I presume you wanted a group photograph?"

"Yep," the black-haired one replied. He pointed to the sign above the shop. "Are you this here Orialley Fountnet?"

"That's Oliole Fontenot. O-lee-o-lay Fon-ta-no. With the emphasis on the *no*."

"Well, the handbill down at the Hair of the Dog Saloon was right," the black-haired one continued.

"How's that?" she asked.

"It said we could get a 'photograph taken by a real live woman!' That you are, ma'am, that you are." His attempt to leer came across as a foolish grin.

"I can see you have a discriminating eye."

"I do?" His mouth dropped open a little. "Maybe you could take a picture of the other side so it won't show."

Did I really work ten-hour shifts at the dress factory and study nights for this? "Gentlemen, tie your horses up at the hitching rail by my shop. There's a pan of water on the front porch if you want to wash your faces. Then hurry back down here. I'll get the camera set up."

"Out here?" the bowler-topped rider protested.

"Yes."

"But we wanted one of them pictures with the backdrop," Mr. Tobacco Juice spewed.

"Oh? Did you want to pose with pick, shovel, and a bucket of huge phony gold nuggets so you

13

could impress the folks back in the States?" she challenged.

"Shoot no, sweet darlin'. We already got our gold to pose next to," the black-haired one announced.

"Well, Pansy, bring it down with you, and we'll set it in the middle."

"My name ain't Pansy! It's Sam Black. And this here's my gang."

"And mine is not 'sweet darlin'; it's Miss Fontenot. If you will call me by my name, I'll be happy to call you by yours."

Red Mustache seemed eager to end the confrontation. "Miss Fontenot, are we really going to pose outside?"

"Yes. Photography is meant to capture the moment — not deceive the viewer. That's why I won't use scenic backdrops. The real thing is always better. And bring that bench off the porch with you when you come."

She had the camera adjusted for portraits as the four straggled down the hill, each carrying a crammed-full heavy bank sack over the shoulder. Two of them also toted the wooden bench.

Oliole propped her shotgun against the wooden box next to her camera. "Now, gentlemen, set the bench in the clearing in front of the camera. I'd like you to place the sacks of gold in the middle of the bench." She waved her hands at them. "Now two of you stand at the ends, and two stand directly behind. It's kind of hard to position you when I don't know the

14

rest of your names."

"Call me, eh . . . Mr. Brown," the one in the bowler announced.

"And I'll be Mr. White," the big man with the partially devoured cigar proclaimed.

"Then I presume you're Red?" She pointed to the fourth partner with the drooping red mustache.

"Yep, that's me. How did you know? We ain't met somewheres, have we?"

"I assure you, I've never met any of you," she said.

"Well, I could make up for that in a hurry," Black insinuated.

She ignored him and surveyed the others. "Well, boys, I could care less what your real names are. But I do want to give you a good quality photograph. Mr., eh, White, stick the cigar in your pocket, and then you and Black slide in a little toward the sacks of gold. Push your hats way to the back of your heads so I can see your charming eyes."

Both men quickly obeyed.

"Now, Red and Mr. Brown, step up right next to the bench and take off your hats. Bend your arms and hold them directly in front of your belts."

When the shorter one pulled off his hat, his red hair sprayed out in all directions.

"Red, that absolutely will not work!" she complained.

"Ain't that hair of mine somethin'? Would you

15

believe I ain't had my hat off for a week?"

I'd believe you haven't had your hat off for a year!

"Red, put your hat back on and trade places with Mr. White. Mr. White, pull your hat off and hold it in your hand." White's sandy-blond hair was highly greased and parted in the middle. "Good, that's much better."

I don't know where they got the bank sacks, but it's a cinch these four don't have the mining savvy to pull that much gold out of the ground.

"Now practice your serious poses, men. I don't want you with foolish grins."

"She's right, boys," Sam Black put in. "This here is a historic picture. Why, a hundred years from now, they'll still be talking about it."

All four men, still frozen in place, began to laugh.

I believe they have a slightly inflated idea of their wealth. She peeked under the black canvas and then pulled herself back out. "Mr. Black, is that your most serious pose? You're grinning like a donkey with a hunk of sugar cane."

"When he's around beautiful women, he usually goes plum crazy," Mr. White explained. "It's a miracle he ain't pinched your derriere or tried to kiss you on the lips."

Oliole patted the shotgun. "Boys, a camera is not the only instrument I'm accomplished at shooting."

"Yes, ma'am," White responded. "I was jist explainin' why Black is always grinning around you."

"Blackie thinks he's quite the ladies' man," Brown chuckled.

"Well, it's true, boys, and you know it," Black insisted. Then he turned toward Oliole. "No offense intended, darlin'."

"Well, I am offended. I'm not at all sure I want your business."

"You mean you'd turn down twenty cash dollars?" Mr. Brown interjected.

"Twenty dollars?" she said.

"We was plannin' on givin' you a bonus," Black informed her.

"I haven't seen any money."

Sam Black opened a canvas bank sack and pulled out a double eagle. He held it high in the air between two grimy fingers. "Now you've seen it!"

"Well, in that case, if you can control yourselves, we will proceed." *They have four sacks of twenty-dollar gold pieces? They didn't dig that out of the ground up at Devil's Canyon! Watch yourself, Oliole. They didn't come by that much honestly. Maybe it wasn't such a good idea to build my shop this far above town.*

Sam Black spat out a brown stream of tobacco juice. "See, Red, I told ya women always change their tune when they see the money, no matter how uppity they act."

I can't believe I put up with this! This is not what I studied years to do. But twenty dollars will buy a lot of supplies. Take the photo. Collect the money. Send them on their way.

"Hold very still until I count to thirty. Abso-

17

lutely do not move," she shouted. "One . . . two . . . three . . ."

She closed the lens at the count of five. *Forgive me, Lord, but I enjoy the power of freezing four men for twenty-five seconds more.* ". . . twenty-nine . . . thirty. That's it, boys. Now mount up, go buy yourself some dinner, and then come back and pick up your photograph this evening."

"We'll jist wait," Black announced.

"Not here you won't. I will sell you a very good photograph, but I do not have to entertain you. Now I need to get this negative into my darkroom before it dries out in the heat. How many copies did you want?"

"Five," the one called Mr. Brown declared. "One for each of us and one for the bank in Cheyenne."

"The bank?"

"He meant the folks back home in Wyoming. His pappy is a . . . eh, connected with a bank," Mr. White explained.

"Fine. I'll have five photographs printed for you. They should dry quickly on a day like this. I'll need half the payment now and the other half when you pick up the photographs."

"Shoot, you kin have it all now, Miss O-lee-o-lay." Black tossed a gold coin off the bottom of her skirt. It fell to the dirt between her boots. She stared down at the coin.

"Sorry about that throw," Black chuckled. "I'll be happy to come over there and pick it up for you."

18

"I bet you would." She kept her knees together and swooped down to retrieve the coin. "Now if you'll mount up and ride back to town, I'll take care of this plate. The longer you wait to leave, the poorer the quality of the negative. I'm not going to the studio until I see you ride off."

"You sure are a cautious lady," Red grumbled.

"Thank you. I consider that a compliment."

Red jammed his foot into the stirrup. "I ain't intendin' it as no compliment."

They mounted their horses and trotted down the hill toward Chan's Laundry and the saloons of Second Street. Halfway down Sam Black stopped and looked back.

Keep riding, mister.

He did.

Oliole scooted up the hill to the studio and into the darkroom. The red-shaded lantern cast a dim glow around the room as she hurried to get the equipment in position. The hand-lettered sign on the wall flickered the words: "And as we have borne the image of the earthy, we shall also bear the image of the heavenly."

Well, Lord, this is about as earthy as I can get — four bank robbers and their plunder. I should get word to the marshal. I'll put up my equipment and run down there before these men return. That is, after I develop these photographs.

She had just finished hanging the fifth photograph up to dry when she heard voices in front of the house. She grabbed a towel to wipe her hands, shoved aside the black canvas tarp, and

19

made her way into the parlor. Sam Black sprawled on the steps of the front porch, his back toward her. He was talking to someone in the yard.

"What are you doing here?" she challenged. Black twisted around at the sound of her boots on the bare wooden floor. After the stuffiness of the darkroom, the porch felt cool.

"Jist waitin' for my pictures." It was not an easy, peaceful smile. The man's right hand rested on the scuffed grip of his holstered Colt.

"Everything all right, Miss Fontenot?" a teen-aged boy called from the yard.

"Eh, yes, thank you, Mr. Johnson. I'm just developing some pictures for this man. What brings you up the hill?"

"Mayor Mandara has called a merchants' meeting at The Marquesa Hotel to discuss the schoolhouse fund. He wanted me to let everyone know."

"Tell the mayor I'll be there."

"Yes, ma'am. Will you be takin' your supper there, too? The Marquesa says she's settin' out a fine spread. She especially wanted me to invite you."

"Yes, tell Isabel I'll be there. She's a very generous lady."

"Not only that, but she likes givin' to others, too. Did you ever notice that?" July said.

Oliole nodded without smiling. *We need to get that school built soon. And I've got to get word to the marshal.* "July, will you be seeing Mr. Parks?"

20

"Mr. Parks? You mean the —"

"I mean Mr. Parks."

"Oh . . ." He glanced over at the man on the step. "Mr. Parks, the one that runs the Mercantile?"

"Yes, that's the one." Oliole nodded.

"What can I do for you?"

"I need you to take a payment to him." She walked right past Black and out into the yard.

"But you always pay —"

"I always pay my debts, don't I?" She slapped the shiny gold coin into the palm of his hand. She watched his eyes flit toward the reclining man. She held out four fingers in front of her, close to her stomach, and winked.

"Yes, ma'am, you always pay your debts. That's what I was telling Mrs. Parks. I said, 'Don't you worry about that tab of Miss Fontenot's.' "

"Thank you for your confidence, July."

"Anything else I can do for you?" he asked.

"Beat it, kid!" Black barked out.

Oliole reached out and held July's arm. "Did you say we were meeting at the Hair of the Dog Saloon?"

"The saloon? Shoot, Miss Fontenot, we ain't never had . . . Oh, no, I said it was at the hotel."

"Oh, yes, of course."

July Johnson trotted down the hillside, and Oliole spun around and stomped back to the shop. As she ascended the wooden steps next to the seated man, Black reached across to the porch post and blocked her way with his arm.

"Oh, excuse me," he bantered, "did my arm slow you up?"

Her fingernails sliced the back of his hand, and he jerked his arm up. "Oh, excuse me," she mimicked, "did I nick you?"

He smeared the blood across his mouth as he sucked the back of his hand. "Ain't goin' to do you no good, sweet darlin'," he blustered. "I got your shotgun and my Colt. This building don't have a back door, so you have to come right back out through here. I figure you and me is meant for each other."

She could smell whiskey on his breath. "Mister, I've been insulted by you just about all I can take. It would be to your great advantage to just get on that horse and ride out of here right now."

He glared at her and then down at his bleeding hand. "I done got my hand scratched, and I haven't even reached into the cookie jar. I might as well taste the sweets before I leave."

Oliole stormed into the darkroom without looking back. *I knew this was coming, Lord. It's a wild land, and I've had a wonderful, peaceful year in Cantrell. There are types like this in every town. I suppose it's my turn to be harassed.*

Leaving only the dim red lantern lit in the backroom, she marched over to the sink and plucked up a pair of scissors. *Mister, you're not tasting these sweets. No man has before, and you are definitely not to be the first.* She grabbed a clean, clear glass two-pint beaker and filled it from the heavy pottery crock next to the sink.

"You might as well come out now, sweet darlin'," Black called.

"I'm working on your photographs," she hollered back.

"They're hangin' out to dry, and you know it. I ain't no ordinary drifter. I'm going to be famous, and the boys are part of my gang. You ain't goin' to forget the day you met the Sam Black Gang. I could make you famous, too. Like Belle Star or one of them women."

"I prefer anonymity," Oliole said.

"Well, he'll just have to wait his turn. So come on out, or I'll put a bullet hole through the lens of this big old camera of yours."

Not my camera! That did it! He touches my camera, and there will be no mercy for him, Lord. Warm up the pits of Hades because you've got another customer.

She marched out to the parlor carefully carrying the glass beaker in front of her. He stood at the doorway grinning, her shotgun in his hand.

"Mister, remove yourself from my porch now and get off my property. This has escalated far beyond what I can endure. If you don't leave, I will be forced to inflict upon you severe, permanent injury."

"You'll what? I have your shotgun!" he sneered.

"But you and I both know you have no intention of using it. A hungry man does not destroy his supper before he's taken a taste, now does he? On the other hand, I have no reason to hesitate throwing this on you."

"Throwing what?"

"This chloric acid, of course."

"What kind of acid?"

"Obviously you have not spent much time around a photographer's studio and are unfamiliar with how potent chloric acid can be when it touches skin."

"What are you talking about?"

"This solution is used to treat the paper before the print is made, but when tossed on human skin in this undiluted form, it will eat to the bone in ten seconds."

"That's hogwash!"

"Hogwash is yellow, I believe. Chloric acid is clear. There are cases of it eating through the skin into vital organs. However, I've always assumed the person would be dead before that happened."

"That's a crock."

"True, I keep it in a crock. That's because it eats through wood and iron."

"I don't believe that," he roared.

"I am hoping for your sake and your children's sake, you'll change your mind."

"I ain't got no kids."

"No, and you won't be having any either. I once met a man who lost his entire nose to chloric acid. Have you ever seen a man without a nose, Mr. Black?"

The man began to back out the doorway and onto the porch. "You ain't bluffin' me."

She followed him as he backed up. "Why should I bluff? Let me prove it to you. I'll pour a little into that jar by the door, and you can stick your finger in it. Then we'll see what happens."

"I ain't stickin' my finger in nothin'!"

"Well, you just lay my shotgun on the step and back out into the yard, and I'll demonstrate what we have here. I'll pour a little on that old harness strap, and you can see what it does to leather. Your face is not tougher than leather, is it?"

"You ain't got nothin' in that jar."

"Lay the shotgun down, and I'll prove it," she insisted.

Black took several steps backwards. "I ain't turnin' loose of this shotgun!"

"Very well, I'll demonstrate it anyway." *May the Lord have mercy on virgins and fools . . . and foolish virgins.*

She tramped across the porch, slammed her boot into the first step, and tumbled toward the ground with a scream. As she fell, she flung the entire contents of the beaker at the startled Black, splashing it in his face.

He cried out and threw his hands to his face. "You blinded me!" The shotgun dropped to the ground.

Oliole scooped it up and rose to her feet.

"It's eatin' through my face!" he screamed. "I can feel it eatin' away!"

The blast from one barrel of the shotgun sailed

far over his head, but the black cloud of gunpowder engulfed the screaming man. He charged down the hill, running, stumbling, falling, with his hands over his eyes.

Marshal Parks, July Johnson, and several others rushed up the street, their guns drawn. They captured Black next to the laundry.

She brushed her skirt off, sat down on her porch, and watched them haul the man down Main Street. The marshal hiked up the rest of the steep dirt street to her shop.

"Are you all right, Oliole?" he called out.

"Everything's fine now, Marshal. Did July get you word about the other three?"

Oliole stood as Marshal Parks marched up to the porch. "The mayor and some others went over to the saloon to arrest them. I presume it has something to do with this gold double eagle?"

"They have four bank bags full and mentioned a bank in Cheyenne."

"It's a cinch they didn't come by that many coins honestly. Does this one belong to you?" he asked.

"Put it in with the others. I will not be paid with stolen money."

"I'll send word down to Cheyenne and see if the description of these men matches anyone they're lookin' for."

"Even better than that," she offered, "I have several photographs of them. Send one down, and they can know for sure whom you're holding."

26

"They really came and posed for a picture?" Marshal Parks asked.

"Yes, and with their stolen money all spread out. They wanted to send one to the bank."

"It's amazing anyone so dumb could have lived this long. The one you chased down the hill is so touched in the head he thought his nose was melting."

"Is that what he said?" She smiled.

"Yeah, he kept screaming that you blinded him with acid and melted his nose. What did you throw on him?"

"A beaker of water."

"Well, if our water starts melting noses, perhaps we should speak to the mayor about the quality of our well." The marshal flashed a dimpled grin. "You sure bluffed him."

"It wasn't much of a challenge. The photos are drying now. I'll bring one down to the meeting tonight."

"Are you going to be all right up here?"

"Ranahan, you know I can take care of myself."

"I know, I know. It's just that Carolina gets worried that you're all by yourself up here."

"Well, tell Sweet Carolina I'm glad she worries about me. She's everybody's big sister, isn't she?"

The marshal shrugged. "I reckon she doesn't know how to be any different."

"Thanks for figuring out that cryptic message I sent down with July. And give the world's cutest baby a hug for me."

"Davy's a handsome lad, isn't he?" the marshal bragged.

"Yes, he looks a lot like his mother," Oliole teased. "Did you and Carolina decide to take me up on that anniversary present?"

"Are you sure you know what you're gettin' into?"

"I'm thirty years old, Marshal. I can take care of a fifteen-month-old baby for three days while you go to Billings."

"I know it. Carolina knows it. But I don't think she can let him go. He's hardly left her side in over a year."

"That's exactly the reason you have to get her away. With that kind of mothering, how's that poor kid going to ever have any siblings?"

"I was thinkin' the same thing." Ranahan blushed.

"I'll talk to Carolina again tonight. Now I've got to get things cleaned up around here."

"You want to come over early and have supper with us?" he asked.

"I've already agreed to eat at the hotel with the Mandaras."

"That's right. I did hear the captain mention that one of his old army pals was coming to town, and he wanted to introduce you to him," Marshal Parks concurred.

Oliole frowned. "I wasn't told that part. In that case, I'm eating with you and Carolina. No, I'm just teasing. But I wish the Marquesa would understand that I'm really not looking for a husband."

"Well, whether you find a husband or not, you're a great addition to our town, and we're glad you decided to stay in Cantrell."

"How could I ever leave? Who else in the world would put up with and constantly feed an eccentric lady photographer?"

"Are you kiddin'? Ever' town in America would be proud to have you."

He really believes that, Lord. That's exactly why I can never leave. "You are a charming man, Mr. Ranahan Parks."

"No one's ever accused me before of being charmin'. I'll see you at the meetin' then."

She turned and hiked back into the photography shop. *And no one has ever accused me of being charming either.*

The pine-scattered limestone ridge behind Cantrell was only a few hundred feet higher than The Image Shop of Miss Oliole Fontenot. The sharp, off-white broken cliffs, dark green pine needles, scattered gray sage, bunches of short brown grass, purple hazes of larkspur, and light blue August sky would make a dramatic panorama, even in black and white, especially when the setting sun hung thirty degrees above the western horizon. After that, the shadows from the cliffs would darken the edges and blur the photo.

At least, that's what Oliole had decided.

29

This time the big-lens camera was placed on a wool blanket on the ground. Oliole crawled on her stomach under the black canvas curtain at the back of the camera and adjusted the angle.

Pine Ridge looks huge from this angle! This is wonderful! I'm going to call it "Summer of the Big Sky." I think I'll have time to take two or three photos.

She crawled out from under the camera tent and scooted across the wool blanket to survey the cliff.

Someday they will invent a process to do color photography. I hope I live that long. Lord, that's my request. You have given me the calling of capturing the image of the things on earth. . . . Well, You created them in marvelous color, and that's the way I should be recording them. But don't ask me to invent it. I'd rather take photographs than invent.

I'd rather take photographs than almost anything on earth.

She hiked down to the studio, packed her wooden tripod and black umbrella, and then plodded back up the hill. She set up the tripod next to the camera and clamped the open umbrella to its top. She moved it over until the umbrella's shadow covered the big camera. She unbuttoned her long, straight skirt up to her knees and then folded her legs under her as she sat down.

Okay, I'm ready. Lord, this is what I live for — not drunken bank robbers, cute babies, or smiling, happy prospectors and bummers . . . but the ability to cap-

ture a single magnificent moment in Your creation. One beautiful scene that is shared between You and me alone — then passed on to all who care to glance at the photograph and stand in awe.

One good photograph makes a good week.

One great photograph makes a good month!

One of her braids dangled across her shoulder, and she reached back and unpinned them both. They stretched like golden yellow ropes down the back of her white blouse to her waist.

They want to know why I live out of town up on the hill. This is why. This is exactly why. I can let down my hair, unbutton my skirt, and lie on my stomach. No one sees me . . . no one cares.

I've got to be this way. How else can I do my work? I do not want to offend or disturb others. I just want the privacy to capture the moment. I don't want to be in the picture. I like just sitting in Your private box, Lord, and looking down on the stage of life.

I especially enjoy the backdrops You've created. Most people get so busy with their lives, they never consider the rest of Your creation. That's where I come in. I'll make them slow down and look at what You've made. And right at this moment I'm going to capture "Summer of the Big Sky."

Oliole slowly surveyed the western horizon from north to south. The only noise she heard was from down the hill behind her toward town. Up ahead the air was still, clear, and the scene peaceful, as if posing for her portrait.

Okay, this is it, Miss Fontenot, the exact image you've waited for!

She flopped down on her stomach and crawled under the canvas curtain of the camera. She could feel the scratch of the wool blanket where her skirt had hiked above her riding boots.

You are neither charming nor graceful, Miss Fontenot. Fortunately, you are alone.

As always.

In the darkness under the canvas she could feel her braids tangle around her neck.

Mama would be shocked to see her youngest daughter crawling in the dirt. I'd probably be shocked. I'm glad I don't have to look at me.

She peered out at the image on the horizon. *Yes . . . this is the image! Yes! Yes!*

Oliole pulled herself out from the back of the camera, opened her black box, yanked out one of the glass plates, and slipped it into the camera. Then she dove back under the canvas curtain.

This just might be my best photograph since moving to Cantrell twelve months ago! Yes . . . yes . . . one . . . two . . .

Suddenly a rumble of hooves, brown horse legs, and muted dust flared up in the viewfinder.

"No!" she cried out. "No! No! No!" *If that's Black, I will murder him on the spot!*

Before she could crawl out from under the black canvas, someone jerked up the camera and jammed it in the dirt beside the blanket. She rolled to her back, blinded by the bright sunlight. Finally she caught sight of big roweled silver spurs and brown tooled-leather chaps.

"What in the world do you think you are

doing?" she screamed.

It was a deep, searching voice. "Missy, how bad are you hurt?"

"Can't you see I was about to take a photograph?" she yelled.

"Where's the photographer? He should never have left you out here with this camera."

"Do you have any idea what you just did!"

"Did it hit you on the head? Honey, where's your daddy?"

Oliole sat straight up.

"Oh, my," he stammered. "You aren't exactly a — a little girl . . . oh, my. Are you hurt?"

"It's not me that will be hurting. I'd like to break every bone in your body. Mister, I don't know how fast you can ride, but you'd better be gone by the time I reach my shotgun because I swear I'm going to send you to your heavenly reward."

He scooted back toward the horse. "The camera didn't fall off the tripod and hit you in the head, did it?"

"Fall off the tripod?" She glanced around at the blanket. "Get my camera off the dirt!"

"What?"

"You put my camera on the dirt. Put it back on my blanket."

"Your camera? You're a photographer?"

"Yes, and I presume you're a cowboy . . . or a complete moron . . . or both! Get my camera off the dirt."

"Yes, ma'am. Are you sure you aren't hurt?"

She stood up as the man replaced her camera on the blanket in the shade of the umbrella.

The man with the unshaved face and sheepish expression stood at least three inches taller than her five feet, ten inches. "Mister, I am sure of only two things — first, I am not hurt, and, second, I will shoot you if you are still on my property when I return with my shotgun. Is that clear?"

"Yes, ma'am . . . so you were just laying down there taking a photograph?" His shoulders were wide, his chin squared off and dimpled.

"I was about to take a photograph until you ruined it. That's what photographers do. You did read the signboard on the front of the shop, didn't you?"

"I, eh, rode in from the north. I didn't get to your shop yet. I've never been to Cantrell before. I'm surely sorry, ma'am. I truly thought you were hurt. I, eh, guess I'll be leavin' now."

"That is the best news I've heard today!" she grumbled.

With the ease of a man who lives on horseback, he swung into the saddle and trotted the horse down the hill.

Oliole spied out the pine-covered ridge and sighed. *I just don't have the heart to set it up all over again. The day's troubles will be sufficient for today. Well, Lord, they were sufficient, all right. Two panoramas ruined and customers who paid me with stolen money. What a successful day!*

It took almost an hour to tote all the equipment back into the shop, properly clean each piece, and put everything away. Then she stood on the front porch, shook out the wool blanket, and gazed down at the town of Cantrell.

Perhaps this is not isolated enough. Maybe I should move. I'll build a little cabin in some outlying mountain range with no one around for a hundred miles. Then I could . . .

She remembered how good it felt to see July Johnson standing in her front yard and Marshal Parks trotting up the hill toward her house earlier in the day.

No, perhaps this is remote enough.

She neatly folded the blanket and stacked it on a shelf in the parlor. Then she meandered into the back room and emerged a few minutes later with a cup of steaming tea. As she strolled to the front porch, she caught a glimpse of her reflection in the swiveling full-length mirror that stood next to the north wall. She backed up and looked more closely.

Little-girl braids dangling down your back.

Dirt smudged on your face.

Skirt unbuttoned.

Knees grimy.

But I do not look like a little girl, Mister Big Spurs. Perhaps I'm not the most feminine thing you've ever laid eyes on, but I'm not always a tomboy.

I enjoy being a lady. I enjoy it very much.

But at that moment I was enjoying being a photographer even more. That is, until you came riding into my life to save me. Some women spend their whole lives waiting for their white knight to come riding into their world. I wish the white knights — and the black knights — would stay out of mine.

She plopped down on the step and sipped the tea. Behind her the sun was setting on the pine ridge.

Dinner at the hotel with the Mandaras! I promised I'd go. This is a good evening for staying at home. I'll just send a note and tell them I can't make it.

Sure. Send it with whom? You're going to go, Miss Fontenot, and you know it. I like the Marquesa. . . . I like the captain. . . . I even like all the children, especially Georgia. She's a firecracker . . . like a young Oliole Fontenot.

But why do they have to invite some old army pal?

Lord, I enjoy making my work the focus of my life. I enjoy living alone. I really do like being unmarried.

At least, most of the time.

Is there any way a thirty-year-old photographer can have good friends who are not worried about her love life? She sipped the rest of her tea and then stood on the steps.

I suppose not.

The Marquesa Hotel dominated the landscape of Cantrell, Montana. At two stories plus a cupola, it was not only the tallest building in town but also the largest. The wide verandas on both the upper and lower levels seemed filled with people night and day. The building was the social hub of the town, at least for those who chose to avoid the saloons on Second Street.

The Mandaras and their four very active chil-

36

dren made each guest feel at home. Lodging at The Marquesa was more like staying with good friends at a huge estate house than checking into a hotel.

To have supper with Captain Mandara and his wife, the Marquesa, at the hotel was not only to have the finest meal in town, but it was also a chance to catch up on the latest news for several hundred miles in all directions. The common joke around Main Street was that there were two ways to get the news of what was happening in the world. You could either subscribe to *The Cantrell Courier* or have supper with the Marquesa. The latter was universally considered far superior.

As she plotted her attire, Oliole Fontenot wondered what tidbits of news she would learn at the supper table tonight.

The topic of conversation will certainly not be my magnificent wardrobe.

Oliole owned six dresses. Four were stored in her trunk under a pile of photographic equipment. The other two hung on hangers on a peg near her dresser and were reserved only for church, weddings, and funerals.

She preferred long, straight denim skirts and long-sleeved white blouses. Her favorite skirt was bleached deerskin, but she had retired it for the season when the weather warmed up in late May.

Her long denim skirts were her favorite for work. Her linen ones were saved for fairly dressy events. But her cotton skirts served for hot, humid summer days.

Like this one.

The violet skirt matched her round amethyst earrings. Her blonde hair was neatly stacked on her head under the straw hat. The lace collar of the blouse tickled her chin. And her brown high-top riding boots were polished.

At least they were polished when she left the shop and began to hike down the hill toward Main Street. She disliked carrying a handbag and had tucked what personals she felt compelled to bring into the deep pockets of her skirt.

The large brown envelope in her hand contained two photographs — one of the four hapless bank robbers and their stash, the other a picture of eight-year-old Grant Mandara waving down at her from the roof of the bell tower cupola on top of the hotel. It was an act that had attracted the attention of the entire town and the wrath of his father.

Although Captain Mandara had built a nice home up the hill on Fourth Street, he had sold it to the Parkses and moved his family into the lower level of the hotel when he married the Marquesa. This made the hotel restaurant their family dining room. When there were no special events planned, they set tables up on the stage at the far end of the dining room. They could draw the curtains if they wanted privacy.

When Oliole entered the crowded hotel restaurant, she noticed that the dark green velvet curtains were drawn. The hostess, sixteen-year-old Nellie Mandara, greeted her at the door.

"Oliole!" She ran over, grabbed Oliole's arm, and whispered, "He is really, really handsome!"

"You have a gentleman friend?"

"Not me!"

"Whom are you talking about?"

"Papa's friend. The one they want you to meet. He is so nice, too. The Marquesa said he was handsome enough to be on the New York stage!"

The only stage I want him on is the one that leads to Billings. Oliole smiled slightly and strolled toward the back of the room, arm in arm with Nellie Mandara. As they circled the drawn stage curtain and approached the long table set with silver and china, fourteen-year-old Georgia Mandara tugged a slightly bowlegged, freshly shaved man in a starched white shirt, black vest, and gray trousers toward her. His thick brown mustache flowed down the sides of his cheeks and accented his familiar sheepish eyes.

"Oliole . . ." Georgia giggled. "This is Mr. Kaid Darrant, Papa's friend."

"Mr. Darrant," Nellie added, "this is Oliole Fontenot. Isn't that just about the most beautiful name you ever heard in your life? She's a real live lady photographer, you know."

Her eyes met his and then glanced down at his big silver spurs.

"Yes, I know. Miss Fontenot and I met a few hours ago," he announced.

"You did?" Georgia gulped.

"My, yes," Oliole added, "didn't he tell you how he saved an ungrateful young girl from getting her head caved in by a tumbling camera?"

"No!" Nellie squealed. "Is that true, Mr. Darrant?"

"Actually I believe I clumsily and completely ruined Miss Fontenot's portrait of the rimrock at sunset," Darrant admitted. "I doubt if she'll forgive me in a thousand years."

"Now that isn't true, girls. I'd be happy to forgive him — in, say, a hundred years or so."

Two

The shutters on the only window in the dark-room of The Image Shop were made of double-thick black canvas framed in oak wood. Mounted on the inside of the window, they were kept closed almost every day.

But they were thrown wide open every night. And in the summer with its mild nights and clear skies, Oliole scooted her brass bed to that side of the room and opened the window to allow the night air in. She lay on top of her covers and studied the stars.

Those nights for her were the highlight of summer.

This was one of those nights.

She wore a long cotton gown with faded yellow daisies barely visible — and thick green wool socks. Her long, unbraided blonde hair made the rough flannel pillowcase feel like silk. The lavender quilted comforter that had topped her bed since she was thirteen always held a smell of her Maine childhood home.

Oliole's large, round eyes opened wide as she surveyed the Montana sky beyond the window.

Thank You, Lord, for this day.

It had high points and low points . . . but it was very full and busy.

The lowest point was Mr. Black. I'll admit it, I was scared. His type behave so ugly, so menacing. Perhaps You should have put limits on man's depravity. But he's safely in jail. But there are others just like him. And some, I am sure, that are even worse. I guess I'll have to trust You one day at a time.

And the high point of my day?

You know the answer to that.

Right now.

Right here.

Just You and me and the Montana night.

No one making demands on me. No one expecting me to live up to their image of what I should be.

I'm just Oliole. Tall. Skinny. Thirty years old and unmarried. On the inside so shy that it hurts. Always wanting to hide behind a black canvas curtain.

Except now.

It's a beautiful sky, Lord. You did a really good job tonight. Of course, You always do a really good job.

I had a pleasant evening. I thank You for that, too. Mr. Darrant is a very nice man, a lot like Captain Mandara, only younger . . . I think. I'm sure he would make a very nice friend. But I don't think he wants to merely be my friend.

Oliole flopped around for several moments and finally turned on her side, facing the interior of the room. She let out a deep sigh and rolled back toward the window.

You see that, Lord? You see what's happening? Already my life is getting more complicated. I visit with him at supper for no more than an hour, and now I'm thinking about him. That's exactly what I don't want to happen.

I have important things to consider. A dimpled-smiling, soft-spoken man with dancing blue eyes is not one of them.

Simplify . . . simplify . . . simplify.

Kaid Darrant, I will allow you to be my friend only if you promise never to bother my night thoughts again. Is that understood? "Yes, ma'am." "Good. Now you'll have to leave my thoughts. The Lord and I have a few things to discuss."

"May I call on you again?" *he asked sheepishly.*

"Only during daylight hours and strictly at my convenience. Is that understood?"

His shoulders drooped, and his head hung low in seeming rejection. "Yes, ma'am. Good night, Miss Oliole."

She scooted under the comforter and pulled it up to her neck. "Good night, Mr. Darrant."

With twelve prints hanging to dry in the back room, the studio straightened and swept, her devotions completed, and a brisk two-mile walk to Wild Horse Point accomplished, Oliole sat on the front porch of the studio/home and gazed down at the fine red dust fog of Cantrell. Her long-sleeved white cotton blouse already felt warm. She thought about rolling up the sleeves to her elbows and unfastening the collar down to her chest.

But she didn't.

I suppose I'll have to wait until another summer

43

squall clears the air to get the perfect picture of Cantrell. Perhaps next time I should mount a sign: "Caution — Photographer at work!" Or maybe, "Danger: Explosion Zone." I will certainly explode if someone ruins my next photographs.

She ran her tongue along her slightly chapped lips. "The wrath of Oliole!" she mumbled aloud. Then she stood up on the porch and faced town. "Beware of the fierce wrath of Miss Oliole Fontenot!" she shouted into the Montana morning.

Now I warned them. They are without excuse.

That's why my house has to be up here. I certainly don't want neighbors within shouting distance. I trust that no one really heard that outburst.

She noticed a man step off the boardwalk in front of the Chinese laundry and stroll up the dirt street toward her house. His wide-brimmed brown hat was pulled low, shading his face.

I hope he didn't hear me. I didn't shout that loudly. She slumped back down on the bench on the front porch and brushed her skirt smooth with her hand.

He's either coming up here or walking all the way to Devil's Canyon without a pack. Of course, he is carrying something in his hand . . . I think.

He was still fifty yards away when she recognized the pleasant smile — and the silver spurs. She fiddled with her braids to make sure they were stacked on the back of her head and then stepped out into the dirt yard, still carrying her chipped flower-print china teacup. "Good morning, Mr. Darrant," she called out.

He tipped his hat and continued toward her. "Mornin', Miss Fontenot."

I trust I do not have jam on my face. I didn't expect him to call on me so soon. I would like to look at a mirror before someone comes to visit. Maybe I should install one on the porch. Maybe I'll put one out in the front yard. Oh, vanity . . . vanity! I'll need to tell him something. Maybe I should pretend I have another appointment. "What brings you up the hill this fine August morning?" she asked.

His long-sleeved white cotton shirt was buttoned at the cuffs and the collar. He wore no tie. "Did you call out to me?"

She brushed a strand of blonde hair with her hand. It immediately flopped back across her eye. "What do you mean?"

His right hand hung down past his holstered revolver. His left hand clutched a large brown envelope. "Just now when I was coming out of the laundry, did you holler something?"

"Did you hear me?" She took a sip from her empty teacup.

"Well, I — I just sort of happened to be lookin' up here and thought maybe I saw your arms move or wave or something. I didn't actually hear anything."

"You were looking up at me?" *I really, really need to look in a mirror.*

His tanned, clean-shaven face offset his mustache and flashed dimples, like parentheses to his smile. "Well, shoot, Miss Oliole, of course I

45

was lookin' up here. Do you have any idea what it looks like when the mornin' sun floods across the mountainside lightin' up your place and reflecting off your golden hair?"

I will not blush. Oliole Fontenot does not blush at anything. "No, Kaid, I'm not aware of how that looks."

"It's mesmerizin' — that's what it is."

"Mesmerizing, huh? I trust that's good."

"Yes, ma'am. Now if you could take a photograph of yourself on the porch on a Montana summer mornin', we could send it back to the States and get 20,000 men movin' to Cantrell overnight."

She tried to cover her laughter with her hand.

He locked his thumbs in his brown leather suspenders. "You think I'm jokin'?"

"Mr. Kaid Darrant, I think you are one smooth-talking, handsome man. But I'm afraid you hiked up here by mistake. I was not calling out to you. I was just making a loud general declarative statement to no one in particular."

His blue eyes narrowed. "You were?"

"Yes. I do that from time to time for no apparent reason at all. Surely the Mandaras warned you that at times my behavior is extremely unconventional."

"Eh, no, I don't reckon they mentioned that. They did say quite a few things about you, but I don't think they mentioned anything about you hollering to the breeze."

Oliole took a fake sip from her teacup. "My

tea's all gone. Would you like a cup, Mr. Darrant? We can sit here on the porch and watch the dust of Cantrell."

He hiked up the steps and turned toward town. "Look at what?"

"Do you see that fine red fog swirl up from horse hooves and wagon wheels?" She pointed toward stores along Main Street.

When he squinted his eyes, she noticed that deep lines formed at the corners. "Eh, yes, I suppose so . . . although it doesn't seem all that dusty."

"Well, it's dusty enough to keep me from getting the exact photograph I want. All Western towns seem to have a haze like this in the summer except immediately after a rain." She stood and motioned him onto the porch. "Now would you enjoy some tea?"

"Yes, ma'am, I think I would."

When she emerged from the parlor, Kaid Darrant sat on the bench on the porch, hat in hand, with his legs stretched out in front of him and his boot heels resting on the big rowels of the silver spurs. His tan ducking trousers were clean but a little frayed at the cuffs.

She handed him a cup of steaming Chinese tea. "Sorry about the dainty flowery cup. I suppose most men don't like them, but that's all I have."

"It don't bother me." He sipped from the scalloped edge of a cup that looked miniature in his large callused hand. "It reminds me I'm in the presence of a pretty lady. I've spent most of my life drinking coffee from a tin cup around a campfire next to a pack of men who smelled worse than the cattle we was drivin'. This is, indeed, a pleasurable civilized lapse."

She sat down in a worn wooden rocking chair on the other side of the porch and glanced down to make sure her denim skirt hung lower than the tops of her riding boots. "Now, Kaid, I'm curious to know exactly what the Mandaras did tell you about me."

He allowed the tea to steam his face, then took a sip. "Well, the Marquesa said it was her opinion that you might be the most beautiful unmarried woman left in America."

"She said that?" *Mr. Darrant, if that was intended to made me blush, it won't work. I don't blush.*

"Yes, that's what she said."

"That's interesting because it's been my opinion for quite some time that Isabel Mandara just might be the most beautiful married lady in the country."

Darrant gazed down off the porch in the general direction of the hotel. "You both have good eyes for beauty."

"Mr. Darrant, it conforms to Rule #6 in the *Handbook for Ladies*."

"Rule #6?"

"Yes. Always say about another woman the things you want her to say about you."

"Do I get to hear the rest of those rules?"

48

"Absolutely not. Now what did the captain say about me?"

"Dawson said you were a firecracker of a photographer — way too good for the likes of Cantrell. He figures you won't want to hang around here very long. Said you would move on to bigger and better things."

She let her cup and hands rest in her lap. "Mayor Mandara said that?"

"Yep, he surely did. And I've never known him in fifteen years to exaggerate."

"Well, that makes my day. Not the part about my leaving. I have no intentions of going anywhere. But I do appreciate a compliment about my work. That is something I received very little of while I was working in New York."

"New York!" He set his cup on the end of the bench and jumped to his feet. "That's why I came up here!" He walked over to her and handed her the large brown envelope that had been lying beside his hat on the bench.

"What is this?"

"Your mail," he explained, retreating back to the bench. "Young Mr. July Johnson was quite excited that you received an envelope from New York City. He asked if I'd bring it to you."

"Then you did have a reason for coming up to see me, other than thinking I was yelling at you . . . which I wasn't."

"Well, he didn't exactly have to twist my arm to get me to bring it to you, if that's what you're fishin' for."

49

She ignored his blush and studied the writing on the envelope. "Well, home delivery service is something the Postmaster General should definitely look into, especially when the deliverer has time to sit and drink a cup of tea. Thank you for your act of kindness."

"Aren't you going to open it? The assistant postmaster was convinced it was extremely important mail." The way he turned his head made Oliole wonder if he had ever broken his nose.

"I know what's in here. Some of my work returned," she said.

"Oh?"

"It's a thick envelope. That means they rejected my work — again — and returned it. I studied photography in New York. I still have a number of good friends active in the business there. So from time to time, I send them samples of my work to see if they can sell them to some of the galleries."

"They have photography galleries in New York City?" Darrant seemed to be staring at her hands. "You mean, just photographs, no paintings?"

"At last count there were sixty to seventy such galleries. They are very popular. But none of them are begging me to send them any samples. They are mainly owned by photographers who want to show only their own work. And some, of course, refuse to show photographs taken by a woman."

"Why is that?"

She gazed at his honest eyes until he flinched and looked away.

I do like the West, Lord. Some prejudices seem to melt away in the vast sparseness of the land. "They said I could display a few if I sign my work 'Mr. Fontenot or even O. Fontenot.' I wouldn't agree to such deception."

"So what's in the envelope?"

"My returned photographs, I presume."

"Are they landscape photos like the one I ruined yesterday evening?" His tone was that of a young boy who had dropped his cookie in the mud.

She rocked back and forth to a muted squeak on every down swing. "No, this is a new series I was proposing. I called it 'Women at the End of the Road.' I've only taken a couple of samples and was waiting to see if they wanted more."

"Sounds mighty interestin'." He gulped down his tea like it was cold water on a hot day.

Oliole studied his face. "Mr. Darrant, would you give me an honest answer about something?"

"Yep."

"Are you sitting here talking to me about photography because you are interested in my work? Or do you have dishonorable intentions?"

He struggled to keep from dropping his china cup as he leapt to his feet. "Dishonorable intentions? What makes you say that?"

"I was merely curious which it was."

"Your bluntness would make a ripe tomato blush!"

"Perhaps. It comes from a father who is a Maine fisherman and years of living in the big city. But you didn't answer my question."

Kaid Darrant shoved his hat on his head. "I am truly interested in your photographs. I've never been around any photographers. I find it very interesting, even if I don't understand the process. But I am truly interested in getting to know you better, whether we talk about photographs or the weather. And I'll try to sit here and not think dishonorable thoughts. Now that's an honest reply."

She leaned her head against the back of the rocker. "I believe you."

"Then you'll tell me about your series of photographs?"

"If you sit over there on that bench." She waved the envelope in his direction.

He plopped back down and once again pulled off his hat. "Now that we have the boundaries marked off, tell me about 'Women at the End of the Road.'"

She continued to rock back and forth, the brown envelope resting on her long green denim skirt. "I want to do a series of photos, each featuring a different woman who has come to the West and settled down — women who have found what they were looking for here. But I wanted twenty-four different kinds of women."

"You mean, you don't want twenty-four farm wives or twenty-four schoolteachers."

"Exactly."

"Or twenty-four lady photographers?" he added.

"There aren't twenty-four lady photographers in the whole country."

"I reckon you're right about that." He glanced down at the unopened envelope in her lap. "So which samples got rejected?"

"I decided to start with the best. I thought if they would want any, it would be these. I sent one I took of the Marquesa and one of —"

"Carolina Parks?"

"I see you've surveyed our female population."

"Well, I haven't made it to Second Street."

"Nor have I," she admitted. "But there might be a photograph there."

"So how did your samples turn out?"

"Very well actually. The one of the Marquesa has her sitting in a rocking chair by the front door of the hotel wearing a black velvet gown and a neck loaded with jewelry. It's a very fetching photo. I call it, 'Isabel Leon Mandara: The Hotel Marquesa.' "

"How about the one with Mrs. Parks?"

She stopped rocking and leaned toward Darrant, waving her hands as she spoke. "This spring the Yellowstone overran its banks and cut us off from Billings for almost two weeks. That meant absolutely no mail. When we finally got a delivery, it took July and Carolina all night to sort it out. Men started crowding around the post office door before daylight. When it came time to open up, there was almost a riot. Everyone was pushing, shoving, fighting to get to the door. So Carolina, with her best authoritative demeanor, told them they'd have to line up single file, or no one would get any mail."

"And they minded her?"

"Mr. Darrant, you're new here. But when Carolina Parks wants something, she gets it, and she gets it quick. She has a penetrating glance that would make Cleopatra jealous. Anyway, I set up my camera right in the middle of the street and took a shot of her standing in the doorway of the post office with her arms folded, while a hundred men stand patiently in single file on down the street, like respectful servants waiting for an audience."

"What do you call that one?"

" 'Sweet Carolina Parks: the Queen of Cantrell.' "

"They sound wonderful! Could I take a look?"

She studied his eyes. Penetrating, yet soft. Inquisitive, but decisive. Leather-tough, yet laughing. Sincere, yet . . . yet . . . something. "Kaid, you are one smooth drover. In New York City when a man said he wanted to come up to my flat and look at my photographs, the very last thing on earth he wanted to do was look at my photos."

"Are you this suspicious of all men or only me, Miss Fontenot?"

"All men, Mr. Darrant."

"Oh, good," he laughed. "Then I won't take it

personal. I would like to see your photographs. And we don't even have to go up to your flat." He pointed at the envelope in her lap. "Perhaps I could look at the rejects?"

"All right." Oliole slowly untwisted the string at the back of the envelope and opened it. She reached in and pulled out the contents, glanced at what was in her hands, and then back into the empty envelope.

"They didn't even send my photographs back," she complained. "That's not right! There's just a long letter."

"I think you dropped something there." He pointed to a small piece of paper on the porch.

Without rising out of the rocking chair, she bent over and scooped it up.

"What is that?" he asked. "It looks like a bank —"

"It's a bank draft for $100!" she gasped as she leaped to her feet.

He stood when she did but stayed on the far side of the porch. "What for? Who's the letter from?"

She glanced down at the stiff papers in her hand. "It's from Lincoln Prince. He's a friend who was going to photography school when I was doing private study."

"They have schools for photography?"

"Yes, they do. Anyway, I send him photos, and he takes them to the galleries for me."

"What did he say?"

" 'Dear Fanny, I hope this letter —' "

"Fanny? He calls you Fanny?" Darrant queried.

I will not blush. "Oh, it's sort of like a nickname."

"Fanny," he chuckled.

"Mr. Darrant, if you so much as breathe a word about that to a living soul, what I'll do to you will make Apache torture seem like a Quaker meeting. Do you understand?"

"Yes, ma'am." He continued to chuckle. "Go ahead and read the letter, Miss Fanny — I mean, Miss Fontenot."

"You have already shortened your life considerably, Mr. Darrant. I trust you plan on living until tomorrow?"

"I promise I won't tell a soul."

"And I will demand that you keep that promise. Now I will continue:

"I hope this letter finds you well and that this news brings good cheer into your life. Two weeks ago I ran across Hobart Greer at a cafe on Madison. Guess what? He's opening a photography gallery on 31st! Some friend of his father has put up the financial backing. He said they would be displaying over 500 images!

"Yesterday I stopped by the studio, and Hobart bought ten of my photographs on the spot. Can you imagine!

"Then, hold on to your padding, Fanny, I showed him your idea for a show, and he wants to buy it! The enclosed bank note is for the two

56

photos you have already sent and a partial advance for the others. Enclosed is the contract for twenty-two more to be delivered by January 1. They will pay twenty-five dollars each initially and then 50 percent of whatever the photos fetch above fifty dollars. I know that might hurry you, but I told him you could do it.

"Guess what else? Your name will be listed as Miss Oliole Fontenot! This is what we've been struggling for all these years, right?

"Jehovah-jirah. The Lord does supply, doesn't He?

"I trust this brightens your day, but as far as I remember, you never lived a dull day in your life.

"Affectionately yours,
"Mr. Lincoln L. Prince, Esq."

"They want the whole show!" she shouted.

"What did he mean, 'hold on to your padding'?" Darrant questioned.

Holding the letter in front of her, Oliole skipped across the porch. "Twenty-two more photographs by the first of January!"

" 'Affectionately yours'?" he quizzed. "Is this Linc fellow your beau?"

She stopped and rubbed her fingers across her lips. "At twenty-five dollars each — that's . . . that's . . ."

"It's $550." He jammed his hands into his back pockets and rocked back on his heels. His spurs jingled on the deck.

She pointed a long finger at him. "Do you

know what this means?"

"Eh, I don't think so."

The bank note clutched in her hand, Oliole danced over to Kaid Darrant, threw her arms around his neck, and kissed him on the lips, leaving a trail of soft pink lipstick. Then she danced out into the yard.

With a slightly bewildered look, he stammered, "But I like it, whatever it means!"

Her hands up in the air, Oliole danced around in circles and then shouted at the top of her voice down at the buildings along Main Street. "Do you see this? Do you see this bank note? Do you know what this means, Cantrell, Montana? It means I am truly a good photographer. I'll have my work displayed in New York City! Miss Oliole Fontenot. That's me! Can you believe it, Cantrell?"

Suddenly the smile slid off her face, and she dropped to her knees right in the dirt. Her chin dropped to her chest. Her eyelids, with long blonde lashes, clamped tight. "Lord . . . thank You. I know all good gifts come down from above. I am eternally thankful. In Jesus' name, amen."

Oliole stood, brushed the dirt off the front of her skirt, and turned toward the porch. An open-mouthed Kaid Darrant stood on the top step. She turned abruptly. "Oh! Mr. Darrant, are you still here?"

"Should I leave?"

"Oh, no . . . it's just . . . you can't imagine what

a thrill this is for me."

He gently wiped the lipstick off his lips onto the back of his hand. "I get the notion you're mighty pleased."

As she approached him, she noticed the pink smear on his hand. "Forgive me for kissing you. I was so excited! Don't take it personal. I would have kissed a mule at that point."

"I'm surely glad you didn't mean anything by it." He backed up onto the porch. "Course, it would have been a shame to waste it on a mule."

She looked down again at the contract. "Oh, my, twenty-two more photographs by January 1. Actually I must have them done by the first of December to be sure they arrive in time. September, October, November — three months! I only have three months! But it will be too cold after the middle of November . . . three months! It can't be done! I mean, it takes time to get them right. You can't just snap your finger and produce a quality image." She glanced up at him. "Do you know what I mean? Of course, you do."

She scurried right past Darrant into the parlor. Grabbing a pencil, she threw herself into the chair at the desk. "Now if I can secure two quality shots per week, that would take eleven weeks . . . a couple weeks to retake any of inferior quality . . . . I'll have to close the shop, rent a wagon —"

"I think I'll mosey back to town," Kaid interrupted from the doorway.

"Yes, well, that will be nice. When did you

want to pick them up?"

"Pick up what?"

"The, eh . . ." She looked up at him. ". . . photographs. Oh, it's you, Mr. Darrant. Are you still here? Yes, well . . ."

"Good day, Miss Fontenot. Shall I report to July Johnson that you enjoyed the mail?"

"Tell him it was the best mail I ever received in my life!"

"I'll do that." He turned and hiked out to the yard.

She glanced down at the paper on the desk. *I'll talk to Carolina. She and Ranahan know lots of people they can recommend as subjects . . . and the Marquesa! She knows everyone! I'll have to travel. . . . The wagon must accommodate a portable darkroom and supplies, sleeping quarters, and . . . Should I hire a team of horses or a team of mules?*

Oliole jumped up from the desk and ran out into the front yard. She hollered at the man ambling down the dirt road toward Main Street. "Mr. Darrant! Mr. Darrant!"

He turned back and pulled off his hat. Even from a distance she could see the dimples in his smile. "Yes, ma'am?"

"I'm glad it was you and not a mule!" she cried out.

"So am I."

She scooted back into the house and snatched up the letter from Lincoln L. Prince. *I can't believe he said, "Hold on to your padding." Linc, that was ten years ago, and it only happened one time*

60

— and you know it!

She sat back down at the desk and picked up the pencil.

Let's see, where was I? I just got a contract for twenty-two photographs; my work will be shown under my own name in New York City . . . and — and I totally humiliated myself in front of a complete stranger!

Not bad for one morning.

I think I'll go for another walk. I couldn't sit still if I wanted to.

The largest store in Cantrell, Montana, was the Cantrell Mercantile and Mining Supply Company owned by Marshal Ranahan Parks and his wife, Carolina Cantrell Parks. It occupied almost a whole city block in the center of town and was the chief supplier for the Devil's Canyon gold diggings in the Big Horn Mountains of Wyoming.

Clerks in starched white linen kept the shelves stocked and the orders filled under the careful eye of July Johnson — when he wasn't fulfilling his role as assistant postmaster or holding hands with a sixteen-year-old beauty by the name of Miss Molly Mae Quincy.

The store was expanded and modernized in the spring, but a few of the old features remained — the cookstove against the east wall and the large oak table in front of it. Most serious business for a 100-mile radius took place over that table.

This particular afternoon was no exception. On one side of the table sat Carolina Parks, her dark brown hair curled across her forehead and swirled past her ears and down her back. Her light wool dress had been tailor-made in Baltimore. The high collar of her starched deep maroon blouse would make any other woman look stiff and formal. On Carolina it looked comfortable, natural.

Carolina Parks was the only woman Oliole had ever met who could look totally organized, without even a strand of hair out of place, and totally at ease at the same time. Whether walking down the street, sitting in church with little Davy on her lap, or just relaxing with a cup of tea, her posture was always perfect. She was, without contest, the First Lady of Cantrell — a town she had personally named after her murdered brother.

Across the table sat an animated Oliole Fontenot, her ever-present riding boots splattered with red dust. Her green skirt sported a small collection of cockleburs near the hem, results of a quick hike to the river and back. The long-sleeved white cotton blouse was unbuttoned at the collar, and there was a blue ink stain on the left sleeve. Her lipstick had not been replaced after lunch. Her long blonde braids, which had started the day on top of her head, now lounged haphazardly across her wide but thin shoulders, which slouched a little as she picked up the cup of tea.

"This is just the most exciting thing that ever happened in Cantrell!" Carolina insisted.

"Well, it's exciting to me."

"No, really . . . our own Oliole Fontenot displaying photographs in New York City. It's wonderful! Have you told *The Courier* yet?"

"You're the first I've talked to, other than Mr. Kaid Darrant."

"Yes. Well, you completely enchanted him. He wandered into the post office mumbling something about never having met a woman like you in his entire life."

"That is not necessarily a compliment."

"Mr. Darrant reads like an open book. Believe me, he meant it as a compliment."

"I got a little carried away. I think I embarrassed him."

"Oh?"

"I ran around the yard dancing and shouting. Did you hear me?"

"No. Not this time. But I can see how he might not be as accustomed to that as we are," Carolina mused.

"That wasn't the part that embarrassed him the most," Oliole admitted.

"My word, what else did you do?"

"I threw my arms around him and kissed him — on the lips."

"You did?"

"Yes, but I didn't mean anything by it," Oliole added.

"To you or to him?"

63

"He understands. He seems like a nice man, doesn't he, Carolina?"

"I really haven't talked with him much. He and Ran had a good visit at the Blacksmith Shop this morning."

"What did the marshal say about him?"

"Ran said Kaid would 'do to ride the river with.' "

"That's a tribute, right?" Oliole prodded.

"It's the absolute highest compliment Ranahan Parks can give a man. There are only two others in this town to receive such an accolade — Captain Mandara and July Johnson."

"And what do you say about him?" Oliole quizzed.

"Mr. Darrant does have a pleasing smile."

"Pleasing?" Oliole rolled her light blue eyes. "When he flashes those dimples, it just about takes your breath away."

"I didn't notice that," Carolina chuckled. "But I'm sure he doesn't smile at me the way he smiles at you."

"No, I guess not." Oliole waved her hand across the table. "Anyway, all of that is a diversion."

"It is? I hoped it meant my prayers for you were being answered."

"So you've been praying for a man to come into my life?"

"Not just any man — a strong man, a God-fearing man of husband caliber."

Oliole snatched up a pencil. "Carolina, that's not why I came over. I need you to suggest

64

women I can take pictures of to complete my collection."

"Where do you want to begin?"

"How about a ranch wife?"

"Try Mrs. Andrews at the Slash-Bar-4."

"Is she the one with the twins?"

"Yes."

"I've seen her at the store several times although we haven't really met."

"What age do the women in your series have to be? Are you going to photograph girls?"

"I promised to do one of Molly Mae if that's what you mean."

"I was thinking of the Andrewses' adopted daughter Angelita. She's about twelve or thirteen by now. If you can get her to sit still long enough, she will give you a Mexican smile that would melt the coldest New York heart."

"As long as I'm at the ranch, I should probably take her photo as well. Besides, I need more than twenty-four so I can choose the best."

"You might as well take Mrs. Odessa's as well. She has the most beautiful long black hair," Carolina said.

Oliole wrote down several names, then looked up. "Just between you and me," she whispered, "I want to photograph a dance-hall girl, too. But I don't want to let that be known on Second Street. No telling what kind of situation I would get into."

"Ask Pepper and Selena for some names of any girls."

"Who?"

"Mrs. Andrews and Mrs. Odessa. They used to work the dance halls."

"You're kidding me! But they seem so —"

"Strait-laced?"

"And devout."

"The Lord has done marvelous work in all our lives, hasn't He?" Carolina ran her finger under the table and inspected it for dust.

Oliole glanced at her list. "I thought maybe I could find a lady homesteader, a laundress, an actress —"

"Be sure and talk with Isabel."

"Yes, I'm stopping there next."

Oliole looked at the perfectly curled ringlets on Carolina's forehead. *How does a woman with a fourteen-month-old boy keep her hair so neat?* "Carolina, do you know a lady doctor out here?"

"I don't even know a lady doctor in the States. Perhaps you'll need to go to Denver or San Francisco for that."

Ranahan Parks shouted above the din of the busy store, "Mama, come get your boy before he toddles into the pickle barrel!"

"It looks like I'm needed." Carolina rose and scooted down an aisle. "And I absolutely love being needed."

Oliole scooped up her list of names and thought about the women she wanted to capture in photographs. *You know, Lord, for the first time in years, I really think I'm needed, too!*

Isabel Mandara strolled the upstairs veranda

of The Marquesa Hotel like a general surveying a battlefield. Although she was married to an ex-officer in the U.S. Cavalry, she had never been an army wife. In fact, she had never been in charge of anything until three newly rich prospectors financed her plan to build the hotel.

After that, everything changed.

Drastically.

She gave constant credit to the grace of the Lord Jesus Christ and, with the counsel of a friend like Carolina Parks, never looked back.

Oliole, who stood a good four inches taller than the Marquesa, hurried to keep stride.

"This is absolutely thrilling," Isabel gushed. "I have many friends in the New York theater. I will write to each of them and demand that they take ten friends each to the gallery and gush over your photographs. I think I know a couple of reporters. . . . Thomas Burstein still works for *Harper's Weekly*. Thomas owes me a favor . . ." She stopped to gaze north toward the Yellowstone River. "He owes me a lot more than just a favor," she mumbled.

Oliole tried to squeeze a word in. "What I need is contact with various women who might be willing to pose for some of the photographs."

"Do you have any actresses in mind?" Isabel asked.

"Not yet."

Philip Mandara, tall and straight for a twelve-year-old, jogged up to the women. They stopped strolling and waited for him to speak. "Hello,

Miss Fontenot. You certainly look handsome today."

"Thank you, Philip. Coming from a young man of such impeccable taste, I take that as a sincere tribute."

Philip bowed and then turned to Isabel. "I'm sorry to interrupt, Marquesa, but I can't find Grant. He's supposed to help me tote supplies from the Mercantile."

"I saw him near the bakery," Oliole offered. "He was packing a gunny sack. He teased me and said he had a cat in the sack."

"He wasn't teasing," Philip informed her. "He must be headed to the river. I'll go find him."

"The river?" Oliole questioned.

"Don't ask," Isabel insisted. "If you find Grant, send him up to talk to me."

"Yes, ma'am."

Isabel grabbed Oliole's arm, and they began to stroll. "Now where were we?"

"Talking about actresses."

"Oh, yes. I understand Adriana Courtney is going to be at the Bella Union in Billings around the first of September. She moved to Nevada when she was twenty and hasn't been back to the States since. She has quite an interesting face."

"That would be wonderful." Oliole scribbled the name on the paper she carried in her hand. "Perhaps you could introduce her to me."

"I'm afraid that won't work, Oliole. First, I do not go to Billings. I had a rather bad experience there last year if you recall."

"I thought that was all settled," Oliole said.

"I don't take chances."

A young man's voice cried out from the street below. "Marquesa?"

Both women sauntered to the railing and looked down at Luke French. "Marquesa, do you want twelve loaves of bread tomorrow?"

"Today's Thursday. No, I want fifteen tomorrow, remember?"

"Yes, ma'am. I'll have them here by 6:00 A.M."

"Thank you, Luke. Is your mother feeling better today?"

"Yes, ma'am."

"Tell her she's in our prayers."

"Thank you, Marquesa. I'll tell her." He glanced over at Oliole and tipped his hat. "Greetings, Miss Fontenot. That surely was somethin' — how you captured them bank robbers yesterday."

"It was the marshal who brought them all to jail," Oliole corrected him.

"Ever'body is sayin' that Sam Black was bushwhacked by a beautiful blonde." The young man trotted down Main Street toward the Mercantile.

"That boy should be writing copy for *The Courier*," the Marquesa mused.

The women continued to saunter along the otherwise empty veranda. "I'll go to Billings and check with Miss Courtney," Oliole announced.

"Yes," Isabel agreed, "and it would be best if

you did not mention my name to her."

"Oh?"

"I'm the reason she won't go back to the States."

"Why's that?"

"I promised to kill her on sight if she ever came into my presence again," the Marquesa announced.

"That *would* be a deterrent. But you've changed."

"Yes, praise God, I have. But some of my old acquaintances have a difficult time believing it."

Nellie Mandara swept out onto the balcony with a small bolt of deep blue cloth draped over her arm. "Hello, Miss Fontenot, how are you today?"

"Very well, Nellie. That is a beautiful dress you are wearing."

"Thank you. I made it myself. Did the Marquesa tell you I'm teaching her how to sew?"

"I don't think she mentioned that."

"I'm not a very good student," Isabel admitted.

"She is too! It's just that she's so busy she doesn't have any time to practice. Marquesa, look at this cloth Mrs. Parks just got in at the Mercantile. Wouldn't this make beautiful drapes for the parlor?"

"Yes, that's exactly what we've been looking for," Isabel concurred.

"That's what I thought. May I purchase the material and make the curtains?" Nellie quizzed.

"By all means."

Nellie whizzed off the veranda and back into the hotel.

"She's quite an industrious young lady," Oliole observed. "Some young man is going to get a wonderful wife."

The Marquesa slipped her arm into Oliole's as they continued to meander along. "She's a prize all right. There is no man on the face of this earth worthy of that young lady. She has the domestic skill of her mother and the organizational skill of her West Point father."

"That reminds me." Oliole kept stride as they circled around a white wicker chair and headed back to the west. "I would like to take one photograph of an army wife."

"Dawson will help you there. Some of his friends are stationed at the Crow Agency. But most army wives I've met have no intention of residing in the West. Perhaps you will want to photograph an Indian woman as well?"

"Yes, if the circumstances are right. With the theme 'Women at the End of the Road,' I'll have to find a scene that shows an Indian woman dispossessed from her homeland and stuck in a distant location."

"That shouldn't be too hard," the Marquesa reflected. "You know whom to check with about Indian families? Tap Andrews. Have you met him?"

"Just once — rather indirectly. Carolina said I should take Mrs. Andrews's photo as an example of a ranch wife."

"Pepper's a jewel. She is one lady I do not ever want to get on the wrong side of."

Oliole laughed. "Some people say the same thing about you, Marquesa!"

The dark-haired Isabel Mandara spun and faced the tall blonde, then broke into a smile. "Talk about a cat fight! Me and Pepper Andrews going tooth and nail. But you get us on the same side, and even Congress would back down."

"I was thinking of trying to find a gunfighter's wife, too."

"That type doesn't have a wife."

"None of them?"

"Well, Lorenzo Odessa and Andrews used to travel on the owl-hoot trail, but that was a long time ago."

"What if I went down to Arizona and photographed Stuart Brannon's wife?"

"He's not married," Isabel informed her.

"But I read in a Hawthorne Miller novel about Brannon marrying a wealthy Mexican señorita."

"That's all fiction. Ask Tap. He's a friend of Brannon's. You might go to Deadwood and see if you can find Martha Jane Burk sober. She'll always pose for a price."

"Who?"

"Calamity Jane. She claims to have been the girlfriend of Wild Bill Hickok, although Marshal Parks says that's the alcohol talking."

Oliole fiddled with one of her braids and then

tossed it over her shoulder. "Perhaps I should go to Deadwood."

The Marquesa stopped and raised her hand to her chin. "Now it has just occurred to me that this project of yours is going to take a lot of traveling."

"Yes, I know."

"You don't plan on going by yourself, do you?"

"I really can't afford to hire anyone. Though I've been promised a good fee for the images, I won't see that money for months."

"Maybe there's someone around who would be willing to wait to be paid."

"Did you have someone in mind?"

"There's a dimpled-smiling drover who's between jobs and seems to like your company."

"Kaid? Why — why, I couldn't . . ."

"You couldn't what?"

"I couldn't, I couldn't . . . and besides, I can't ask him to be a flunky. What I need is someone to drive a wagon, take care of the team, help me set up equipment — things like that. That would be insulting to a man like Mr. Darrant."

"Oh, in that case why don't you ask one of the unemployed drunks over on Second Street?"

"Never!"

"Then whom will you ask?"

"Perhaps I can find an older refined gentleman."

"Around here? Look, Oliole, you do plan on going to remote places, correct?"

"Yes, my goal is to capture 'the image of the

73

earthy,' as in 1 Corinthians 15:49."

"Okay, let's say you're rolling along some remote rut of a road trying to find a homesteading woman, and up rides Sam Black and his gang. Whom do you want sitting beside you in the wagon? Some gray beard with rheumatism in his joints or the likes of Kaid Darrant?"

"Marquesa, you are a very persuasive woman."

"Then at least ask him. My guess is it wouldn't take much convincing. He really is smitten by you."

"That's what I keep hearing from others."

"Give him time. He'll get around to telling you."

Eight-year-old Grant Mandara shuffled out on the balcony, his brown hair flopping down into his eyes. "Did you want to see me, Marquesa?"

"Say hello to Miss Fontenot."

"Hello, Miss Fontenot. Have you captured any men today?"

Oliole looked over at the Marquesa.

"I'm sure he means bank robbers," the Marquesa explained.

"Oh, not today, Grant." Oliole smiled.

The boy scooted between the two women and took the Marquesa's hand. "Did you want to see me?"

Isabel put her arm around his shoulder. He stood only a few inches shorter than she. "I want you to go help your brother tote supplies from the Mercantile right now."

"Yes, ma'am. Is that all?"

"You promised your father and me you had retired from the cat extermination business."

"This was someone who had paid me in advance. I had to keep my word, didn't I?"

"Do you have any others paid in advance?" the Marquesa questioned.

"No, ma'am."

"Then you are officially retired. Turn in your gunny sack."

"Yes, ma'am. Can I go help Philip now?"

"By all means. And please tuck in your shirt."

"Yes, ma'am."

The women stopped by the railing on the balcony that faced Main Street and watched a freight wagon roll along in a swirling fog of red dust.

"So what about asking Kaid Darrant to assist you in the photography project?" the Marquesa quizzed.

Oliole raised her thick blonde eyebrows. "I thought of another large problem hampering that idea."

"An unmarried woman traveling with an unmarried man?"

"Yes."

"Then marry him." The Marquesa shrugged.

Oliole exploded with laughter. "What? Marry a man I don't know just so it would be acceptable when I travel?"

This time it was the Marquesa who burst out

with peals of laughter. "Okay, okay . . . that was a foolish idea."

"Have you got any other suggestions?"

"Well, they aren't nearly as adventuresome. But how about taking along a chaperone?"

"You mean, have Mr. Darrant assist me and hire another person just to ride along to add respectability? Now it's beginning to sound like a circus. I think I'll do it on my own. I took care of Black the other day. I can do it again."

"Next time there could be four of them. And they won't always be that dumb."

"Excuse me, Mrs. Mandara!" a high-pitched female voice called out from the boardwalk beneath them. They both leaned far over the railing to see a woman in a long black dress peering up.

"Mrs. Montgomery, how are you today?" the Marquesa greeted her.

"My gout's acting up, and I have a touch of the quivers again — not to mention my ankles are swollen . . . but one shouldn't complain. That's my motto."

"What can I do for you, Helen?"

"Did you check your calendar for the 24th?"

"Yes. It will be fine to hold the Schoolhouse Fund Drive Committee meeting in the hotel parlor."

"Will you be attending?"

"Yes, I will," Isabel said.

"And how about you, Miss Fontenot?"

"I'll be there if I can, Mrs. Montgomery. I might have to take some photographs out of town that week."

"Very well. Good day, ladies!"

Oliole and Isabel watched Helen Montgomery disappear into the grocery store next door.

Oliole whispered, "What in the world are the quivers?"

"I have no idea, but I wasn't about to ask," the Marquesa chuckled. "Listen, I just thought of what you need for your photography trips."

"What's that?"

"You need an apprentice — someone you're training."

"What protection would an apprentice be?"

"No, I mean Mr. Darrant and an apprentice," the Marquesa explained. "You don't have to pay someone you are training, and that person could act as an unofficial chaperone. You can hire a driver for you and your assistant. That sounds proper."

"All of this is very speculative. I don't know anyone who would fit that category."

Fourteen-year-old Georgia Mandara stomped across the veranda toward them. "Marquesa, we need to hire a new housekeeper for upstairs. Do you have anyone in mind?"

"Why? Did Rosie quit?"

"No." Georgia leaned over the rail of the balcony and stared down at the street below. "I fired her."

"You did what?" Isabel gasped.

"Her work did not meet Mandara standards. You said so at supper last night, so I fired her."

Then she turned to Oliole. "Did you know my brother Grant can spit off the balcony and hit a nickel out in the street?"

"Eh, no, I didn't know —"

"You can't fire the hired help!" Isabel fumed. "Where's Rosie now?"

"I knew you were talking to Oliole, and I didn't want to bother you. Miss Fontenot, I heard you kissed Kaid Darrant right on the lips. Is that right?"

"You didn't want to bother me!" the Marquesa grumbled. "Everyone else in town doesn't hesitate to bother me. Why should you be different? Where's Rosie now?"

"Last I saw of her she was in Room 21. I trust she's packing her things by now."

"How did you know I kissed Mr. Darrant?" Oliole pressed.

Georgia slipped her arm into Oliole's. "Grant was in the cupola with his spyglass, but don't tell Father. Grant's not supposed to go into the cupola, and he's not supposed to use Father's spyglass."

"I'd better go talk to Rosie," the Marquesa announced. "We are not going to fire her. At least, not yet."

Georgia brushed two wild strands of dark brown hair out of her eyes. "I think I'll go down and inspect the kitchen. I told Charles he would have to keep it much cleaner than he has been or else."

"You are not to inspect the kitchen again!" the

Marquesa ordered. "Go out and play or something!"

"I'm just trying to help! You act like I'm just a little girl. I'm not a little girl anymore! I'm old enough to . . . to . . ."

"Yes?" the Marquesa said.

Georgia clutched Oliole's arm more tightly. "I'm old enough to be a photographer!" Her small round nose was pointed high in the air.

Oliole looked into the Marquesa's deep brown eyes.

"Oh, no," the Marquesa warned. "There is no way you want to do that."

"Why not? I think it would be delightful," protested Oliole.

"It would be a nightmare."

"That's ridiculous. She's only a child," Oliole countered.

"What are you two talking about?" Georgia demanded.

"She would make a good chaperone."

"Oh, sure," the Marquesa argued, "after two days, Mr. Darrant is liable to go running off into the brush screaming and never come back."

"You exaggerate. If I can talk him into it, I want Georgia to come with me," Oliole proclaimed.

"Go with you where?" Georgia asked.

"Would you like to be my apprentice?"

"Oh, yes! Yes! Yes! Really? Will we travel?"

"Sometimes." Oliole nodded.

"To New York City?"

"Hardly, but we might go to Billings."

"Billings? I've been to Billings lots of times," Georgia sighed.

"Perhaps Deadwood."

"Oh, yes. Wild and wicked Deadwood! I hear there are ten men to every woman there."

Oliole rolled her eyes toward the Marquesa. "Perhaps we won't go to Deadwood. But what do you say, Miss Georgia? Do you want to be my apprentice when I travel?"

"Just you and me?"

"I'll need to hire a driver for the rig."

"The Frenches have a fifteen-year-old son who is good with horses. I'll go see if we can hire him!" Georgia offered.

"Oliole will do the hiring," the Marquesa insisted. "You come with me and apologize to Rosie."

"Do I have to?" Georgia whined.

"Yes."

"Do I really get to travel with Miss Fontenot?"

"If your father agrees. It's his decision."

"He does everything you tell him to."

"Not always. I told him not to spank you when you tossed that tantrum at the Fourth of July celebration, but he went ahead and did it anyway."

Georgia rolled her big brown eyes. "Well, he should have listened to you! Can I go ask him now?"

"No, he's busy helping roof the church. We'll talk to him at supper."

"How are we going to travel, Oliole? Will we

have a fancy coach?"

"That's a very good question, Georgia. I think I'll go down and talk to Mr. Parks about that. We'll need something that I can set a developing booth on top of, yet I don't want it to be too cumbersome."

"Will it be drawn by six white horses?" Georgia pressed.

"No, but we might get a couple of old mules. How does that sound?"

"Boring. But don't worry, Oliole. I'll try to keep things lively."

Three

They reached the Musselshell River after the sun dropped below the bluff on the western horizon, but they still had plenty of twilight to set up camp. A large grove of scattered cottonwood trees on the south side of the stream covered several acres, providing some protection from the wind and a good supply of grass for the livestock.

The evening sky held only a few clouds that now reflected down to earth the unseen sunlight, like huge glowing electric street lamps of the kind Cheyenne, Wyoming, now boasted.

Oliole slid down from the wagon seat and dusted off her brown denim skirt. Georgia Mandara plopped down behind her, a straw hat hanging on her back by a violet ribbon now clutched in her teeth.

"Are you going to take a photograph of the sunset tonight?" she asked.

Oliole removed her straw hat and laid it on the wagon seat. "No, it's a little late for that. Besides, it wouldn't be as spectacular in black and white." She reached back and unfastened her long blonde braids, letting them flop down her back. "The Musselshell is not as big as I expected it to be."

Kaid Darrant unharnessed the two dark

brown mules and led them across the clearing. "Well, Boss Lady, what kind of camp do we want tonight?"

"I'm going to leave all the photographic equipment in the wagon. So we'll just have a little supper and a campfire. I thought maybe I'd hike up to that bluff to the west."

Kaid rubbed his square chin. His hand found a seven-day stubble that now blended into his mustache. "I thought maybe you would. Take your shotgun." He pointed to the wagon box.

Oliole glanced down at her dusty brown boots. Her feet felt sweaty. "I'm not going out of sight of the wagon."

"Take your shotgun anyway." His tone was that of one who assumed his orders would be obeyed. He gazed beyond the river at the grassy, treeless rolling hills to the north. "I hear the Sioux have been known to drift up the Musselshell in the summer, trying to pick a fight with Blackfeet. They'll respect a shotgun."

Oliole pulled a handkerchief out of her skirt pocket and carefully wiped her forehead. "I really don't see that I'll need to." Her tone was that of one who didn't like being told what to do.

Georgia tugged at the high collar of her chocolate brown dress and then rubbed her nose with her palm. "Can I hike with you? I'll carry the gun."

Oliole slipped her arm around Georgia's shoulder. "Kaid, do you need either of us to help you make camp?"

He handed her the lead ropes to the mules and retrieved the short double-barreled shotgun from under the wagon seat. "Not until cookin' time. Little darlin' promised to bake us a pan of biscuits." He cracked the shotgun open, checked the chambers, and then snapped it shut before handing it to Oliole.

She waited while Georgia relaced her black high-top shoes. Then they hiked up the gradual incline away from the river. Georgia reached down and yanked up a wild grass stem and began to chew on it. "Oliole, how come you want to go on a hike every evening?"

"Because hours of riding in that wagon make me stiff." Oliole slowly stretched her neck back and forth. "Besides, I'm always curious to see what's on the other side of a hill."

"Won't it just look like everything on this side of the hill?"

"Perhaps, but until I get to the top of that bluff, I won't know for sure." Oliole stopped and took several deep breaths. "Georgia, what do you smell?"

"I don't smell anything. Is there a skunk? What do you smell?"

"Grass, dirt, sage, and a warm westerly breeze."

"Oh, that," Georgia said.

"It's the smell of summer in the West. It doesn't smell like this in New York City. Now breathe deeply and remember this smell. Someday you'll be too busy to smell this. Then all you'll have is a memory."

Georgia slipped her hand into Oliole's, and they continued hiking up the hill. "Do you realize we've been gone for a whole week?"

Oliole could feel the wide heels of her boots sink into the soft, dry dirt. "Yes. Do you miss home?"

"Sometimes. I mean, I don't miss Nellie or Philip or Grant . . . but I miss the Marquesa and Papa."

"Well, we'll take a photograph of Mrs. McMillin at Roundup and then turn south toward Billings. That means we're over halfway done with this trip."

"This has been the most exciting journey in my life!" Georgia exclaimed.

"I'm glad to hear you say that. I was afraid this week was going to be too boring for you."

"Are you kidding? I loved the Slash-Bar-4 ranch. Mrs. Andrews and Mrs. Odessa had so many stories to tell. It was incredible. I didn't know Mr. and Mrs. Andrews were the ones that captured those bank robbers in Cheyenne! I read all about that in *Frank Leslie's Illustrated*." Georgia used the shotgun to point out a hole in the dirt. "What do you think lives in there?"

"Either a snake or a prairie dog."

"I hope it's not a snake. Did you know Mrs. Odessa once had a pet snake she kept in her dresser?"

"Eh, yes, I heard her say that. I didn't realize Selena would share so many stories of her days as a dance-hall girl. I certainly trust you will not repeat some of them to your father and the Marquesa. They might never let you come with me again. You will need to be discreet."

"I'm certainly more discreet than that Angelita Andrews," Georgia boasted.

"I thought you two got along well." Oliole reached down and plucked two tiny blue flowers as they continued to hike.

"Are you kidding? All she ever talked about was herself. How she had a boyfriend named Peter, and his stepfather had a gold mine, and she was going to be very wealthy someday, and how she had helped Mr. Andrews capture outlaws on more than one occasion, and how many considered her the cutest girl in Montana."

Oliole tucked a flower into her hair above her right ear. "She said all that?"

"More or less."

"She didn't lack confidence, did she?" She handed the other tiny flower to Georgia Mandara.

"She's not all that cute." Georgia stuck her flower behind her ear.

"Other than her pretty brown skin, I thought the two of you looked very similar."

"Are you kidding?"

"No." Oliole took Georgia's hand and pulled her up a steep part of the hill. "I think you two could be quite good friends. I hope she comes to visit you in Cantrell sometime."

"Do you think I'm cute, Oliole?"

"My goodness, yes!"

"Nellie's really the pretty one in our family. She looks just like Mama, you know. Our mother was very beautiful. I look too much like Papa to be very cute."

"That's not true at all."

"Do you think when I grow up and fill out, I'll be beautiful like you?"

As the hill steepened, they slowed their pace and walked single file. "Oh, don't set your goals too low. I think you will far outshine me. I was quite tall, thin, and tedious-looking when I was your age. I was always the last girl in school any boy asked to dance with him."

Georgia tried to brush her dark brown hair out of her eyes, but it immediately flopped back down. "You were?"

"Yes. But that might have been because I always turned them down."

"You didn't like dancing?"

"I love to dance. It's boys I have trouble with."

Georgia's chin sank to her fairly flat chest. "I like dancing with boys," she murmured.

"That's quite all right," Oliole insisted. "Most girls do. I was always extremely bashful around boys."

"I like dancing with boys, except for my brothers. Every time I dance with Grant, he shoves something slimy down the back of my dress. But brothers aren't really boys, if you know what I mean."

"I think I do." They stopped by an outcropping of basalt rock. "But I don't have any brothers. Just one sister who used to live in Deer Lodge, but she moved to New Mexico last fall."

Georgia leaned against the rock and set the gun down. "Would you like to dance with Mr. Darrant?"

"Perhaps," Oliole mused. "I haven't given it much thought." Georgia put her hands behind her head. "Nellie said you're going to marry Mr. Darrant someday."

"Nellie has a very romantic mind."

"Is that bad?"

"I hope not," Oliole responded. "But it's not something I think about much. I suppose I have more of an analytical mind. I have so many practical things to think about that I don't have much time for romantic thoughts."

Georgia locked her fingers together and placed her hands on top of her head. "What kind of mind do you think I have?"

"Look back down at camp," Oliole instructed. "What do you see?"

"A canvas-topped army ambulance that has been converted to a portable photographic studio and a tall, handsome man with square shoulders all by himself building a campfire," Georgia reported.

"You have a romantic heart."

"What do you see, Oliole?"

"Two mules."

"What?"

"See that grassy spot by the river? The two

mules are picketed, but they have switched end for end so that the tail of one is swatting flies for the other. I'd like to get a picture of that with the sun going down in the west."

"Oh, wow! Are we going back down and set up the camera?" Georgia asked.

"No, there's not enough time. But that's what I see down there."

"If you took that picture, what would you title it?"

Oliole hiked along the base of the summit of the hill. "How about . . . 'Partners to the End'?"

Both began to laugh.

"I'll race you to the top of this bluff!" Oliole challenged.

Georgia took off running before the sentence was complete. When they reached the top, they flopped down on a rock escarpment that had broken through the crust of the mountain.

"Oliole, you are the most fun woman I've ever been around. Most old ladies — I mean, most women your age are so serious all the time. You still know how to laugh and have a good time."

"Thank you, Miss Mandara. I consider that a compliment. But I think the Marquesa is a woman who knows how to enjoy life, too."

"She and Papa sure laugh a lot in their room at night when all the lights are out. Sometimes we creep up to the door and listen. Do you laugh at night when the lights are out?"

"Sometimes."

"All by yourself?"

"I'm never by myself."

"You aren't?"

"No. At night in the dark is when I have some of my best discussions with the Lord."

"You mean that's when you ask God for things?"

"Sometimes we just visit."

"You visit with God?"

"Yes. And sometimes we laugh," Oliole said.

"I never thought about God laughing." Georgia shrugged.

"Well, believe me, He does. Usually we laugh about the stupid things I've done or said."

Georgia pointed straight west into the broad sloping grassy valley. "Oliole, look out there! Are those antelope or deer?"

"Where?"

Georgia leaned close until her hair brushed against Oliole's. "Look down there, right on the other side of the river. . . . I can barely see them."

Oliole stood up on the rock and stared west. The stiff breeze that was blowing in a small flotilla of clouds still felt warm. "Stand up here, Georgia."

"Can you see them better from up there?"

"No, but you can lean into this breeze," Oliole said.

Georgia took Oliole's strong grip and struggled up to the top of the rocks.

"Did you ever go on a boat ride?" Oliole asked.

"You mean like a little boat in a lake?"

"No. I mean on a big boat out on the ocean. A

steamboat or a sailboat at full sail."

"No, not really. I was on a riverboat once, but it was to hear a band concert in St. Louis."

"My father's a fisherman. My grandfather was a sea captain. When I was young, I spent a lot of time going out on boats in the Atlantic Ocean. My favorite thing to do when it wasn't storming was to go right up to the front, called the bow, right at the point where the two sides of the boat come together, and then lean into the wind and close my eyes. This is almost like that." Oliole leaned into the breeze and tugged Georgia with her. "Now close your eyes," she instructed.

"Why?"

"Because then you can imagine all sorts of things."

"What kinds of things?"

"My favorite is to imagine that Jesus has swooped down and grabbed my hand, and I'm flying with Him right up to heaven."

"Really?" Georgia said.

"Wouldn't that be wonderful, Georgia? If we could just open our eyes and be in heaven?"

"Yes, but —"

"Are you ready for heaven, Georgia?"

"Today?" she gasped.

"Why not?"

"Well, I believe in Jesus," Georgia replied, "but I don't think I want to go to heaven right now. I mean, I haven't even — you know — I haven't even kissed a boy or anything. I kind of wanted to try that before I went to heaven. Nellie says there's no kissing and stuff like that in heaven."

"Well, I do suppose it's different from here, all right," Oliole said.

"Oliole, how old were you when you first kissed a boy?"

"That was a long time ago." *It was the summer I was fifteen, and it happened in Murphy's boathouse.*

"Did you like it?"

"Yes, I did." *But not nearly as much as Teddy Murphy did.*

"Nellie likes it, too."

"She does? Who is she kissing in Cantrell?" Oliole kept her eyes closed and swayed back and forth into the wind.

"Not in Cantrell. There was this boy, Gerald, back in St. Louis. I used to crawl out on Grandpa's roof and watch them in the backyard."

"Oh?"

"They used to kiss, and then Gerald would —"

"I've got an idea," Oliole blurted out. "Georgia, let's pretend we're those antelope or deer sprinting across the prairie with the wind in our faces." *I don't think I want to know what Nellie and good old Gerald did in the backyard.*

"Okay! Are we girl deer or boy deer?" Georgia asked.

"Girl deer, of course."

"Then we don't get to have a pretty rack of horns."

"Those old things? They must be heavy, hot,

and cumbersome. We don't need them. We're sleek, fast, just running with the wind in our faces."

"I don't think they're deer," Georgia announced.

Oliole opened her eyes, stood straight up, and stared down at the twilight glow in the vast valley. "Oh?"

"I think they must be elk."

"Why is that?" Oliole quizzed.

"Because they look too big to be deer."

"That might be. Why don't we ask them?"

Georgia wrinkled her nose. "How do we do that?"

Oliole began jumping up and down and waving her arms. "Hey, you wild animals!" she screamed. "Are you deer or elk?"

"I don't think they heard you," Georgia giggled.

"Maybe you'd better help me. You're not jumping and waving."

"But what if someone sees us?"

"Who would see us?"

"Maybe Mr. Darrant," Georgia warned.

"Can you see him from here?"

Georgia turned back and looked the other way. "Eh, no."

"Then he can't see us. That's what I love about the West, Georgia. It's so wide open and empty I can shout, wave, dance, holler, and no one cares." Oliole jumped straight up and waved her arms. "Hey, elk! Is that you?"

Both began to jump, scream, wave, and giggle.

Then Georgia stopped and grabbed Oliole's arm. "I think they're coming toward us."

Oliole stopped and stared at the distant animals. "What?"

"They swam the river and are coming toward us. They look big even for elk."

"Oh, no!" Oliole moaned, staring down the mountain slope.

"Are there people riding the elk?" Georgia questioned. "Those aren't elk, are they? They're horses!"

Oliole tugged Georgia off the rock. "Grab the shotgun, Miss Mandara. I think it's time we get back to camp."

"Were we waving at some men on horses?"

"I believe so."

"What are we going to do?"

"Hurry back to camp," Oliole said.

"What do we tell Mr. Darrant?"

"That we spotted some men headed this way."

"Do we tell him we waved to them?"

"Not if we can help it." Oliole nudged Georgia down the escarpment.

"Maybe they didn't see us."

"Sure. They turned around, swam their horses across the river, and are riding up this bluff just for the fun of it."

Oliole and Georgia trotted down the hill. For the first fifty feet the rocky terrain kept them to a slow jog. Then the trail smoothed out to brown grass and dirt. Oliole, carrying the shotgun, raced down until she nearly stumbled.

"Oliole! I can't stop!" Georgia shouted a few feet behind her.

Never run down a steep hill. Never run carrying a loaded gun. Never let a child get between you and potential danger. Nice work, Miss Fontenot. You succeeded in doing everything wrong.

"Give me your hand, Georgia." Oliole reached back and felt a warm hand clutch hers. "Hang on to me!"

Oliole leaped up and then dug the heels of her boots into the soft dirt of the hillside. She felt instant pain shoot up into her calves, thighs, and hips. Georgia slammed into her back and threw her arms around Oliole's neck. The sudden impact sent Georgia Mandara over the top of Oliole Fontenot. But with the girl's arms still wrapped tight around Oliole's neck, both tumbled head over heels on down the side of the smooth mountain.

Oliole hadn't realized her finger was on the trigger of the shotgun until the barrel jammed into a hole in the ground. The explosion from the shell caused her to abandon the gun. Dirt, grass, and rocks ground into her face, her hair, and her back.

They didn't stop tumbling until they reached the edge of the cottonwoods. Both sucked air, trying to grab a breath.

"Are you hurt, Georgia?" Oliole gasped.

"No. Are you, Miss Fontenot?"

She looked over at the girl lying on her back.

"No. Is my face as dirty as yours?"

"I don't know," Georgia replied. "But yours is as dirty as your blouse!"

Oliole glanced down and wiped at her blouse with a dirty hand. "That was quite a fall."

"I've never had anything like that ever happen to me," Georgia said.

"Me either." Oliole sat up, then collapsed back on the dirt. "You want to do it again?"

Both broke out in uncontrollable laughter.

Oliole was only vaguely aware of Kaid Darrant's jingling spurs as he ran to where they were lying. "Are you two all right?" he called out.

Both continued to sprawl on their backs in the dirt. "Oh, yes, Mr. Darrant. Why do you ask?"

"Why do I ask? You just fired a shotgun into the mountain and then rolled in the dirt halfway down the hill. Don't tell me you did it for fun."

"We are laughing, aren't we?" Oliole declared. "We decided to see who could roll the farthest."

"I won," Georgia giggled. "But I think Miss Fontenot gets the prize for being the dirtiest."

"Laugh all you like," Darrant huffed. "I thought you were both injured or worse."

"You're too serious," Oliole giggled. "Don't you think he's too serious, Georgia?"

"This is funny, Mr. Darrant," Georgia insisted.

"That might be, but we have visitors." He pointed to a gang of horsemen cautiously descending the mountain.

Oliole sat straight up and stopped laughing.

"Indians? We didn't know they were Indians."

"Are they the reason you started running?" he probed.

"Yes, but we didn't know they were Indians. We saw some men down by the trees next to the river on the other side of the bluff."

"They must have spotted you. My fire isn't putting out any smoke. Did you send them a warning shot?"

"No, the gun went off by accident."

"I hope they believe that. Where is your gun?"

"It's stuck in a snake hole," Georgia piped up.

He stared at Oliole.

"I'll explain later," she offered. "Kaid, I'm sorry they saw us." Oliole stood and tried to brush off the dirt. "I should never have —"

"Don't worry about it. They have eyes like eagles. They probably would have seen you no matter how carefully you snuck up on that ridge."

"We didn't exactly sneak," Georgia mumbled.

"What?"

"Eh . . . nothing," Oliole put in quickly. "What should we do now?"

"Little darlin', you get that extra handgun out of the box under the wagon seat. Keep it in the pocket of your dress. Oliole, go tend the fire as if you were the one cooking. Keep my carbine within reach." Kaid pulled out his Colt .44 revolver and slipped a sixth cartridge into the cylinder.

Oliole scooted next to the campfire. She felt

pain in her ankles, legs, and shoulder. "Are you expecting trouble?"

"Nope. I'm preventin' trouble. Ladies, keep between me and the wagon. Just go about like you were making camp as usual."

Eight buckskin-clad men with dark complexions and long black hair braided down their backs rode down the hill on a mixed remuda of mostly wide-rumped horses.

All had McClellen saddles on their horses.

Carbines across their laps.

None wore feathers.

Nor war paint.

The lead rider had a red bandanna around his neck. He stopped his horse only a couple of feet from Kaid Darrant. "Howdy," the round-faced rider called out.

Kaid tipped his hat but left his right hand on the grip of his holstered revolver. "Howdy, friends!"

"It sure is hot, isn't it?" The Indian pulled off his bandanna and wiped his forehead.

Darrant glanced at the fluttering cottonwood leaves. "That wind seems to make it worse."

"You're telling us. We've been trailing a herd of pronghorns for three days. They catch our scent three miles away. Just the time we circle them, the wind shifts. Last night they bolted north, and we've decided to give up the chase and go home."

He waved his arm toward Oliole and Georgia. "Are your wife and daughter always that dirty?"

"Eh . . . no, they were playin' a game," Kaid murmured.

The man looked back at his friends and grinned. "Is that what they were doing up at Coyote Point? We heard them scream and wave their hands and thought they were in trouble."

Kaid stared back at Oliole. "They were doin' what?"

"We thought they might be signaling for help," the Indian explained.

A heavy man with a wide, easy smile rode up to Kaid and handed him the shotgun. "I guess your wife was huntin' snakes for supper." All the others broke into laughter.

The first man pointed to the light green grass between the cottonwoods. "That's a mighty nice little meadow for only one horse and a pair of mules."

"Plenty of room to graze your horses, boys. Why don't you come on down and make camp with us?" Kaid offered.

Oliole peeked into a pot containing nothing but boiling water. She stirred it with a large wooden spoon and then replaced the lid. *I can't believe he invited them to stay here! What was he thinking? There's a woman and child to protect — even if we aren't his wife and daughter.*

Georgia scooted near her. "Miss Fontenot, I'm scared."

Both of them stared as Kaid Darrant loped over to the other Indians and continued the conversation beyond their hearing.

"Everything will be fine. Mr. Darrant knows what he's doing, and the Lord is with us," Oliole tried to assure her. *Lord, this is a little more excitement than I wanted. It might be a nice time for the cavalry to ride over the mountain ... or any other solution You have in mind.*

"I hope Mr. Darrant is good with a gun," Georgia continued.

"I hope we don't have to find out," Oliole said.

"They think you and Mr. Darrant are my mama and daddy. That's quite absurd, isn't it? You aren't nearly old enough."

"Thank you, young lady, but I am more than old enough to be your mama."

"Really? I didn't know you were that old! Nellie said you were only a few years older than she is."

"I'm probably old enough to be her mother, too."

"You sure do look good for a woman that old."

"Except that right at the moment I'm covered with dirt and have aches and pains all over my body."

"Here comes Mr. Darrant. Everything must be okay. I think he's smiling. He has a nice smile, don't you think?"

"Yes, you are certainly right about that."

Kaid strolled to the fire and squatted down on his haunches, his back toward the Indians who were pulling their saddles off their horses and making camp only thirty yards away. "We'd better fry up some more biscuits, little darlin'. I invited them to join us for supper."

Georgia's brown eyes widened. "You did?"

"Do you think that's safe?" Oliole reached over and patted the carbine that lay beside her.

"Yep. But I had to promise them one thing."

"What's that?" Oliole studied his dancing blue eyes.

"That I wouldn't let the two of you help with cookin' until you went down to the river and cleaned up." Darrant's dimpled grin burst into a laugh.

Oliole stared down at her dirty blouse. "Us?" she fumed, her hands on her hips. "Of all the insulting remarks!"

"You do look frightful." He shrugged, still hunkered by the fire.

"Oh? Well, if I have dirt on my face, it's totally my business and no concern of theirs. They can just eat by themselves. I'm not about to have strange men ride up to camp and order me to clean up."

"You mean, we aren't going to wash our faces?" Georgia pressed, her brown eyes peering out of circles of dirt.

"Oh, we'll clean up, all right. Will we ever! But not because some tribal hunting party and a handsome man with a dimpled smile tell us to. Come with me, Miss Mandara!" Oliole stomped toward the Musselshell River. Then she turned around. "Mr. Darrant, since you are so spotlessly clean, you may cook supper!"

Eight Indians and Kaid Darrant were sitting around the campfire when Oliole and Georgia finally emerged from the back of the wagon almost an hour later. Twilight was fading to shadowy night. When they strutted toward the fire, all the men turned and stared. Oliole wore one of her two Sunday dresses, and her blonde hair was neatly stacked on her head. Her earrings sparkled, her skirt swished, and her light pink lipstick was in place.

Georgia Mandara wore a ruffled lavender dress with a wide purple ribbon in her dark hair. She, too, had a touch of lipstick and wore one of Oliole's necklaces.

"Now that is quite a change!" Kaid Darrant proclaimed.

"Oh, this? Why, this is just my typical supper attire. Where is your tie, Mr. Darrant?"

"My what?" he gulped.

The Indians slapped their knees and snickered.

"You made your point." Kaid waved at a thick log that had been dragged up next to the campfire. "We saved you the bench." Then he pointed to the main Indian spokesman. "Ladies, I don't remember everyone's name, but the sergeant's name is Jim Crocker."

The one Indian with black hair cut above his shoulders tipped his hat.

"A sergeant?" Oliole questioned.

"These men are army scouts who live over at

the Crow Agency when they aren't busy with the boys in blue."

"Or trying to bring some fresh meat home for our families," Crocker added. "Are you the lady photographer from Cantrell?" He pointed at the sign that hung from the side of the black canvas-covered wagon.

"Yes, I am. You've heard of me?"

"We were told that a handsome yellow-haired lady had set up a photography business at Cantrell. I didn't recognize you at first."

Again all the men laughed. "The reports were accurate. You look quite handsome," a heavy man to his right concurred.

"Thank you, sir."

"You're welcome," he replied.

"You should come out to the Agency some time and photograph us and our families."

"I'd like that." Oliole felt self-conscious. She glanced down to see if her dress was completely buttoned.

"We can put on our ceremonial gear and pretend to be mighty hunters!" another one laughed.

"The hunting is getting worse every season," Crocker reported. "Look how far we have to go. Someday we will give in and eat nothing but tedious beef, like all of you. It is tasteless meat but better than starving."

There were several mumbles and a chorus of nodding heads.

"If you come out," the heavy man offered, "I

will have you take a photograph of my entire family. I have six daughters but none with yellow hair or fancy dresses."

Oliole felt the inspecting eyes of every man. *Why did I dress up? Why didn't I just stay covered with dirt?* "Well, eh, just who told you about my photography shop?"

"I've got a friend who lives over in Cantrell," Crocker reported. "From time to time he rides out to the Agency."

"Who's that?" Oliole took the plate of biscuits, beans, and beef that Kaid Darrant handed her. "Perhaps I know him."

Crocker scraped his knife across his nearly empty blue-enameled tin plate. "Captain Dawson Mandara. We rode together on several campaigns."

Georgia leaped to her feet. "He's my papa!"

"He is?" Crocker squinted his dark brown eyes and looked her over closely. "Are you Nellie?"

"I'm Georgia!"

Crocker shook his head. "Well, I'll be. It doesn't seem like it was that long ago. I was there at Fort Rob when you and your sister were born."

Georgia's round eyes opened wide. "You were?"

"Do you know who this pretty young lady was named after?" Crocker waved his knife like a pointing stick.

Oliole shook her head.

"She was named after the best general I ever

rode with," he reported.

"You were named after an army general?" Oliole asked.

Georgia shrugged and sat back down. "We all were. I was named after General George Crook."

"You tell your papa you had supper with Jimmy C. and the boys from Otter Creek. He'll know who you mean."

Oliole tugged her lace cuff up out of her plate. *Lord, a few minutes ago I was concerned that my life was in danger. Now I feel like we're dining with family friends. Your surprises are truly endless.*

The talk around the fire bounced from battles to hunting, from weaponry to good horses. When Oliole and Georgia finished washing the tin dishes and pans, they retired back to the wagon and left the men around the fire.

"Do you want me to light the lantern?" Georgia asked.

"Perhaps we should slip on our gowns in the dark," Oliole suggested.

"That's what I was thinking. But I'm not nearly as scared of those men as I was."

"It has been a rather exciting evening." Oliole stuck her foot out toward Georgia. "Can you see to help me with my boots?"

"I wish Papa would let me wear riding boots like yours."

"He won't let you?" Oliole held out her other foot.

"He says they're not practical. He says if I want them, I'll have to buy them with my own money. It will take me forever to save up seven dollars."

"That gives you an adventure to look forward to."

"The past week of traveling with you and Mr. Darrant has been the most thrilling in my whole life!"

"Well, Miss Mandara, you are still young. You have lots more days in your life for other exciting things."

"Can you tell if this is your gown or mine?" Georgia asked.

"Does it have a collar?"

"Yes," Georgia said.

"It's yours. Mine is more scooped at the neck."

Georgia Mandara was already under her blanket as Oliole combed out her long blonde hair.

"Do you think Mr. Darrant will sleep under the wagon again tonight?" Georgia asked.

"I suppose so." Oliole rolled back her blanket and crawled in beside Georgia. "That's all right with you, isn't it?"

"Yes. I like knowing there's an armed man down there looking after us. Did you know Mr. Darrant sleeps with his mouth open?" Georgia whispered.

"How do you know that?"

"I peeked. There's a little hole in the wagon floor, and if I roll my blankets back, I can look through and see him . . . if the moon is bright."

"Georgia, don't be sneaking a look at a man

106

while he sleeps!"

"Can I peek at him when he is awake?"

"No. You wouldn't want a boy peeking at you, would you?"

"I guess it depends on the boy," Georgia giggled.

"Go to sleep, young lady."

"Good night, Miss Fontenot. Pleasant dreams."

"Pleasant dreams, Georgia." *But not too pleasant.*

Stretched out in the wagon next to Georgia Mandara, Oliole went to sleep long before the conversations around the campfire ceased. Sometime after midnight she awoke and found her face toward the wagon sideboard, with a girl's thin arm across the wool blanket that covered her back.

She slowly peeled down the blankets and canvas that served as floorboard covering and mattress. Then she jammed her eye right against the slight crack in the unpainted, weathered boards.

The hair on the back of her neck stood up when she heard a young voice next to her whisper, "See, I told you he slept with his mouth open."

Kaid Darrant spurred the gray roan saddle horse just ahead of the team of mules as Oliole Fontenot drove the wagon toward the first building they had seen since leaving the Slash-Bar-4 ranch.

"This is the town of Roundup?" Georgia asked as they stopped the wagon in front of the two-story rectangular building surrounded by an unpainted picket fence that was broken down in several places.

Oliole adjusted her floppy straw hat and retied the ribbon under her chin. "We knew it wasn't as big as Cantrell."

"You can't have a real town with only one building, can you?" Georgia questioned.

Oliole pointed to the south. "There's another one over there."

"Where?"

"Down among the trees near the river."

"And look up on the bluff." Georgia waved her arm straight ahead of her. "Isn't that a log house?"

"Now see? I bet there are half a dozen buildings scattered around here. And you thought there wasn't a town!"

"The Slash-Bar-4 had more buildings at their headquarters than this," Georgia protested. "You don't suppose they have a bathhouse here, do you? I wouldn't mind having a hot bath."

"That does sound nice. But we might have to wait until we get down to Billings."

"Who is that?" Georgia pointed at the steps of the two-story building.

"I believe it's a young man waving at you."

Georgia ducked out of sight behind the black canvas. "Tell him I'm not receiving callers today," she squealed.

Kaid Darrant rode back to the wagon. "While you two are visitin', I'll go check out those corrals." He pointed toward the trees. "This must be the post office. I'll be back and help you unload the gear as soon as you make plans for the photograph. These clouds won't hurt your work today, will they?"

"As long as it doesn't rain," Oliole responded.

The dark-haired young man with the thin face and hawk nose strolled out toward the wagon. "Hello!" he called out as he approached. "I'm Luke Richards, but everyone calls me Slick."

Kaid tipped his hat and spurred the horse toward the trees.

The young man wore a neatly ironed, starched white shirt, black tie, creased wool trousers, and tattered black boots. His hair was parted in the middle and heavily greased. "I said, my name is Slick."

Oliole studied his hair. *If you use any more of that stuff on your hair, they could call you Lard.* "Hello, Mr. Richards. Would you mind holding these reins while I get down?"

"Yes, ma'am!" Instead of clutching the reins, he reached out and grabbed Oliole's arm above her elbow and squeezed it. "Let me help you down."

"Thank you, but I'd rather you held the mules. I'm quite capable of making it to the ground without your clutching my arm."

He jerked his arm back and grabbed the reins of the mule team. He looked her over and shook

109

his head. "I just cain't believe how this day turned out. I was expecting another wearisome day. I walk out of the post office, glance down the road, and in rolls a vision of perfect feminine loveliness."

Oliole glanced up at the black canvas that closed off the front part of the wagon. "Well, Miss Perfect Feminine Loveliness is not taking callers today."

"I'm feeling a little faint," Georgia called out.

"Yes," Oliole echoed, "I believe she's feeling a little faint and has decided to rest."

"Are you talking about your little sister who was riding with you?" Richards rubbed his wispy chin whiskers.

"I'm not her sister," the still-hidden Georgia blurted out. "And I'm fourteen years old."

"That's nice. I'll send my little brother to see you. He's fifteen." Then Luke "Slick" Richards stepped close to Oliole and whispered, "I'll be nineteen next year."

She noticed several pimples on his cheeks. "You're eighteen?" she quizzed.

"Factually, I'm seventeen until December 4. But I'll be nineteen next year. Old enough to have been around, if you catch my drift." He reached out and held onto Oliole's arm.

Oliole leaned within two inches of his face. He smelled like lilac water. "Mr. Luke Richards, have you ever had your nose broken?"

Without pulling away from her, he reached up with his free hand and rubbed his nose. "Eh, no."

She yanked his hand off her arm. "If you grab me one more time, I can guarantee you will have."

His hand dropped to his side. "Maybe I'm actin' a little brazen. But once you get to know me, you'll warm up to me. Some girls — I mean, some women call me winsome."

Georgia stuck her head out but kept the black canvas wrapped around her neck. "I call you a clod. Mama, why don't you just have Papa shoot him like the others!"

The young man jumped back. "What? Your mother? She's your . . . and he's your . . . Oh, man, I think I'm going to . . ."

"Perhaps you should go somewhere, lie down, and keep out of our sight until we leave Roundup," Oliole suggested.

Luke Richards trotted up a trail in the general direction of the log house on the hill. Georgia climbed down off the wagon. "I can't believe he was flirting with you!"

Oliole took the reins and tied them to the brake handle of the wagon. "He probably has bad eyesight and is too vain to wear spectacles."

"He sure fooled me." Georgia studied the town. "When I first saw him over there, I thought . . ."

"You thought you'd like to get to know him better?"

"Yeah, sort of," Georgia said.

"Well, you got to know him better. What do you think of him now?"

"I think he's a worm."

111

"He's a little conceited and slightly girl-crazy," Oliole said.

"Slightly? Any boy that tries to get fresh with someone twice his age is touched in the head."

"I'm not exactly twice his age."

"You know what I mean. But how was I to know what he was like from a distance?"

"You can't. But when we found out his nickname had to do with how much oil he combed into his hair, it should have given us a clue."

"How did you like that line about you two being my parents?" Georgia asked.

"I think it was a lie and unnecessary."

"But effective?"

"Oh, yes," Oliole chuckled. "Very effective. But no more lies. You stay with the team while I go see if I can find Mrs. McMillin."

"What if good old Slick comes back?"

"Are you afraid of him?"

"Not me," Georgia laughed. "He's only interested in you."

"Why am I so lucky?"

"That's what you get for being a perfect vision of feminine loveliness!" Georgia giggled.

"Remind me to leave my face covered with dirt next time we roll down a hill," Oliole laughed.

Following the sound of wood being chopped, Oliole rounded the two-story house and faced a large broad-chested woman swinging an axe.

"Mrs. McMillin?" she questioned.

"You the photographer lady from down on the Yellowstone?"

"Yes, ma'am, I'm Oliole Fontenot."

"O-lee-o-lay? What kind of name is that?"

"My mother's neighbor had that name. She told me it meant 'The Golden One.' "

"Your hair's golden, all right. But how about your life?"

Oliole stepped closer to the woodpile. "I don't understand."

"Is your life golden?"

"Golden? Well, I'm not wealthy, if that's what you mean."

"You're old enough to know there's more to life than money. I'd say you're around thirty. Am I right?" the lady pressed.

"Yes, you are."

"I can tell it in your voice."

"My voice?"

"Miss Fontenot, every heartache, every bruise and pain, every trial, every temptation, every victory, every moment of bliss . . . they all show up in the voice. But you didn't answer my question. Is your life golden?"

"Well, I have peace with God, plenty of food for tomorrow, a purpose to accomplish in life, good friends . . . lots of challenges. I'd say that's golden, wouldn't you?"

"Have you got a husband and kids?"

"No. But I believe my life is golden anyway."

A wide smile broke across Mrs. McMillin's face. "I do believe you're right." She let the axe handle rest on her shoulder. "Now what about the photograph?"

"As I mentioned in my letter, I'm taking a series of images of women in the West to capture what life is like for them out here. I call it 'Women at the End of the Road.' "

"Sounds good to me. I won't have to stop splitting wood, will I? I mean, until you're ready to open the shutter."

"Do you want me to take a photograph of you chopping wood?"

"Why not? It's what women do out West."

"You're right about that. Would you like to change dresses or anything?"

"Why? What's wrong with this one? I haven't worn it a week yet."

"It looks fine to me. I just want you to be happy with the way you look."

"Miss Fontenot, I haven't been happy with the way I look since I was twelve. I'm not about to start being happy now. But dressing up won't change who I am. This is me."

"May I drive my wagon around here to the side of the house? I'd like to have my developing equipment as close to my camera as possible."

"Be my guest. You said in your letter that others might be coming with you."

"I have an assistant and a driver."

"You are planning on staying the night, aren't you?"

"We can take care of ourselves," Oliole insisted. "I wouldn't want to be a burden, seeing that you're so busy with chores."

"You call making firewood a chore? It's a pleasure, a pleasant diversion that gets me out of the house. You didn't get that color in your cheeks by being in a darkroom your whole life, did you?"

"No, I like being outdoors, too," Oliole said.

"Back in the States most women are pale and sickly. And they call that beauty? It's a disgrace, I say."

"Mrs. McMillin, you're quite a lady."

The older woman wiped the sweat off her forehead and winked at Oliole. "That's what Mr. McMillin always says." Then she took another full swing at a thick log. Oliole watched it crack and then pop in two.

In the background of the photograph an unpainted two-story, clapboard-sided, rectangular house in a clearing surrounded only by a battered unpainted picket fence.

In the foreground a middle-aged woman with mostly gray hair loosely pinned on her head, dressed in black from her wrists and neck to the toes of her lace-up black shoes. One foot rested on a two-foot round of pine log. Near the other was a scattered pile of split wood. Across her shoulder lay a hickory-handled axe. A polite smile played on her face. A slight twinkle shone in the eyes framed by deep lines from a lifetime of hard work.

The minute Oliole hung the print out to dry, she knew what she would call it: "The Recreation of Mrs. Alexander McMillin." *Lord, this is the most fulfilling project I have ever had. Someday . . . twenty or fifty years from now, people will see these and know a little of what it was like to be a woman in the West of the 1880s. The photographs tell the story. Mrs. McMillin's face reveals more than a dozen diaries.*

After a huge supper of fried chicken and home-grown sweet corn with the McMillins, Oliole once again found herself watching the sunset from a bluff, this time just a mile and a half west of Roundup. She perched on a stump in a stand of scattered scrub pines and glanced down at her hands folded in her lap.

They are not pale and delicate, but they aren't callused and strong either. She reached back to unfasten her coiled braids. They tumbled down her back as she rubbed her neck. *Lord, I'm not sure how my hands are supposed to look. I'm not sure how You want me to look. I know how I want me to look. Usually I know how others want me to look. But I guess I've never asked You how You want me to look. I suppose I've always imagined that You love me no matter what. I'm glad about that.*

It's hard to please others all the time.

And it's impossible to please me.

"Well, is this providential or what?"

Oliole knew whom the voice belonged to even before she spun around. "Mr. Richards, what brings you up here?"

"I'd like for you to call me Slick." He now wore a light gray suit coat over his white shirt and tie.

"I'm sure you would, Mr. Richards."

116

"Say, if you scoot over a little, we could both sit on that stump," he suggested.

"Why would I want to do that?"

"So we can talk."

"Are you unable to talk standing?" she asked.

"Well, it surely seems so formal."

"Why don't you pull up a log? There's really not room enough for two on this stump."

"Eh, I reckon I'll just stand," he said.

"You didn't answer me. What are you doing up here?"

"What are you doing up here?" he challenged.

"Mr. Richards, never answer a question with a question. It is impolite."

"It is? Well, eh . . . I saw you up here and I —"

Oliole glanced back down the hill. "How could you see me from down at the river? The trees totally block the view."

"I didn't actually see you. I talked to that little girl, and she said —"

A vision of Georgia and Slick flashed into her mind. "Did you talk to a little girl, or did you talk to Miss Mandara?"

"That's who I meant. She said you went for a hike. She wouldn't tell me where, but I figured a photographer would like sunsets. I ain't no dummy, you know. So I hunted around for your tracks and trailed you up here. I'm good at that sort of thing."

Oliole folded her hands in her lap. *He reminds me of Charlie Garvane who lived across the hall in New York.* "I'm not sure we really have anything else to talk about."

"Sure we do." His grin bordered on total silliness. "I found out that you ain't that girl's mother, and the drover isn't your husband. So that sort of makes you unattached. Like me."

"I wonder if you have a dietary imbalance?" Oliole mused. "Do you eat your greens?"

"What does that have to do with you and me sparkin'?"

"Sparking? Mr. Richards, you are becoming insufferable."

"Thank ya. I kind of grow on you, don't I?"

"What I meant is, you are intruding on my time and my range. Let me say this clearly. I'm sure you are a pleasant young man, but you are twelve years younger than I am, and I choose not to spend this sunset with you. Good day, Mr. Richards."

"You're thirty?" he gasped.

"Yes, I am."

"You really are old enough to be that girl's mother!"

"Precisely. As you can see, this would be a good time for you to leave," she said.

"Well, I, eh . . . never had no partiality against older women," he stammered. "But I cain't believe you're that old."

"Amazing, isn't it? Now if you did track me up this hill, then you must have noticed a man's boot prints walking with me."

"Eh, well, I didn't actually, eh . . ."

"Aren't you curious about who that man is

and where he might be right now?"

"You ain't goin' to bluff me again." Luke Richards looked back over his shoulder. "There ain't no man up here."

"You're wrong. There is one man. And one boy. It would probably be best if the boy ran along before Mr. Darrant returns."

"I ain't a boy. And I say, there ain't nobody else within shoutin' distance."

Relax, Oliole. He's just immature, that's all. "But what if you're wrong?" she probed.

"What do you mean?"

"What if you continue to annoy me to the point that I cry out for help, and what if Mr. Darrant comes running with his gun drawn? There is a possibility that you could end up shot."

"Shot?" He spun around and surveyed the hillside again. "You're just trying to scare me. That won't work. I say it's providence that brought us together."

"Did you get a chance to see Mr. Darrant today?"

"Yeah, so what?"

"Does he or does he not look like the type who would defend a woman's honor?"

"Defend your honor? I ain't goin' to do nothin' like that."

"You didn't answer my question. Do you think Mr. Kaid Darrant would pull a gun and use it?"

"Yeah, I reckon he would."

"Then it might be to your advantage to be

gone when he returns."

"I don't see him nowhere," he said.

"I'm only saying, you can be a gentleman and exit amicably. Or you can play the rogue and be forced from the scene. That's your choice. Either way, you will have to leave." Oliole tilted her head and spoke with a soft, calm voice. "By the way, Mr. Richards, have you ever been shot before?"

"Of course not."

"I understand the pain is quite incredible. Of course, if you die quickly, I presume there's not much pain."

"This is dumb. I don't have to stand around and listen to things like this. I'm going to find someone who will be more pleasant. Good day, Miss Fontenot!" Luke Richards turned and stomped down the hill.

Oliole glanced up at the bright orange semicircle that was slowly sliding into the western horizon. *Lord, I'm not sure what that boy's problem is, but he's going to get himself in trouble if he doesn't get a little self-control and wisdom.*

She heard boots approaching from behind her, the big silver rowels on the spurs singing a familiar tune.

"Say, was that the kid from Roundup with the greased-down hair?" he asked.

She glanced back at Kaid Darrant, who toted his carbine over his shoulder. "Yes, it was."

"What did he want? There isn't some trouble in town, is there?"

"Not that I'm aware of. No trouble anywhere." She stretched out her legs and sank her boot heels into the soft dirt. "He's just a little confused. Now what took you so long?"

"I trailed that buck into the cedars and lost him there. Never even got off a shot. We might have to wait two days until we get to Billings to have more fresh meat."

"I'm sure we'll manage on salt pork. Mealtimes don't seem to be a major concern to any of us."

"I'll find something along the trail tomorrow." He squatted down next to her.

Oliole slid over. "Kaid, I think there's room for two on this stump."

He tipped his hat. "Thank you, ma'am. Don't mind if I do." He scooted next to her, and she could feel his ducking-covered thigh brush against hers as their shoulders touched.

Oliole didn't pull away. "Isn't it beautiful?" she exclaimed.

"The sunset?"

"The sunset, the mountains in the distance, the rolling hillside, the rocks, the river, the cottonwoods, the sagebrush — it's all beautiful."

"I guess I don't think about it much. You sure must like sunsets. Ever'day you seem to be up on a hill starin' at them. Don't you ever get weary of that?" he asked.

"Absolutely not."

"Did you do this when you were a little girl?"

"Never. I grew up in South Bristol, Maine. It's

right on the ocean at Muscongus Bay. When I woke up early enough, I could look out my dormer window and watch the sun rise over the Atlantic. But at night the sun would just drop behind the maple trees in the backyard. I never really saw it go down on a vast horizon until I came to the West. Now I'm trying to balance out all those sunrises I've seen."

"I suppose it's part of having the eye of a photographer."

"That's true. Everything God creates is so marvelous. That's what I like about the West. I can see more of creation with one glance."

"And no people," he said.

"I do have a fondness for landscapes. But God does a good job of creating people, too. We have to do some awfully dumb things to mess His work up."

"I thought your photograph of Mrs. McMillin turned out quite pleasing," he added.

"Yes, it did. I hope I'm that satisfied with all my work."

"How many keepers do you have now?" he asked.

"You mean, how many photographs go into the New York collection?"

"Yeah."

"Counting the two the gallery's already purchased, I believe I have seven," Oliole said.

"If you get one in Billings, that will make you one-third of the way there."

"I'd like to end up with some extras so I can be

more selective in what I send."

Oliole thought he might reach over and hold her hand.

But he didn't.

"Are we heading back to Cantrell after Billings?" Kaid asked.

"Yes. Carolina gave me a name of another farm wife along the river. They have some corn growing that might make a nice backdrop. Provided they haven't harvested it by now."

"Well, when we get to Cantrell, I'm going to miss these evenin's. It's been a peaceful time for me," Darrant admitted. "Ten years of army life and ten years of driving cattle doesn't give a man too much time for relaxing at sunset."

"You'll go with me to the Crow Agency and over to the Black Hills, won't you?"

"I reckon if you'd ask, Oliole Fontenot, I'd probably do most anything. Course, I'll work the fall gather in a month or so. But this has been like a vacation. I'm beginnin' to like being a lowly teamster."

"You are not a lowly teamster. You are my associate in charge of transportation and safety," she said.

Kaid pulled off his hat and twirled it in his hand. "Do you know what I'd like to be in charge of?"

"You aren't going to act like Slick, are you?"

"Who?"

She thought about putting her hand on his knee.

But she didn't.

"That boy with the greasy hair likes to be called Slick. But tell me," Oliole insisted, "what would you like to be in charge of?"

His voice was deep and strong like the waves breaking on a deserted section of beach. "Hand-holdin'."

"Oh," she said. "That can be arranged."

"It can?"

"Certainly. Let me show you." She reached over and grabbed his left hand, then his right, and pushed his two hands together, lacing the fingers. "There you go," she laughed. "You're holding hands with yourself."

"That isn't what I had in mind," he mumbled.

"No? Oh, Mr. Kaid Darrant, were you suggesting holding hands with me?"

"You know I was."

"Well!" She jumped to her feet and reached back for his hand. "I do believe I can do something about that." She pulled him to his feet until he stood beside her. "Do you waltz, Mr. Darrant?"

"Do I what?"

"Waltz. You know, dance?"

"I'm not proficient, but I reckon I do," he said.

"Good!" Oliole held the edges of her skirt and curtsied. "Why, thank you, Mr. Kaid Darrant. I'd love to waltz with you all the way down the hill clear back to Roundup!"

"Dance down the mountain?" he gulped.

"And I thought you'd never ask! Of all the men at this dance, you were the one I hoped would ask me." She laid her left hand on his shoulder and slipped her right hand into his callused one.

Kaid stared around at the otherwise empty mountaintop and then slipped a strong arm around her waist. "But — but there's no music," he protested.

"Hush, Mr. Darrant." She squeezed his hand. "If you really listen carefully, there's always music!"

Four

The blue cotton dress she wore was as pale as her eyes. She left the off-white enameled wooden buttons unfastened down past the base of her neck. Her slightly damp hair hung straight against the sides of her head as Oliole stroked the wide-toothed ivory comb through the blonde tangles. She thought that the only time her hair truly looked golden was when it was wet. The crack in the corner of the large unframed dresser mirror distorted the view as she glanced back across Room 21 at the England House Hotel in Billings, Montana Territory.

The cool polished wood floor felt clean and comfortable on her bare feet. The leather upholstered stool she straddled had very little stuffing left and felt like the wagon seat that had been home to her backside for most of the previous ten days. In the mirror she could see the big tightly framed Chinese silk screen with its hand-painted picture of a setting sun. The screen stood between the dresser and the far wall and separated the two occupants of the hotel room.

"Is your water still hot enough?" she called out.

"Oh, yes, thank you," Georgia replied with the bubbly enthusiasm of a fourteen-year-old. "I don't think I've ever enjoyed a bath so much in my life."

Oliole stared in the mirror at the dark semicircles under her own eyes. She attempted to brush them away with her finger. "Sometimes we need to go without for a little while in order to appreciate what we have."

"That includes family, too," Georgia murmured.

Oliole tugged at the skin at the corners of her eyes until the wrinkles disappeared. "Are you homesick?"

"I think I am."

When Oliole released the skin at her eyes, the wrinkles returned. "That's quite normal, you know. It's healthy." *You look thirty, Oliole Fontenot. I am thirty, thank you.*

"Miss Fontenot, were you ever homesick?" There was a musical tone in Georgia's question.

"Yes, it was quite terrible actually. When I went to New York to learn to be a photographer, I used to cry myself to sleep every night." Oliole continued to examine herself. Shoulders back, chest out, chin demurely lowered.

From behind the screen Georgia Mandara continued the interrogation. "Really? How long did that last?"

"About two years." Oliole batted her eyelids at the mirrored image.

At times Georgia's voice sounded deep for her age. "You cried for two years?"

"It seemed that way." *Good . . . with work and a*

youthful hairstyle I could look . . . twenty-eight!

Oliole could hear water splash in the porcelain tub. "Is this yellow towel mine?" Georgia queried.

"Yes. Can I bring you anything?" Carrying her comb, Oliole shuffled across the room.

"No! You stay right over there!" Georgia's panicked voice sounded about ten years old. "I have everything I need!"

Including a healthy dose of modesty. Don't ever lose that, Miss Mandara. Oliole returned to the short stool and continued to comb out her hair. She could hear bath water dripping on the floor. The air in the room felt humid, steamy.

"I think I'll open the window a little," she announced.

"No one can see in, can they?" Georgia demanded.

"Not a soul. You are completely safe, young lady."

"Good. I'm a little shy about some things." Georgia cleared her throat. "Anyway, why were you homesick for so long?"

Oliole returned to the mirror and once again stared at her reflection. *When I was eighteen, I might have had red, puffy eyes on occasion, but I didn't have dark circles under them.* "Oh, I suppose it was a combination of things. It was really difficult to pack up and leave my beloved Maine. My mama and daddy gave my sister and me a very good home. They loved us dearly, were devout Christians, sheltered us from many hardships. I didn't have a very accurate view of what life was like in the city. So when I was eighteen, I decided to leave my job teaching school and become a photographer."

"You were a schoolteacher?"

A scene of thirty-one students squirming in oak desks in a fog of chalk dust, trapped in a small, hot room, flashed through Oliole's memory. "For two years."

"You can't see me, can you?" Georgia's voice was high-pitched.

"Of course not."

"Good. I didn't know you were a teacher. Did you like it?"

"Most of the time. But I liked the adventure and creativity of being a photographer even more."

"So you just quit teaching and moved out of Maine?"

"Neither of my parents wanted me to move to New York. But they were gracious enough to encourage me to be all God wanted me to be. So they saved up some money and sent me off on the train."

"That must have been really scary. The biggest city I've ever lived in is St. Louis. And I've never ridden the train by myself. Did you know anyone in New York?"

"I have a cousin there. He works at a bank. I stayed with him and his family for two days and then found a tiny room to rent on the fifth floor of a big brick building. I hiked over to the photography school on the following Monday. But when they found out I was a female, they refused to let me attend classes, even though I had a letter of acceptance."

"They didn't know you were a girl when they accepted you?"

"I suppose they were confused by the name Oliole."

"Did you know that women in Paris sometimes paint their toenails?" Georgia asked.

"Eh, no, I suppose I never thought about that before."

"It's true! Nellie read it in a book one time. Why would anyone want to paint their toenails? No one would ever see them."

"Perhaps it's for their, eh, husbands."

"Husbands don't want to look at your toes, do they?"

"I suppose not." *I can't tell if her answer is very naive or very sophisticated.*

"Anyway," Georgia probed, "what difference did being a girl make at photography school?"

"They didn't think a young lady should get into photography for a profession. Besides, they said I would put undue social pressure on the male students." Oliole could still feel the cold rebuke of Dr. Patrick Sullivan and the uncomfortable ogle of Prof. Mackensie.

"Does that mean they thought all the boys would spend more time courting you than studying?" Georgia giggled.

"You're a pretty perceptive young lady."

"Thank you. I can figure things out quickly, too. What did you do then? Did you cry right there at the photography school?"

"Not there. I wasn't about to have them see me break down. But I cried all the way back to my room. I just knew photography was supposed to be my whole life, and they didn't even give me a chance. But I couldn't go home to Maine. My parents had to sacrifice a great deal to get me to New York. If I went home, I knew I would spend my entire life teaching school in New England. I felt the Lord had something more in mind for me.

"So I took a job at a dress factory across from the Del Romane Restaurant. I knew it was a cafe where many of the photography students ate. I'd go over there for meals and visit with the students. As I got to know them better, I started quizzing them on what they were learning. A couple of the men smuggled me out books and study notes. I read everything and began to buy as much equipment as I could afford. But most of the day, I merely sewed. And at night, with neighbors screaming through thin walls and babies crying, I'd study on my own and sob myself to sleep."

"What were their names?" Georgia asked.

"Whose?"

"The two men who sneaked books and study notes out to you."

"One was Lincoln Prince and the other Nathanael Scott." Oliole thought of Linc's ner-

131

vous grin and the spectacles perched on the end of Nathanael's nose.

"Were they cute?"

"Never in my life did I ever meet a cute photographer." Oliole glanced in the mirror and could see Georgia, now in front of the screen, pull on her petticoats. Their eyes met.

Georgia swung away. "Don't look at me! I'm ugly."

"Miss Georgia Mandara, do you say that because it's what you believe in your heart? Or are you trying to elicit a compliment from me?"

Georgia dropped her head and turned back toward the mirror. "A little of both, I reckon."

Oliole twirled around on the stool, her hands folded in her lap. She stared at Miss Mandara from foot to forehead. The petticoat-clad Georgia blushed but didn't try to hide.

"You're a refreshing kind of cute."

"Some parts of me are too skinny, aren't they?"

"Not for a fourteen-year-old. But there is one thing that might improve your looks."

"What's that?" Georgia scooted next to the mirror and peeked at herself. "I need to dye my hair, don't I? Papa would never in a thousand years let me do that. But my hair is so monotonous. Mrs. Parks said she would curl it for me if Papa agreed. I'm afraid to ask him."

"I was not thinking about your hair. What you need is to forget your looks and throw yourself into some fun, exciting, and challenging things to do. When you get so busy learning, growing, being yourself, and seeking God's direction for your life, you'll radiate that inner beauty that catches others' attention. Especially boys."

Georgia's brown eyes widened. "Really?"

"Try it. Just let loose and thoroughly enjoy the life the Lord's given you . . . and see what happens. That's what I try to do."

"Like the other day in Roundup when you and Mr. Darrant waltzed all the way down the hill?"

Oliole began to laugh. "I guess that looked kind of wild. But it was fun. Not every man would have done that with me. I'm fortunate that Mr. Darrant has strong arms. Several times he had to keep me from falling."

"Do you know what Mrs. McMillin said?" Georgia snatched Oliole's ivory cameo necklace off the dresser and held it up to her chest. "She said that was the most romantic thing she'd ever seen in her whole life. She should know. She's really, really old. I bet she's fifty."

Oliole reached over and fastened the necklace behind Georgia's neck. "Don't let Mrs. McMillin's looks fool you. She's a very romantic lady."

Georgia held out her arms and danced around the room with a pretend partner. "What made you think of waltzing down the mountain?"

"I don't know. It just seemed to be a fun thing. I believe if it's not unbiblical, immoral, or illegal, it's probably all right to do, even if no one has ever done it before."

"It might have been funner if you and Mr. Darrant fell down."

"I considered it."

Georgia stopped dancing and returned to the dresser. "I'd like to be that way when I get older, too."

"Well, make sure you enjoy being fourteen."

"Did you enjoy being fourteen?"

"I hated it most of the time," Oliole admitted.

"Good. That means I'm not the only one. But I sure have enjoyed the last ten days." Georgia strolled over to the silk screen and pulled on her yellow dress. Then she began the arduous task of fastening dual columns of tiny black buttons. "What are we going to do after our hair dries?"

"We'll go talk to Miss Adriana Courtney and then join Mr. Darrant for supper."

"Do you think Miss Courtney is as good an actress as the Marquesa?" Georgia plopped down on the edge of the bed and tugged on her long white cotton stockings.

"What do you think?"

Georgia flopped back on the bed and stared up at the once-white ceiling. "I think the Marquesa is the best actress in the whole world."

"Well, don't mention that to Adriana Courtney," Oliole cautioned. "I understand there are always professional jealousies among actresses."

"Is that why the Marquesa said I shouldn't mention her name at all?"

"Probably jealousy had a lot to do with it." Oliole glanced down at her unpainted toenails.

Adriana Courtney was staying in the President's Suite at the Occidental Hotel.

The President wasn't.

A white-uniformed middle-aged woman with bright red lipstick opened the door when Oliole knocked. The woman's graying hair was pulled back so tight her eyes almost looked slanted. A small handbag dangled from her arm. She glanced at the visitors with the expression of a matron who had found mice in her pantry.

"Hello, I'm Miss Fontenot, the photographer. And this is my assistant, Miss Mandara. I wrote for an appointment with Miss Courtney."

Before the woman could speak, a melodious female voice shouted from the adjoining room, "Who is there, Esther?"

With a voice like a fenced dog, the woman hollered back, "A photographer without a camera."

"Have him wait in the lobby. I'll be down shortly. This is hardly the time to entertain company."

"A lady photographer!" the woman shouted back. "At least, she claims to be a photographer."

"Oh. . . yes . . . the letter. In that case send her in." The voice seemed to be closer now. "Have you picked up my dress from the laundry?"

"I'm on my way." The older woman motioned for Oliole and Georgia to enter. Then she disappeared down the hall, closing the door behind her.

Thick sandy-blonde hair was stacked in curls on her head as the actress barged into the sitting room wearing only a green silk and black lace undergarment that revealed her legs up to her thighs and her chest well below her neck. Oliole tried to focus on the woman's green eyes while Georgia just dropped her mouth open and stared.

"So you are Miss Oliole Fontenot, the lady photographer," Miss Courtney gushed as she swooped across the spacious room and plucked a letter from a stack of mail. "I was intrigued when you wrote to me about having my photograph in a New York gallery."

Oliole remained motionless near the door, clutching her purse in front of her with both hands. "I appreciate your agreeing to be photographed."

The actress glided on bare feet from one side of the room to the other. "Oh, I haven't agreed to pose yet. But I did agree to talk to you about it." She suddenly parked herself in front of a full-length mirror mounted on an oak stand. "How do you like this costume?"

"That's a costume?" Oliole fought the urge to throw her shoulders back and her chest forward. "I thought perhaps it was an undergarment."

Adriana strolled over to Oliole. "Oh, it is, but in the final scene the general tears off my dress and —"

"He does what?" Georgia gasped.

Miss Courtney eyed the young girl from head to toe.

"Oh, this is my assistant, Miss Mandara," Oliole explained.

"Yes, well, please have her close her mouth and quit staring." Adriana marched back to the dresser and ran her finger down the letter. "Tell me about the gallery. Where is it?"

"It's a new gallery on 31st Street. I understand it's —"

Adriana interrupted, totally engrossed in her own thoughts. "Oliole? What a delightful name." She scooted quickly over to Georgia, who now stared down at the actress's painted toenails. "She has a name like Oliole and blonde hair that I only dream about having. I'd trade a year on the stage in San Francisco for that hair and that name, wouldn't you?"

Georgia looked up at the woman's smooth-skinned face. "You would?" Then she quickly dropped her eyes.

"Yes." Miss Courtney reached out and tapped Georgia on the shoulder. The young girl flinched. "Will you hand me that black silk robe?" Adriana's gold-ringed hand waved at a nearly empty coat rack on the wall by the door.

Georgia Mandara retrieved the gown, visibly relieved to see the actress finally cover up.

"Now exactly what kind of photograph did you have in mind?" Miss Courtney swept by in front of Oliole, leaving a trail of strong, sweet gardenia perfume. She motioned for them to sit on a green velvet settee while she continued to prowl the suite.

Oliole rubbed her thin ringless hands as they rested in her lap. "My series is a collection of photos of women who have chosen the West as their home. I want a varied selection of different activities and occupations. I understood you've made a career of acting out here."

Miss Courtney stopped her pacing and rested her hands on her hips. "Not by my own choosing."

"Oh?"

"Don't get me wrong. I have no intention of returning to the East." She resumed her stalking. "At least, not anytime soon. In New York even a great actress has a limited amount of time to enjoy her fame before someone else comes along. Those of lesser skills are hardly noticed at all. Out here they love you forever. It's not just your looks." She glanced down at the front of her black silk robe. "Though heaven knows I was blest with those. Nor is it your talent. All you have to do to succeed here is show up and smile."

Oliole surveyed the entire room. The furnishings were elegant, though slightly worn. *And have your dress torn off by the general.* "Then you will agree to the photograph?"

Miss Courtney rolled the letter into a tube and held it like a spyglass to her eye. "Just how much is the sitting fee?"

"Oh, no," Georgia piped up. "Miss Fontenot

won't charge you anything for the photograph."

Adriana Courtney turned the paper telescope toward Georgia and began to laugh. "She's a cute little girl."

Georgia's bangs-covered forehead drew tight. "I am fourteen years old. I am not a little girl. Did I say something funny?"

Oliole reached over and patted her on the knee. "I believe Miss Courtney was asking what we would pay her to pose for us."

Georgia wrinkled her nose. "We pay her?"

Oliole stood and strolled close to the actress who was standing in front of a full-length window covered by thin, sheer curtains. "If I would be allowed to stage the photograph I want, I will give you five publicity prints for free and agree to sell you ten more at my cost if you need them."

Adriana tapped her long crimson fingernails on the wooden windowsill. "What size will they be?"

"Nine by twelve."

"You have a large camera."

"Yes, I do."

"Just where will they be shot?"

"At the Bella Union Theater tonight right before your early performance of *The General's Little Lady*."

"Indoors?" Adriana turned to face Oliole. They were only a couple of feet apart, but Oliole was several inches taller. "Will you have enough light?"

"Yes, the setting sun will come through the window on the west wing, and I'll use some flash powder. There will be shadows, of course, but that's part of the image I want."

"Did Mr. Goldstein, the manager, agree to this?"

"He agreed to it if I promise not to take more than three minutes for the shots. And I can only use the flash powder once."

"Are you that good?" The question seemed to come from the actress's eyes.

"Yes, I am." The answer came straight from Oliole's heart.

Adriana stared at Oliole and then held a hand out to her. Oliole took the hand. It felt a little damp, as if rubbed in cold cream, but very warm and soft. "I like you, Miss Fontenot. You have a confidence based on your ability, not merely in your image." Adriana peered back out the window but continued to hold Oliole's hand. "I wish I had that confidence," she murmured.

"You have self-doubts?" Oliole thought she saw sadness in Adriana's green eyes.

"My word, yes! Every day . . . every performance . . . will they like me? Will they love me? Will they get up and walk out? Did I disappoint them? Were they expecting something else? Someone else? It haunts my life."

Oliole thought about putting her arm around the actress's shoulders.

She didn't.

"I always imagined all actresses were supremely confident."

Adriana dropped Oliole's hand and once again prowled the room. "We all pretend to be. Very few are. In fact, the last one I knew who was totally sure of herself was a black-haired half-Puerto Rican hellion who bodily threw me out of a theater and threatened to kill me if I ever returned to New York."

Georgia's eyes blinked wide. "Really? I don't think I'd like New York."

"Good choice. But that was years ago. I'm sure the Marquesa has died a violent and painful death from the hands of a former lover by now." As she swooped by the coat rack, Adriana snatched up a man's silk top hat.

"The Marquesa?" Georgia gulped.

"You've heard of her?" Adriana didn't bother looking back at Georgia but stopped in front of the mirror and shoved the hat on her head. It slipped down to her ears and half covered her eyes.

Oliole glanced at Georgia, held her finger to her lips, and shook her head. "Oh, we've all heard of the legendary Marquesa," Oliole explained. "I, eh, thought she had retired."

"No actress ever retires. We just run out of work — that's all. I'm sure she's prowling around somewhere, or she's dead." She cocked the hat sideways. "When I'm old, I think I'll do comedy. Anyway, I don't know why I'm telling you this. You give me five prints, and we'll call it a fair trade. You did say it would just take three minutes, correct?"

141

Oliole remained perched at the window. "Yes."

"What is this great photograph going to look like?" Adriana parked beside her, glanced out the window, then moved on, replacing the hat on the hat rack. "I wonder if he's coming back for his hat? Perhaps I should just hand it to his wife!" she muttered.

Oliole refused to look at Georgia. "I want a theater photograph. On the side of the stage at the Bella Union, on the west wing, there is a large mirror. I plan to —"

"Yes, that's my last stop each night before I enter." Adriana perched in front of the full-length mirror.

Oliole strolled over to her. "I want to set up my camera on an angle so I can see a few rows of the audience in the background, and you will be in costume at the mirror with that one final reflection. You and your mirrored image will show in the photograph."

A wide full-lipped smile broke across the actress's face as she continued to examine herself. "My, that sounds dramatic."

Georgia rose and strolled toward the women. "Miss Fontenot is a very good photographer. You ought to hear what she wants to call your image." For a moment all three were lined up in the mirror.

Then Miss Courtney broke for the door to the bedroom. "You caption the photographs?"

Oliole stayed put. "Yes, they seem to like that best at the galleries."

Adriana spun around in the doorway and ran her fingers up and down the formal white molding. "So what will mine be called?"

"If I can get the correct angle, I'm titling it 'Both Sides of Adriana Courtney.' "

"I love it!" The actress's green eyes sparkled clear across the room. "I go on at 7:15 P.M."

"I know. I'll be set up and ready at 7:00. If you would come to the west wing about five minutes before you normally go on, we can take the photograph."

"You said three minutes."

"I thought maybe you'd need a couple of minutes afterwards to review your lines before you went on."

"Are you joking? I could step on the stage right now and tear into that part." She reached over and grabbed a startled Georgia Mandara by the shoulders. "Just answer me one thing, General. When the cannon ball sailed so close to your head that you thought you would surely die, were you thinking of me . . . or were you thinking of her?"

Startled, Georgia rocked back on her heels and murmured, "I . . . I was thinking only of you!" Then she blushed and stepped closer to the window. "Oliole! There's July Johnson!"

Fontenot pushed the thin curtains aside. "Where?"

"Down there on the other side of the street." Georgia pointed.

"Are you sure?"

"Of course I'm sure!" Georgia insisted.

"Who's this Mr. Johnson?" Adriana asked as she, too, peered out the window.

"He's a nice-looking, industrious young man who lives in our town," Oliole reported. She dropped the curtains and put her hand on Georgia's shoulder. "Go on down and visit with him. I'll be right there."

Miss Mandara didn't move. "I'm not going to see him by myself."

"Why not?" Oliole asked.

"Because Molly Mae Quincy told me and Nellie if she ever caught either one of us visiting with July by ourselves, she would personally break our noses."

"That must be quite a young man," Adriana laughed.

"How about you and me going together then?" Oliole suggested. "Miss Courtney, if you'll excuse us, we'll see you at the Bella Union later."

"Would you like me to get you some tickets for the play? You might as well stay and watch the whole performance."

"Thank you. That will be delightful. We'll need three tickets for the second show. I'll have darkroom chores right after I take the photographs."

Adriana slipped her black-silk-robed arm around Georgia's shoulder. "Will the young man be going to the theater with you?"

Georgia stared at the gold rings only inches from her eyes. "No. Kaid will go with us."

The sandy-blonde eyebrows raised high as she folded her arms across an ample chest. "Kaid?"

"Kaid Darrant." Oliole retreated to the settee and picked up her leather purse. "He's a friend who's driving the team and . . . well, he's sort of a handyman. A handyman who takes care of things."

"A handy man who takes care of things? I'd like to have one of those myself," Adriana Courtney mused.

The oak staircase flowed in a quarter circle down to the hotel lobby. Georgia led the way. Neither spoke until they almost reached the ground floor.

"Did you see her toenails?" Georgia asked.

"I believe we saw almost everything."

"Was she talking about our Marquesa?"

"I presume so."

"I wonder why the Marquesa threatened to kill Miss Courtney? Maybe it was just some lines from a play. She didn't really mean it, did she?"

They stepped through the tall hotel doors onto the raised covered wooden sidewalk. "Well . . ." The noise from the traffic in the street made Oliole raise her voice. "That's certainly one way of looking at it. Now where is July?"

Georgia surveyed the street on her tiptoes, her round eyes squinting. "Do you think Molly Mae is with him?"

Oliole tugged her dress sleeves over her wrists. "I can guarantee her father would never agree to

145

her coming to town with July!"

"Maybe they eloped!"

"I don't think so," Oliole laughed. "Last summer, before you moved to Cantrell, I took Molly Mae and July up to the bluff behind town to get a sunrise picture. Molly Mae's father thought they had run off and was so angry he was ready to kill July. I have a feeling July'll be careful not to rile Mr. Quincy ever again."

"Was that when you broke your leg? The Marquesa told us all about it."

"Yes. Don't remind me."

The street in front of the hotel teemed with freight rigs and farm wagons. The summer dust swirled as rapidly as the conversation on the crowded, covered boardwalks. They stepped out of the flow of foot traffic to the corner and peered across the street. Georgia stood on a packing crate and jumped up and down trying to spy past a wagon drawn by six brown mules. "Do you see him?"

Oliole pointed across the street and down the block. "Isn't that July in front of McGuire's Hardware?"

"That's him!" Georgia confirmed. "Do you think he would hear us if we yelled?"

"Probably not." Oliole stuck two fingers between her teeth and whistled so loudly Georgia jumped back off the crates. Every rig in the street instantly drew up to a halt.

"Wow!" Georgia gasped. "Where in the world did you ever learn to whistle like that?"

"In New York City. It's the only way to signal a hack." Oliole grabbed Georgia's arm and tugged her into the middle of the street. "Sorry, boys," she apologized to the teamsters on the wagons. "I just need to see Mr. Johnson over there."

"July!" Georgia hollered.

Traffic resumed about the time they reached the boardwalk on the other side of the street. The gangly young man sprinted up to them. New leather suspenders held up his faded duckings. "Georgia! Miss Fontenot! I was hopin' maybe I'd see you here."

"What are you doing in town?" Georgia asked.

"I had to come get supplies. Some prospectors came down from Devil's Canyon two days ago and almost cleaned us out of mining gear. I reckon it's still booming up there."

"Will you be in town long enough to dine with us?" Oliole asked. "It will be my treat." *Last summer he was two inches shorter than me. Now he's two inches taller.*

"No, ma'am." July tipped his floppy broad-brimmed hat. "They should have my order loaded now. I'll be pullin' out and drivin' into the night. I promised Ranahan and Carolina I wouldn't dally none."

Oliole looked into his lively brown eyes. *And I wonder what you promised Miss Molly Mae Quincy?*

July gave them a slow, shy smile. "You two sure do look purdy for being on the trail over a week."

Oliole tilted her head and placed her finger on

147

her chin, as if posing for a photograph. "We just had a hot bath and washed our hair. Good thing you didn't see us this morning."

"Or up on the Musselshell when we rolled down the hill and got covered with dirt when those Indians rode up," Georgia added.

"Really? When will you be gettin' back to Cantrell? I want to hear all about your adventures."

"We'll be home in two days," Oliole assured him.

July glanced up and down the sidewalk. "Is Mr. Darrant still with you?"

"Oh, yes, we haven't chased him off . . . yet." Oliole waved her arm toward the east. "He took the team to the livery and went to visit with some old drover friends of his."

"Well, you might want to make sure he stays a tight," July suggested, his face reflecting worry.

Oliole stepped closer to him until their eyes were only inches apart. "Why's that?"

"Well, it's a horrible injustice, Miss Fontenot — that's what it is. It got Marshal Parks so aggravated that he sent a five-page telegram to the governor in Helena. Five whole pages. I seen it myself. Then he sent another to the U.S. Marshal's office in Denver."

"What are you talking about?"

July slipped his fingers into his back pockets. "About Sam Black and his gang."

"Why? What happened to them?" Oliole asked.

"Did they get lynched?" Georgia gasped. "Did their eyes bug out?"

"Georgia!" Oliole scolded.

"I hear their eyes bug out when they get hung."

"No one got hung. Two or three days after you left, two U.S. Marshals and a bank inspector from Cheyenne came to town," July said.

"To pick up the bank robbers and take them to Wyoming?"

"Nope. To pick up the money and take it to Wyoming."

"What about the men?" Georgia demanded.

"They said the Territory of Wyoming didn't want them. I reckon their prison is already full so they refused to extradite them."

Oliole shook her head. "What did they do — turn them loose?"

"Yep." July nodded. "Marshal Parks said he had no choice."

"Are they loitering around Cantrell?" Georgia questioned.

"Ranahan kicked Black out of town. The marshal said that since he harassed you, he was declared a detriment to the town and not allowed to return. His compadres stayed down by the river two, maybe three days and then rode off."

"I imagine getting chased out of town didn't sit well with Mr. Black," Oliole remarked.

"No, ma'am, I reckon it didn't. He rode down Main Street screamin' about how he was going to get even."

"Get even? He is a violent man. Does he intend to seek revenge on Marshal Parks or upon the whole town?"

"Neither." July's voice was almost a whisper. "He said he was going to get even with you!"

Georgia swallowed hard. "With Miss Fontenot?"

"That's what he claimed."

Georgia clutched Oliole's arm. "What are we going to do?"

"I suppose we should get back to Cantrell as soon as we're finished. I don't want any of them to get drunk and decide to burn down my studio."

"That's the exact same thing Marshal Parks thought," July reported. "He and the captain have been takin' turns sleepin' on your porch ever' night."

Oliole rubbed the back of her neck. It felt tense. "By all means, tell them to go inside and use the bed or the sofa."

"Yes, ma'am, I'll tell 'em."

"Has anyone in Cantrell spotted any of the gang in the last few days?" Oliole pressed.

"No, ma'am. Carolina thinks they've gone to Deadwood or someplace like that to rob another bank. I don't think they'll hang around Cantrell, what with the whole town on the prod."

"Thank you for that report, Mr. Johnson. We're much obliged."

"Yes, ma'am. I surely hope them men aren't in Billings today. Like I said, you ladies ought to have Kaid with you."

"Thank you for your concern, Mr. July

Johnson. We'll be very careful."

"Well, I've got to hit the trail. You take care of yourselves. Ever'body in Cantrell really misses you two."

Georgia raised her eyebrows. "They do? Even Miss Molly Mae Quincy?"

July blushed. "Well . . . at least she does hanker for Miss Oliole's return."

Oliole Fontenot parked her wagon in the alley next to the stage door of Bella Union Theater. She thought that the photographic session had gone extremely well. While Adriana Courtney completed the first performance of *The General's Little Lady*, Oliole huddled in the soft glow of her portable darkroom developing photographs on the egg-white-coated albumen paper.

She had a cotton towel draped around her shoulders and repeatedly used it to wipe the sweat off her face. The smell of chemicals hung in the air in the stuffy black canvas-covered wagon. The first two poses had not come out with the light, clarity, or drama that she had envisioned.

But thanks to flash powder, photo number three was haunting. Adriana's bold yet timid, confident but unsure, attitude reflected from the mirror.

Thank You, Lord. It's nice to know after bragging all afternoon about needing only three minutes to get the photograph, that I could actually do it. It is exactly what I wanted!

She put away her materials and straightened the clutter of her miniature portable developing room. Then she grabbed a small mirror. In the flickering lantern light, she scanned her face.

Well, Miss Oliole, it's difficult to believe you were clean, neat, and fresh only a few hours ago.

One of her long braids had fallen off the back of her head and now dangled over her shoulder and down across her chest. The other braid remained coiled in place.

I should take a photograph of my hair looking like this. I'd call it "One Up, One Down."

She unfastened the other braid and tossed the pair to her back. Then she wiped her forehead once more with the towel and laid it across the narrow bench that served as a table in the back of the wagon. After buttoning up the collar of her light blue dress, she searched in a wooden box marked "Dangerous Chemicals." She pulled the cork from the frosted white glass bottle with her teeth and splashed a little on her hand. Replacing the cork, she rubbed the liquid on her neck and behind her ears.

I refuse to go to the theater smelling like sweat. Although smelling like a Garden of Lilies might be just as offensive.

Kaid and Georgia haven't returned. I presume they're still eating supper at the England House. She dug a gold-chained necklace watch out of a small, worn brown leather case. *It's forty-five minutes until Adriana's next performance. It's too stuffy to wait in here. Perhaps there's a bench in front of the theater. Kaid said that if I went anywhere, I should tote the shotgun. Surely, he didn't mean while sitting in front of the theater.*

Even though it was after 8:00 P.M. and the sun had set, it was not dark when Oliole climbed down across the seat of the wagon and onto the dirt street of Billings. She left the shotgun in the wagon. Compared to the stuffy air inside the developing tent, the dusty summer drift felt almost like a cool breeze. She brushed her skirt down over her riding boots and then stood and stretched her arms. She could hear the hum of conversations on the boardwalk out on the street and the squeaking sounds of a slow-moving wagon around the corner.

I like the pace of the West, Lord. No one's in a hurry. It's like everyone wants to let sights soak in, afraid they'll miss something. I don't want to go back to the city. Well . . . perhaps just to view my show and then come right back.

The dirt crunched beneath the heels of her boots. Her calf and thigh muscles relaxed as she took long strides out of the alleyway. *Maybe I'll just go on over to the England House and have a cup of tea and a cracker while they finish eating.*

The sidewalk in front of the theater was empty. The once-busy street was almost deserted. Horses and rigs lined the sides, but most of the people had retreated into the saloons, theaters, and restaurants. The oak double doors were thrown open, and she heard a roar from the mostly male crowd.

I wonder if that's the scene where Adriana gets her dress yanked off? I'd sit down, but it would seem strange, I suppose, for a woman to be sitting at sundown . . . alone on a bench . . . outside a theater.

I think I miss home, too.

Lord, I really like a place where I can sit out on the porch undisturbed and watch You bring down the curtain on another day. Just a couple more days and we'll be there.

She lifted up her braids and let the brief breeze cool the back of her neck. Oliole had started across the street when she heard a man's voice call out from behind, "Hey, girlie . . . where's the best dance hall in this town?"

Girlie? Mister, you don't know who you're talking to!

She spun around to face the man back on the raised boardwalk. "You!" she gasped. The dark chaps and boots were well worn, the hat pulled low across his eyes; a week's beard was on his face, a sneer on his lips.

"Well, I'll be," he growled, drawing his gun out of his holster. "If it ain't Yellowstone County's lady photographer. If I was a prayin' man, I'd say my prayers have been answered. Course, I ain't a prayin' man."

"Mr. Black, you ought to be standing trial in Cheyenne for bank robbery," she said.

"And you ought to be horsewhipped and hung for getting us caught in Cantrell. They took all our money."

"Whose money?"

154

"You lied to me! You didn't have nothin' in that glass but water."

"I assure you I won't make that mistake again," she snapped.

"Get over here in this alley." He waved the Colt .45 at her. "You and me need to — talk."

"I most certainly will not!" She turned and started to march across the street. *"Yea, though I walk through the valley of the shadow of death, I will fear no evil . . ." Keep walking, Oliole.*

"Where do you think you're goin'?" he screamed. "I could shoot you down right in the street!"

Lord, I can't die here. Not now.

"I told you to come over here!"

I have a photographic project to complete.

"Look, I'm warning you for the last time!"

Heavy boot heels crashed off the boardwalk onto the dirt street.

You told me I was to capture "the image of the earthy." Well, I haven't done it yet.

"Nobody can bluff Samuel Black and get away with it. You stop right there!"

So it can't be here that I die. Can it?

Black's hand made a pinching grab for her shoulder blade and yanked her back on her heels. When she saw the gun in his hand shove past her on the right, she dropped her head to her chest.

The odor of sweat and whiskey swept over her. "Maybe it's time you and me got better acquainted! This time I ain't takin' no for an answer." His voice sounded only inches behind her head.

With all the strength she could muster, Oliole threw her head straight back. The sound of the impact was like an axe handle slamming against a tree trunk. Instant pain flashed through her head as it cracked into his face.

Black's grip fell off her shoulder. The Colt discharged into the dirt, causing her to jump forward and spin around. Deep-red blood trickled out of both nostrils and across his fat, dark lips.

"You broke my nose!" he screamed.

At the sound of the gun discharging, people scurried out of shops and buildings and crowded the boardwalks. Most stayed back in the shadows and watched.

With his blood-smeared left hand, Sam Black grabbed one of Oliole's braids and yanked her across the street. "You ain't ever goin' to see daylight!" he growled. "You've insulted me and abused me for the last time." He dragged her toward the theater alley. Blood dripped off his chin as he waved the revolver at the crowd.

Oliole struggled to keep from stumbling and swung her arms wildly at him without landing a blow. Several men approached, guns drawn. "Let her go, mister!" one of them shouted.

"Back off, or I'll shoot her. I swear to God, I'll shoot her!"

The men stopped their advance but kept their revolvers drawn. "Let her go," another one demanded.

"I'll let her go dead! Ain't no woman alive that can put one over on Sam Black." His voice seemed to roll up from the pits of hell.

The pain in Oliole's head was so severe that all she could do was clutch her head and try to keep the hair from being pulled out of her scalp.

Suddenly the crowd of men huddled around the boardwalk in front of the Bella Union Theater surged forward and divided while Adriana Courtney strolled out into the street, wearing only the skimpy costume from the scene where her dress was ripped off by the general. Long black silk stockings graced her legs to her thighs, and the green silk garment, trimmed in black lace, dipped improperly low at the bodice.

Every man on the block eyed the plucky partially clad actress.

Sam Black included.

At that precise moment, Oliole jerked her braid free and made a run for the crowd at the side of the street. *Lord, I am not going to die today. I've simply too much left to accomplish.*

To her right a man sprinted into the street and dove at the gun-wielding Sam Black. Upon reaching the boardwalk, Oliole heard another shot explode behind her. She spun around and saw a powerful fist slam into the bank robber's jaw. Black's revolver dropped to the dirt, and when the second blow caught him in the already battered nose, the gunman crumpled.

Georgia Mandara threw her arms around Oliole. They clutched each other and stared as

Kaid Darrant slammed two more powerful punches into the downed man and then abandoned Black to a deputy marshal and strolled back to them.

"Are you all right, Oliole?" he drawled.

"Yes, I think so. How about you, Kaid?"

Darrant held his hands out in front of him. "Well, I got a little blood off his face on my knuckles. But that will wash up."

"You took a horrible chance diving at a man holding a gun."

"So did Miss Courtney," he added. "But neither of us were in as much danger as you."

"I didn't have a choice," Oliole confessed. "That is twice that I've had a confrontation with Mr. Black. I am not amused."

"You've got blood all over your hair!" Georgia exclaimed, still clutching her arm.

The mumbling crowd filtered back inside the buildings as Adriana Courtney marched toward them, now wearing a borrowed long beige duster that dragged the dirt. "I trust you are all right, Miss Fontenot?" she called out as she approached.

"Oh, yes. Thank you. Thank you for that diversion," Oliole said.

Courtney kept her eyes on Kaid Darrant as she spoke to Oliole. "Diversion? I have no idea what you are talking about. I just wasn't about to let some novice actress steal center stage. That was mostly my theater crowd. If they stare at anyone, it should be me," she laughed. Finally she glanced at Oliole and then back at Kaid. "Say, is this the man who takes care of you?"

"Oh, yes . . . this is my — my, eh . . ."

"I'm her driver, Kaid Darrant." He tipped his hat.

"I was afraid of that. Well, if you ever get tired of taking care of her," Adriana drawled, "I know where you can get a new job."

"Really?" Georgia pressed. "Where?"

"It was a joke, honey." Then Miss Courtney turned back toward the theater. "I have to go salvage act three. Try not to steal my crowd again."

Kaid observed the actress retreat. "She's quite a lady," he mumbled.

"Are you speaking of her costume or her gumption?" Oliole challenged.

Kaid began to blush. "Eh . . . her spunk, mostly."

Georgia slid in between the two of them. "Did that man Sam Black come find you at the wagon?"

Oliole felt her racing heart finally begin to slow down. "No, I was on my way to find you two and had just passed the theater when he suddenly appeared and grabbed my shoulder."

Georgia rubbed her nose. "Yeah, but what happened to his face?"

"I bumped the back of my head into it."

"On purpose?" Georgia quizzed.

"As a matter of fact, yes, it was on purpose. I needed to persuade him to turn loose of me."

Georgia put the palms of her hands on her

cheeks. "I wish I could have seen that."

"What on earth for?"

"So I could try it some time on my brothers when they tease me! Were you afraid?"

"Afraid and mad," Oliole said.

"Mad?"

"Yes, I kept thinking I couldn't let some demonic dolt keep me from completing my photography project."

Kaid Darrant rubbed his ten-day-old beard as he glanced down the street. "You know what I'm thinkin', ladies?"

"Does it have to do with Miss Adriana Courtney?" Oliole challenged.

"Of course not," Kaid blustered. "I was thinkin' the sheriff will hold Black overnight for being drunk and causing a public disturbance."

"Disturbance? He was trying to kill Miss Fontenot," Georgia protested, her voice high-pitched.

Kaid tugged off his red bandanna and wiped the blood from his knuckles. "What I'm sayin' is, no matter what the charge, they won't hold him in jail too long. They'll just turn him out and maybe hurrah him out of town. I figure if we left for home now, we could get to Cantrell while old Black is sobering up in jail."

"We can't go straight there," Oliole maintained. "I've got to take one more photograph along the way."

"It could wait, can't it? I'd surely like to get you back safe. In Cantrell you'd be surrounded by friends. That gang wouldn't dare show up in town again."

"I appreciate your concern, Kaid, but I have the session arranged." Oliole jammed her hands on her hips and could feel her neck muscles tighten. "I will not be chased out of any town, including this one, by ruffians and renegades."

"In that case," he proposed, "I'll sit out in the hallway of your hotel throughout the night to make sure you're safe."

"You'll do nothing of the kind. With Samuel Black in jail, we'll be safe at least for tonight," she informed him. "I choose not to live in fear. If I can survive life in New York City, I can certainly survive in Billings, Montana Territory."

"Black's got friends. As far as I know, they aren't in jail."

"If they didn't help him just now, I doubt if they're in town," she reasoned.

"I reckon you could be right about that. But will you take the shotgun to your room?"

"Only if you insist."

"I insist," he said.

"All right, but we aren't going to our room until after the play. I promised Adriana we'd attend the second performance."

Kaid scratched the back of his head. "Does she really wear that outfit in the play?"

"Yes, but if you'd rather not go, I'm sure —"

"Oh, I'll go," he murmured. "I wouldn't want you to be in any more danger."

Georgia rolled her eyes at Oliole. "We better

go to the room and clean you up before the play. You really have quite a bit of blood in your hair, Miss Fontenot."

"I'll drive the rig back to the livery," Kaid reported.

"We'll meet you in front of the theater a little before the show begins," Oliole said.

"We'll meet in the lobby of the England House, and I'll walk you two over," Kaid replied.

"You're a very cautious man, Mr. Darrant."

He tipped his hat. "Thank you, ma'am." He wandered down the quickly darkening street that now showed absolutely no trace of the earlier confrontation.

Oliole was already dressed when Georgia peeked out from under the covers the next morning. "Good morning. Is the general gone, Miss Fontenot?"

Oliole grinned as she combed her hair. "Did you dream about the play?"

"Yes. Wasn't Miss Courtney about the best actress you ever saw in your life?"

"She certainly seems to enjoy the role, doesn't she?"

Georgia climbed out of the bed with its thick mattress and yanked a sheet around her flannel-gown-covered shoulders like a shawl. Then she strutted across the room. "Just answer me one thing, General," she announced in a pleading, almost whiny voice. "When the cannon fire sailed so close to your head that you thought you would die, were you thinking of me . . . or were you thinking of her?"

Oliole held a strand of her long blonde hair under her nose like a mustache and growled in a deep voice, "You know exactly what I'm thinking about, Constance, my dear — even when I'm not thinking about it!" She grabbed the sheet, tugging it off Georgia's shoulders.

"My name's not Constance!" Georgia replied with suppressed laughter.

Both of them flopped on the bed and began to giggle.

Georgia rolled over and poked Oliole in the ribs. "Did you see that man in front of me draw his gun? I thought he really was going to shoot the actor that played the general."

Oliole brushed Georgia's bangs out of her eyes. "Perhaps the customers should be a little more sober when they watch a stage drama."

Georgia stood straight up on the bed and peered down. "Do you think I could ever be an actress?"

"Perhaps so. You seem to have a lot of public skills," Oliole said.

"Papa says I can't be an actress."

"What does the Marquesa say?"

"In front of Papa? Or just to me when we're alone?"

"How about when you're alone?"

"She says she'll let me act in some of the plays she has at the hotel," Georgia said.

"That might be a good place to learn."

"To learn what?"

"How to be an actress."

"I already know how," Georgia insisted as she stomped around on the unmade bed. "I just need to have someone give me a part to memorize. Do you think I could play Franchesca in *The General's Little Lady*?"

Oliole pulled herself off the bed and looked at Georgia. "Not for a few years."

"Why?"

"Are you ready for the general to pull off your dress while you waltz around in silk underwear?" Oliole waved her arm at Georgia's flannel nightgown.

"I forgot about that part. I could never, ever do that!"

"Then perhaps your acting career should move slowly."

Georgia stalked around on the bed as if it were a stage. "Yes, you might be right, my dear. Now would you be a real sweetheart and run down to the laundry and pick up my gown?"

Oliole curtsied. "Yes, Miss Georgia. Is that your gold gown or your silver gown?"

"Both," Georgia giggled.

"May I polish your shoes? Fetch your breakfast? Mend your stockings?"

"You will not touch my black silk stockings! But you may polish my toenails," Georgia demanded. She waved a finger at Oliole and was immediately struck in the face by a feather pillow.

For several minutes both ladies belted each other with pillows and then collapsed on the bed in laughter.

"I changed my mind," Georgia announced. "I don't want to be an actress. I want to be just like you. I've never known anyone who had more fun."

Oliole held her stomach as she caught her breath. "That scene last evening with Mr. Samuel Black wasn't all that much fun."

"Okay, I want to be just like you, except I don't want anyone to ever get mad at me and treat me mean."

"That, my dear Miss Mandara, will never happen."

"Why not?"

"Because just when your life is peaceful, someone will come along and do this!" Oliole bopped Georgia with a pillow, and the ruckus resumed.

They were dressed, their valises packed, and the unneeded shotgun propped at the door. Oliole sat in a straight-backed wooden chair reading her Bible. Georgia stared out the window. Suddenly she shouted, "Here he comes!"

Oliole tucked the Bible into her brown leather purse, then stood, and retrieved her valise.

"Should we wait here for him to call? Or should we go down and meet him out front?" Georgia asked.

"Let's go down. There's no reason to make him hike up these stairs."

They gathered up their belongings and tramped down the wooden stairs. "I like Mr. Darrant," Georgia announced. "Do you like him, Miss Fontenot?"

"Yes, I do."

"Do you like him enough to kiss him?"

"Do you?" Oliole challenged.

"Kiss him? Me? He's too old for me. But you didn't answer my question."

"Yes, I believe I just might like him enough to kiss him. But don't you tell him that." *Did I just tell a fourteen-year-old girl to keep a secret?*

"Are you planning on kissing him today?" Georgia quizzed.

"Not that I know of. Why all this talk about kissing?"

"When Randolph kissed Miss Adriana last night at the end of the play, I thought my toes would melt. You know what I mean?"

"I think I'm getting you back to your papa at just the right time!"

"Whoa . . . look at Mr. Darrant! What happened to him?"

Kaid Darrant climbed down off the wagon seat and scanned the street. His right eye was black, and his jaw showed deep scratches. Both hands had white cotton strips wrapped around the knuckles, and he limped a little as he hiked to his saddle horse tied to the back of the converted army ambulance.

"Kaid, did you have an accident?" Oliole quizzed.

He pulled off his brown hat and gingerly rubbed his face. "Ain't I a handsome fellow?"

"You look horrible!" Georgia gasped.

"I had a little run-in with Samuel Black's compadres."

Oliole held onto his strong arm. "They *are* here in town!"

"They're in jail with Black right at the moment."

"Jail?" Georgia stuffed her valise into the wagon and climbed up onto the rawhide-covered wooden seat. "What did they do?"

"They showed up at the wagon last night intending to bust up all your gear," Kaid reported.

Oliole felt her heart race and her breath grow short. "My camera! My negative plates! What did they ruin?"

"Just my face. I figured somethin' like this could happen, so I checked out of the Drovers' Hotel and night-guarded the wagon."

Oliole continued to clutch his arm. "You fought three men?"

"It wasn't all that much of a fight. I coldcocked one of 'em right off with the barrel of my carbine. So it was kind of fair after that."

"Two against one is kind of fair?" Oliole asked.

"At least it gave me a chance," Kaid explained with the tone of a teacher illustrating addition to a first-year grammar school class. "We pounded on each other until the deputy came down and arrested the lot. Said he'd keep them in jail until the judge fines them at 11:00 A.M. But don't worry, I didn't let them touch any of your gear."

Oliole gently touched his cheek. "Kaid, you need to see a doctor!"

He winced. "Ever'thing will heal up in a few days. Reminds me of a time when a cinch broke during a stampede, and I fell off my horse."

"What happened then?" Georgia pressed.

"I shot a big, old brindled bull and hid behind him till they all passed by. I think I had ever' square inch of my body kicked or stepped on."

"I don't know how to thank you for taking such good care of us." Oliole lifted his callused hand and kissed the back of it. She refused to look at Georgia.

Kaid didn't pull his hand back. "I guess we ought to hit the trail, ladies. I think we could all use a little rest back home in Cantrell."

The sky was blue.

The grass brown.

The sun a pale summer yellow.

The juniper trees on the bluff were grayish green.

The water of the Yellowstone River was September clear.

But Oliole Fontenot saw nothing beyond the rear ends of two chocolate brown mules.

Lord, this man has put his life in jeopardy to save me. And to save my equipment. I can never repay him. What can I say? What can I do? I don't deserve that kind of sacrifice.

He acts like it was nothing at all. Mr. Kaid Darrant, you have complicated everything. I can take care of myself. I do not need to be beholding to anyone, especially a strong, handsome, principled man with a tender yet adventuresome streak.

Lord, I'm not so independent, am I? I want to be on my own. I want it to be just You and me. Then You send people into my life to look after me.

You did send Kaid Darrant into my life, didn't You?

What can I do to show him my gratitude?

I've got to think of something.

Something moral, biblical, and legal.

Five

Twelve large photographs blanketed the surface of the oak table in the parlor of Oliole Fontenot's studio.

Different hair.

Different ages.

Different clothing.

Different backgrounds.

Different amounts of wear and tear on their faces.

But they were sisters.

Each one had come to a sometimes beautiful, sometimes brutal, nearly empty land.

Each had chosen to stay where violence sometimes went unchecked.

They faced danger, deprivations, and sometimes dirty diapers.

But they had found their spot. Their place. Their purpose. And they had no intention of leaving.

Sisters of the Western spirit.

Twelve pairs of intense eyes.

Twelve expressions of measured independence.

Twelve chins held proudly.

Oliole prowled around the table, scrutinizing each photograph from every angle.

Lord, these might not be prize-winning photographs, but these are prize-winning women. I'm proud to call each one a friend. Look at Pepper Andrews. Do you see those eyes? They had to face it all, night after dance-hall night. But look at those twin babies on her knees. That's what you told me: "And as we have borne the image of the earthy, we shall also bear the image of the heavenly."

But I'm only halfway through.
I need to find twelve more.

Customers crowded the Mercantile as Oliole peeked through the doorway before picking up her mail at the post office. Carolina, dark curls perfectly in place, swooped by with three tattered and greasy prospectors trailing after her like coal cars tugged by a polished silver locomotive.

"Will you still have time to come up for lunch?" Oliole called, feeling a little sloppy in the presence of Carolina Cantrell Parks.

Carolina looked over the top of a stack of neatly folded tan canvas trousers. "Most definitely! I have to get out of this store. Ran's off with a posse chasing bank robbers, and David decided this is a good day not to stay in the playpen and mind his mother."

The moment Oliole stepped into the building, she could smell cinnamon and sweat. "Can I take Davy with me?"

Carolina handed each bearded prospector a pair of ducking trousers and then glided across the smooth wooden floor toward Oliole. "You're kidding me."

"No. Let me take care of him this morning, and you can pick him up at lunch." Even though she stood several inches taller than Carolina, Oliole felt overshadowed.

Carolina's wedding-ring-clad left hand reached out and held Oliole's wrist. "Perhaps you've had a sunstroke, Miss Fontenot."

Oliole patted her hand. "Carolina, do I get to take Davy with me or not?"

"You're crazy. Unmarried and crazy." Carolina stood on her toes to hug Oliole's shoulders.

A scent of lilac perfume wafted to Oliole from Mrs. Parks's hair. "I'll take that for a yes."

"Let me gather a few of his things after I take care of this sale."

Oliole squeezed her hand and let it drop. "I'll go to the post office and be right back."

When Oliole returned, Carolina Parks met her on the big uncovered front porch of the Mercantile. In one arm squirmed a grinning, fat-faced fourteen-month-old baby with an unmanageable shock of fine, dark brown hair. By her feet sat a small green satchel that had once seen the great cities of Europe but lately held diapers, oil, and powder.

"Good morning, Davy! Why don't you come to my house and play with Aunt Oliole?"

Carolina handed her the baby and then folded her arms in front of her. "There will be rewards for you in heaven, Oliole."

Oliole cradled him on her left hip. Davy Parks settled into the position like a seasoned mommy-rider. "I have never seen this child when he wasn't smiling."

"Ran claims he smiles even when he cries." Carolina licked her fingers and tried to brush down Davy's cowlick. "Remember, if he starts giving you trouble or behaves badly, bring him back."

"Relax, Mama Parks, we'll get along just fine." Oliole scooped up the satchel. "Of course, every woman in town will be jealous that I get Davy all to myself. He is the pride of Cantrell."

Oliole strolled up the dusty dirt street. She felt like dancing, but she could still sense the inspection of an anxious mother behind her. Although the air was a trifle dusty, there was a freshness in the Montana summer morning. She was walking past the bank when she heard a shout echo over the noise of the street: "Miss Fontenot!"

Georgia Mandara was leaning over the railing of the second-story veranda of The Hotel Marquesa. Oliole waited for a wagon to roll by and then hiked across to the hotel.

Georgia's wide grin was framed by long dark brown hair. "Good morning, Oliole!"

"Well, good morning, Georgia. You look like you have your working clothes on." Oliole studied the girl's laughing eyes. *It won't be long until drovers and drifters will be fighting to ask you to the dance, young lady.*

"Yes, we were full last night, and I need to help

Nellie clean rooms." She waved a short feather duster over the railing. "Are you actually baby-sitting little Davy?"

Oliole turned so the infant could look up at Georgia. "Yes, until noon."

"Wow, I didn't think Mrs. Parks let anyone take care of him." Georgia rubbed her nose with the back of her hand, leaving a slight smudge on her cheek.

"It's a rare treat. We'll have fun. He's always such a happy boy." Davy let out a delighted squeal, and Oliole turned to see him staring at an old man leading an unsaddled grulla-colored horse.

Georgia leaned her elbows on the railing, her chin in her hands. "I wish I could come play with him."

"When you finish your chores, come on up to my house."

Georgia stood straight up. "Really?"

"Ask the Marquesa." Oliole squinted as she stared up at the girl.

"Ask me what?" Isabel Leon Mandara stepped out onto the veranda on the street level. She wore a white cotton apron over a taffeta dress and held a wooden rug beater in her hand. "Did you kidnap that baby?"

Oliole put her nose in the air. "I get to baby-sit Davy all morning."

"Well, aren't you the privileged one! I wondered if this day would ever arrive. It might be the first time in that child's life that he was more than five feet away from his mother."

"Ran's out of town, and Davy was being naughty, so he got banished to the south side of town — to 'Aunt' Oliole's. It will be fun. Georgia wanted to ask you if she could come up and help me — after she finishes her chores, of course."

"Marquesa?"

It was a young lady's voice calling down from the upstairs veranda.

But it was not Georgia's.

Nellie Mandara stood next to her sister, her long, dark hair pulled back and stacked neatly on top of her head.

Isabel scooted next to Oliole and took the baby from her arms. Resting the happy boy on her hip, she shaded her eyes and looked up at the veranda. "Marquesa," Nellie continued, "Georgia is spending too much time visiting with the hotel guests. She is way behind on her rooms. I'm having to do her work and mine as well."

"I am just being polite to paying customers, unlike some of the other workers," Georgia huffed.

"Girls! I need you both to get back to work immediately. We will all have to work hard to get things ready for tonight. Now go on." Isabel dismissed them with the wave of a rug beater. "And no dawdling, Miss Georgia Mandara."

"Yes, ma'am." Georgia's shoulders slumped as she and her older sister disappeared back into the hotel.

Isabel stared at the baby's wide brown eyes. "Next time, precious, you're going to have to come stay with 'Aunt' Isabel." She handed the infant back to Oliole and turned away as she wiped her eyes.

"Are you all right?" Oliole asked.

Isabel sighed and turned back. "I love Dawson's children dearly. But I wish — just for one moment — I could cuddle my own child. But some things are not meant to be." She wiped her eyes again and flashed the professional smile that could dazzle a crowd of a thousand theater-attenders. "Enough of this maudlin talk."

Grant Mandara sprinted up, wearing long trousers held up by suspenders over his cotton shirt. He ducked right between the women, hurriedly looking back over his shoulder.

"You're out of breath," the Marquesa observed.

He threw his arms around her waist and nodded his head. "Yeah, I've been chased by a Wolfe."

Oliole set the valise on the step of the hotel and bounced the baby on her hip. "Chased by a what?"

"By Jeremiah Wolfe. He wants his nickel back. But I think I lost him."

Oliole stared at the boy's mischievous face. *Is this Davy Parks seven years from now?* "Why does Jeremiah Wolfe want his nickel back?"

Grant pulled away from the Marquesa and looped his thumbs into his suspenders. "Because

176

he thinks I cheated him out of it."

The Marquesa brushed his thick bangs out of his eyes. "Did you?"

"Nope," he declared. "I shot the tin can out of the tree just like I bet him."

Oliole raised her thick blonde eyebrows. "Shot?"

Grant yanked a forked stick out of his back pocket. "With my slingshot."

The Marquesa tilted her head, arms folded. "You were betting?"

Grant's chin fell to his chest. "Just a nickel."

The Marquesa tapped his shoulder with the rug beater. "Your father told you not to bet anymore, young man."

"Not even a lousy nickel?"

"Of course not," the Marquesa lectured. "Now go give Jeremiah back his money."

"Do I have to?" he whined.

The Marquesa lifted up his chin until their eyes met. "Yes." Then she turned to Oliole. "Georgia can't go today. She'll have to stay and work. We really need her."

"Go where?" Grant inquired as he kept an eye on Main Street's foot traffic.

Oliole brushed a strand of blonde hair back over her ear and shifted the baby to her other hip. "Up to my house to help me baby-sit Davy. Would you like to come, Grant?"

His eyes lit up as if given a pardon by the governor. "Yes!"

The Marquesa reached out to Oliole's free

arm. "I don't think you want to try that."

Oliole's deep breath brought freshness to her mind. "Of course I do." *At this moment, Lord, I do believe I can do anything!*

"Oh boy, really?" Grant shouted.

"But you have to take the nickel back first," Oliole insisted.

"I do?" He shifted his weight from one foot to the other. "Okay, I'll be right back!" He took off running down the street.

Isabel Mandara stepped up beside her until their arms brushed. "Miss Fontenot, do you have any idea what you have just agreed to?"

"Of course I do . . . sort of." Oliole reached down and plucked up the valise. "It will be a grand adventure."

"Are you sure you're thirty?"

"Yes," Oliole chuckled, "why?"

"Because sometimes you act about sixteen."

"Is that good or bad?"

"That, my dear Miss Fontenot, is what I'm trying to figure out. Anyway, why don't we have lunch here at the hotel instead," the Marquesa offered.

"Oh, no, I have everything purchased already," Oliole insisted. "Carolina's going to try to get up there about 12:15. How does that sound for you?"

The Marquesa shook her head. The thick, wavy black hair flagged from side to side. "If you don't come running down the hill stark raving mad before that time, then I'll be there."

"Good. Davy's a little chunk. I think I'll start to my place before my arm wears out. Send Grant up when he gets back."

"You don't plan on doing any other work this morning, do you?" the Marquesa called out.

Oliole waited while a dark-skinned man and a dog herded a dozen sheep up Main Street. "I have one appointment this afternoon and another about dusk — that's all."

Oliole hiked across the street and turned the corner by the bakery and Chan's Laundry where the wooden sidewalk ended. Before she was halfway up the hill to her studio, which marked the upper limits of town, eight-year-old Grant Mandara caught up with her.

"Are we going to play some games?" he puffed, tugging at the valise in her hand.

She released it into his grasp. "Sure. What would you like to play?"

Grant looked up at her with penetrating brown eyes. "Do you have a faro layout?"

"Faro?" Oliole laughed as she thought of smoky saloons and oilcloth-covered tables. "Do you know how to 'buck the tiger'?"

His eyes widened to the size of silver dollars. "Yeah, but don't tell my papa."

"I won't tell him. But I don't have a faro layout. Let's see . . ." She hiked ahead of him, then stopped, and waited. "I have a Parcheesi game. Have you ever played that?"

He marched right past her, never slowing. "Nope." Grant carried the green valise in front

179

of him with both hands and made a game of bouncing it off his knees as he walked.

"I think you'll like it. It's quite popular in New York."

His eyes sparkled. "Do you play it for money?"

"I don't," she announced.

"Good, 'cause I'm broke." Grant raced to her front porch fifty feet away, then spun around, and ran back to her. "Wow, where'd you get the pig?"

"What pig?"

"There's a pig tied to your front porch. Over there. See him?"

Oliole stubbed the toe of her riding boot on a rock protruding in the path. She readjusted the infant on her hip. "What's he doing?"

"Nothing yet. But it could get messy if you leave him there too long."

She cautiously approached the porch, looking for intruders in her house. "He's not my pig."

"Then why's he tied on your porch?"

"I have no idea in the world." Oliole surveyed the mostly barren hillside around her place.

"What are you going to do with him?"

Why would anyone tie a pig to my porch? It this a joke? "Well, I'm sure he doesn't know how to play Parcheesi, so why don't you lead him out to the yard and tie him to the little juniper tree."

"Wow, it's like a miracle pig that just appeared out of the blue!" Grant exclaimed. "Maybe the Lord sent it."

"Eh, I don't think pigs just appear." Oliole

stood at the bottom of the porch stairs and looked at the muddy 200-pound hog. "What's that note over there?" She pointed to the post next to the animal.

"It's your note. It says, 'I'll be right back,' " Grant reported.

She shook her head. "It's not my note."

"It must be from the pig's owner."

"I suppose so."

"Do you want me to feed him?" Grant asked.

"He doesn't look hungry, and I have no intention of feeding someone else's pig."

As Grant led the porker to the juniper, Davy Parks began to cry. Oliole jiggled him on her hip. "It's all right, darling. You don't have to be scared of the piggie."

"He isn't scared, Miss Fontenot," Grant called back. "I think he wants to play with the pig."

"Play with it?" Suddenly a vision of Davy Parks and a pig rolling in the mud together while Carolina approached flashed through Oliole's mind. *She would die on the spot!*

"You know how little kids are with animals," Grant added.

Wisdom from the mouth of an eight-year-old? Oliole toted the whimpering yet smiling baby into the house. "Come on, little punkin', let's see what else Aunt Oliole has that you can play with." She shoved the door to her house/studio open and glanced around. Everything was just where she had left it. *Kaid would be mad because I didn't lock my door, but I refuse to let Samuel Black and friends frighten me out of my freedom.*

Grant Mandara tramped in behind her. "Boy, that's a big pig. I wonder what his name is?"

"Why don't you name him?" *I need to put up my photographs if I'm going to entertain two active boys.*

Grant tugged at the collar of his off-white shirt. "I was thinking of calling him George — after my sister."

"In that case, perhaps you shouldn't name him." Oliole smiled and shook her head. "Georgia might not appreciate having a hog named after her. Grant, grab that buffalo robe off the settee, and let's stretch it out on the front porch. Then why don't you sit down and play with Davy for a minute while I put up my photographs."

He gazed around at her studio/parlor. "What will we play with?"

"What did you like to play with when you were little?"

"I liked to play poker," Grant reported.

May the Lord be gracious to the Marquesa and the captain. This child is precocious beyond belief. "No poker, but take that bag of clothespins." She motioned toward the counter. "Perhaps you can build a fort or something."

Within a few moments David Cantrell Parks sat with a big smile in the middle of a ten-foot buffalo robe on the front porch, sucking on an unpainted wooden clothespin and watching Grant Mandara build "a genuine replica of Fort

Union." Both were under a bright Montana summer sun and the watchful eyes of a 200-pound hog.

While Oliole Fontenot sat cross-legged on the buffalo robe, Davy Parks slept on the folds of her long blue print skirt that draped her lap. Across from her, an intense Grant Mandara studied the Parcheesi board.

"I can't believe you beat me three games in a row," he moaned. "Did I happen to mention to you that I don't like to lose?"

Oliole raised her eyebrows. "Neither do I!"

"One more game?" Grant begged.

"Or until Davy wakes up." Oliole could feel her leg falling asleep beneath her. "I do believe it's about time we changed his diaper."

Grant's face reflected sheer panic. "What do you mean, we?"

"I'll tell you what." Oliole unfastened her pig-tails from the back of her head and let them drop to her back. "The loser of this game has to change his diaper."

Grant violently shook his head. "Not me! It's no bet."

"Why, Mr. Grant Mandara, here I thought you were a wagering man," Oliole teased.

He swallowed hard, his Adam's apple signaling his intense concern. "Not when the odds are stacked against me."

"Okay, one more game. Then I'll change him. After that, you play with him while I cook lunch for his mommy and the Marquesa."

Grant scooped up the wooden playing pieces from the circle in the center of the board. "How come you ladies have lunch together every week?" he asked.

"That way I can find out what you've been doing all week. The Marquesa gives us a full report."

His mouth dropped open. "Really?"

"Certainly."

"Well, eh . . ." He tugged on his suspenders as he searched for a word. "Maybe you and me should have lunch every week so I can tell you my side of the story."

Oliole reached over and tousled his thick, dark hair. "I'm joshing you, Grant Mandara. We mainly just talk about women stuff."

"What kind of stuff is women stuff?"

"Oh, things like dresses, recipes, children, church . . ." *Men, suffrage, health, theology, politics, and monthly depression.*

"Sounds boring." Grant peered around at the sleeping pig.

"Well, it's not. Your Marquesa and Carolina Parks are two very fascinating, widely traveled women for such a small town. They are delightful friends for me."

Grant glanced down the hill toward town. "I think that's Mr. Darrant, and he's headed this way."

A slightly bowlegged man with dark felt hat pulled low in front plodded up the footpath to her house. "I believe you're right."

Grant glanced down at the game and then back down the trail. "Maybe he wants to play Parcheesi with us."

"Perhaps so," Oliole mused. *Chances are he has no idea what's waiting for him.*

"When are you going to marry him?" Grant blurted out.

Oliole flinched, and the baby murmured, then dropped back off to sleep. "Marry him?"

"Georgia told us all about you dancing down that mountain with Mr. Darrant up at Roundup. Nellie said that was just like being engaged." Grant shot the words out with one breath and then gulped for air.

"Nellie said that?"

"Yeah, she knows all about that girl and boy stuff."

"I see," Oliole said.

"I bet Terry Lee Farquat ten cents that you'd marry Mr. Darrant before the fall gather. So if you are going to do it anyway, maybe you'd like to do it before the roundup begins."

"I can't promise you that." *Why did I let my hair down? I should have it pinned for gentlemen callers. . . . Of course, it is only Kaid.* "Please don't make any more bets."

Grant leaned toward her with a whisper that sounded more like a growl. "But you are going to get married, right?"

Oliole hurriedly tried to pin her hair back. "You sure are in a hurry to marry me off."

Both continued the conversation while staring

185

down the hill at the approaching man.

"And you sure are avoiding the subject."

"You are a very perceptive young lad."

"Yeah, and I can figure things out quick, too," Grant triumphed.

Kaid Darrant took long strides up the hill, his tan canvas ducking trousers still showing a crease of newness. His collarless, long-sleeved off-white cotton shirt was buttoned at the neck. His suspenders were as old as his boots. Even with the wide-brimmed felt hat pulled low in front, Oliole could see the square jaw and the half smile that was a permanent fixture. The silver rowels on his spurs announced his approach.

"Miss Fontenot," he called out as he approached, "looks like you all are havin' a party."

"Yes, we are, Kaid. Would you care to join us?"

He surveyed the yard as he stepped up to the bottom of the porch. "Did you invite the hog for lunch, or is he lunch?"

"We don't know," Oliole replied. "Is he a friend of yours?" She remained seated on the buffalo rug.

Kaid stared out at the hog, now lying on its side in the shade of the juniper. "I can't say that I know him, but his face looks familiar. Did he ever serve with Col. Wastoon in the Dakotas?"

A wide smile crept across Oliole's face. "I'll ask him when he wakes up." *Mr. Darrant, you are the easiest man I've ever talked to in my life . . . and that includes my father. Especially my father.*

"He's just a pig," Grant insisted.

"That's what they said about Col. Wastoon," Kaid laughed. It was a deep, effortless laugh. He pulled off his hat as he stepped up on the porch.

Oliole found herself staring at his mouth. *It's what I call a Western laugh. They don't laugh out here unless they mean it.*

"Never thought I'd see young Davy so far from his mama," Kaid announced.

Oliole felt like hugging the baby but didn't want to wake him. "Amazing, isn't it?"

"You look mighty fine with a baby in your lap, Miss Oliole."

Just exactly what did you mean by that, Mr. Kaid Darrant? "Thank you kindly. He's an easy baby to take care of. All he wants to do is eat and play and sleep."

"Me, too," Grant put in.

"Did you come up here for a reason, Kaid? Or did you hear there was a hot Parcheesi game and wondered if you could sit in?" *I should have used some of that perfume like Carolina's. Something stronger than dirty diaper.*

"I was thinking about a little visit, but I wasn't expecting quite this reception. Maybe I should call later."

"You're welcome to stay, cowboy."

"In that case, I reckon a Parcheesi game would be just fine."

"Good. I'm glad. Would you hold Davy for a minute?" She lifted the sleeping baby toward the standing man.

The leather-tough face paled instantly. "Me?"

"You do know how to hold a baby, don't you?"

"Well, I, eh, don't think . . . I mean, what if I . . . I've never had any kids of my own," he stammered.

"Nor have I," she shot back. Davy woke and squirmed in her extended arms.

"Anybody can do it," Grant insisted.

"Just cradle him in your arms like you do a sick newborn calf you're trying to get back to the barn out of the cold," Oliole instructed.

Kaid shoved his hat to the back of his head. "Oh. That's all?"

"I think that will work," she said.

Darrant took the baby, holding him like a sack of barley in front of him. Oliole stood up and brushed her dress down. "See, I knew you could do it."

"Eh, well . . ." Kaid swallowed hard and tried to hand the baby back to Oliole. "It's the first time I've ever done this."

Oliole plunked her hands on her hips. "You look real good with a baby in your arms, Mr. Darrant."

"What exactly do you mean by that?" Kaid demanded. He held the now kicking Davy Parks straight out in front of him.

"I suppose the same thing you meant." She reached out and took the baby and rested him gently on her hip.

"Oh, brother," Grant moaned. "If you two are going to start talking all that boy and girl stuff,

I'm going out to visit with George."

Kaid peeked in through the open door of the front room. "George?"

Oliole pointed out toward the juniper tree. "The pig."

Kaid gently punched Grant's shoulder. "Stay here. We aren't going to talk about boy and girl stuff."

Oliole raised her blonde eyebrows. "We aren't? Well, in that case I might as well go change a diaper and cook. I've got the ladies' club coming for lunch."

"I thought we were going to play another game of Parcheesi," Grant insisted.

"Perhaps Mr. Darrant will play with you. Either that or he can change the diaper and cook lunch for the ladies."

Kaid stared down at the game on the buffalo robe. "Eh, I'll play Parcheesi," he offered.

"Would you like to hold Davy while you play?" she asked.

Kaid just stared at her.

"I was teasing, Mr. Darrant."

"He knew that," Grant asserted. "Didn't you, Mr. Darrant?"

Davy Parks teetered and toddled from the bed to the table and back to the bed, dragging a string with six clothespins fastened at one end.

Oliole fussed over the cookstove oven that was seldom used. *Why didn't you just meet at a cafe, Miss Fontenot? Why did you have to say you wanted to cook? It's not your best feature. What is my best feature?*

I take good photographs.

No. I take great photographs.

And . . . perhaps singing on the front porch when no one can hear me might be one of my better features.

Oh, and dancing down mountainsides when there is no orchestra. I'm quite good at that, too. Provided there's a handsome man holding my waist.

Cooking?

It's behind sewing.

So why did you agree to cook lunch for the ladies?

Pride.

"Come on, Davy darlin', let's go see Uncle Kaid."

He reached up and clutched her finger and then waddled his way by her side out into the parlor and to the open front door.

Kaid Darrant sprawled across the buffalo rug in front of the Parcheesi board. Grant Mandara sat cross-legged next to him. "How's the game going?" she asked.

"Great!" Grant exploded, rolling the dice across the board. "Mr. Darrant taught me how to play Sergeant's Bend."

"What kind of game is that?" She glanced down at a pile of small pebbles in front of the boy.

"Look, Miss Fontenot, I won again!" he shouted. "Mr. Darrant said they play it a lot in the Deadwood saloons."

"Mr. Darrant, what are you teaching him?"

"We got tired of hoppin' those wooden pegs around in circles," Darrant explained. "It was either this or go out and practice roping a hog. So how's the cook and her helper?"

"I believe we almost have everything fixed. The scalloped potatoes are still in the oven."

Darrant laid back on the buffalo rug and stretched his arms. "Perhaps I could call on you later this evening."

She glanced at Grant, wrinkled her nose, and then looked back at Kaid. "Did you want to talk to me about that girl and boy stuff?"

Darrant stared north, over the top of town and out toward the Yellowstone River. "Yep, I reckon I did."

"Good," she said.

"Oh, brother! You two are beginning to sound like Papa and the Marquesa."

"That's bad?" Kaid said.

Grant rolled the dice again. "It sure isn't as much fun as playing Sergeant's Bend."

Kaid sat up and pointed down the dirt trail to Main Street at three men on horseback. "Looks like you have company." He swung his legs around, dropping them off the front of the porch. His right hand dropped to his holstered revolver. With his left hand he shoved his hat back on.

Oliole snatched up the baby and positioned him on her narrow hip. "Can you tell who they are?"

"It isn't Sam Black and that gang. Just looks like some goldfield miners." Kaid scratched the back of his neck and let his hand slip off the pistol grip.

"You visit with them," Oliole urged. She set Davy down on the rug. "I need to check on the potatoes. Grant, you watch the baby, but don't take that string away from him. He'll pitch a fit."

With the front door wide open, as well as the canvas curtain separating the back room from the parlor, she heard the men ride into the yard.

"Howdy, mister," a voice raised in the deep south drawled.

"Howdy," Kaid replied. "You boys headin' for the diggin's, or are you coming from them?"

"Both," a deep voice boomed. "We been there, and we're goin' back."

Kaid continued to question. "Have any luck?"

"Jist enough to buy supplies and keep diggin'," the first man replied.

"But not enough to pack up and quit," a third man added. "You surely got a cute baby there, mister."

I wonder what kind of expression is on Mr. Kaid Darrant's face now? Oliole smiled.

"Thanks. He looks a lot like his mama, of course."

Oliole tried to peek out to the front yard but couldn't see anything. *Is he going to tell them some big windy story?*

"You ain't the photographer, are ya? We wanted to git our picture taken. We heard there was a purdy photographer lady."

"Yep, she's handsome all right. But merely saying she's purdy might be a few miles short of the trail. She's in the back room trying to get the twin babies to sleep. I'll go fetch her."

"Twins! You got one that age and twins?"

"And then there's Grant here, our eldest."

Kaid Darrant, why are you stringing them on? You're a scoundrel!

"You've been a busy man."

I think I'd better put an end to this. She marched out to the porch and folded her arms across her apron.

All three men stared at her and then tipped their hats. "You're right, mister, that baby surely does favor his mama. But he's got your hair."

Oliole looked over their varying degrees of grubbiness. "Don't believe everything this drifting drover tells you, boys. He has a tendency to let the truth wander off and get lost in the brush. Now did I hear you say you wanted a photograph?"

"Yes, ma'am," the one with the thinnest face and the thickest beard replied. "We wanted to send something back home. But we ain't rich men. How much would it cost?"

Oliole noticed that her braids were hanging down the front of her apron. She brushed them to her back. "You want three photographs or one?"

"Three if we can afford it," the southerner replied.

193

"It will be one dollar for a set-up fee and one dollar for each photograph." *I could stair-step them down the hill with the bay horse toward town and the dun closest to the camera.*

"That's four cash dollars," Grant reported.

"Sounds fair enough. You willin' to take it in trade?"

"What do you want to give me?" *Perhaps they want portraits. But they're too gamey to get close to the camera.*

The man pointed to the sleeping pig. "Half of that hog."

"That's your hog?" *It might be fun to take a photograph of them with the pig.*

"We left him here to show our good intentions. You wasn't home at the time."

"Yeah. Then we went downtown lookin' for ya," the man from the south replied.

"But you weren't in any of them saloons," the one with the crooked nose laughed.

She turned to Darrant. "What's a hog like that worth, Kaid?"

"About ten to twelve dollars," Grant piped up.

"I reckon the boy's right," Darrant agreed.

"The Chinaman at the laundry is takin' the other half. He said he'd butcher it for you if we'd give him the hide, head, and feet. What do you think?"

Oliole stared at the three dirty men on broken-down horses. *I suppose it's all right, provided the pig isn't stolen. I wonder what my friends in New*

York would think of this? *"How did you do today, Miss Fontenot?" "Not bad. I made half a hog . . . and you?"* "Okay, but here's what I want. Let Mr. Chan at the laundry have the entire hog, and have him give me four dollars worth of credit off my cleaning bill. How does that sound?"

"I reckon he'll go for that."

"Can we take that picture right now? We want to get back to the diggin's."

"Yes, but the photographs won't be ready until tomorrow morning," Oliole said.

"Kin we jist pick them up when we come to town next?"

"Certainly. When will that be?" *Lord, this isn't very glamorous work, but it's four honest dollars.*

"Our order will be in at the Mercantile next week. One of us will have to come back then."

"Okay, boys, the photographs will be here waiting for you. Do you want to be on the horses or on foot? I suggest on the horses. It gives more of a rugged-frontiersman look."

"I ain't never thought about being on horseback. That would make a mighty fine picture," the main spokesman replied.

"Good." Oliole waved her hands as she gave instructions. "I'll set my camera up here on the porch. You boys can stay right in the saddles. That way I'll be high enough to get a good angle on your faces and still have downtown Cantrell in the background."

"You don't suppose our kin will think we look like drovers, do you?" the one with the southern

195

accent pondered. "We surely don't want to look like no drovers!"

"No chance of that," Kaid jibed. Then he turned to Oliole. "What can I do to help you, dearest?"

"Well, darlin' . . ." She dragged out the word so long that a smile cracked across his leather-tough face. "Grant can watch little Davy. Why don't you go in the back room and check on the twins while I take these boys' photographs."

"The twins?" he mumbled.

She stepped up close enough to brush against his arm. "You started this," she whispered. "Go check my stove and make sure my potatoes aren't burning."

Kaid sighed, shook his head, and meandered into the back room.

Within ten minutes she had her camera set and glass plates ready. She positioned the three men together with their horses in the center of the yard. After setting the lens, she stepped out from under the black canvas and surveyed the scene.

Kaid appeared at the doorway between the porch and parlor. "The twins are sleeping like newborn foals in tall grass in late May," he reported.

Grant played on the steps of the porch, trying to balance dice on his nose. Davy Parks sprawled on the buffalo robe, chewing on a corner of the Parcheesi board. Three men, hair slicked back by six months of campfire smoke and bacon grease, held their hats in their hands. They tried to keep bored horses from fidgeting. And one about-to-be-chow-mein hog basked in the noontime sun.

In the background, Oliole spotted two well-dressed women strolling up the trail.

"Here come my luncheon guests. So, boys, try to hold those mounts still until I count to thirty. Are you ready?"

"Yes, ma'am — let 'er rip!"

After a delightful luncheon of fried summer squash, bacon, scalloped potatoes, and honey-baked custard with Carolina, the Marquesa, and a sleeping Davy Parks, Oliole washed her dishes and straightened up the studio. She waited for a 3:00 P.M. appointment that didn't show up, then loaded her camera and supplies into a borrowed wagon driven by Kaid Darrant, and rode three blocks down the hill to Second Street.

There were only one or two first-class saloons in Cantrell. The Imperial was one. Maybe the Drover's Den could be considered another. But the Aces & Eights, while one of Cantrell's oldest, was also one of the wildest and dirtiest.

Everyone who carried a sneak gun or wanted a fight or had a wheel or two missing from his cerebral wagon ended up at the Aces & Eights. Most came in from the diggings with gold in their pokes. Very few left with the same. Like circling buzzards, gamblers seemed drawn to the unpainted single-walled wood-frame building with bullet-riddled ceiling and bloodstained floor.

The resident captain of the professional gamblers at the Aces & Eights was Conrad Bishop. With three tens, he won the saloon on a hand of five-card draw the day he rode into town. But he refused to stake a claim to more than the eight-foot circular table in the back of the narrow building. From his chair in the corner he could see everyone in the room.

One ivory-handled Colt .45 lay on the table at all times. Another was tucked into a custom vest holster that allowed him to draw without standing. There were all sorts of stories about what he carried in his boots, but no one knew for sure since the two ivory-handled revolvers had settled every dispute.

Bishop's neatly trimmed gray-speckled black beard and tailored St. Louis suit would make him look like a banker in some other environment. His clean, neat appearance, clear blue eyes, and proper use of English made him stand out like a sheep in a wolves' den in the Second Street saloon. But the minute he touched his hands to a deck of cards, anyone sober knew he was not the one who would be fleeced.

Of course, very few in the Aces & Eights were sober.

"Are you sure you want to do this?" Kaid asked Oliole as he parked the rig at the side of the saloon and swung down to the packed dirt alley. "This isn't exactly a place for a lady."

"I've been in saloons before, Mr. Darrant."

She climbed out of the wagon.

He tied a rawhide lead rope to a post planted in the ground next to the edge of the boardwalk. "But this one's nastier than most."

She pulled a brown leather case out of the wagon. "And just how do you know that?"

Kaid strolled to the back of the wagon and hefted the camera to his shoulder. "I had to check them all out just to make sure I knew which ones to avoid."

"I appreciate your appraisal, but I cannot afford to turn down a twenty-dollar portrait."

"Never?" Kaid prodded.

She brushed down the front of her dress. "I told Mr. Bishop that I would not photograph sin. He assured me there would be nothing sinful about the pose. In order to take the photographs I want, I need to photograph many that are . . . well, less than inspiring. It's a job. I don't agree with their chosen profession any more than Carolina does, but she sells them shoes and boots nonetheless."

Kaid whistled. "Whoa! You convinced me! Or is it me you're tryin' to convince?"

"Both of us, I suppose. Well . . . here goes." Oliole sucked in a deep breath.

She swept into the dimly lit saloon amid shouts, curses, and arguments. But the cacophony seemed to die gradually with each step she took toward the corner table. There was total silence by the time she reached it.

The well-dressed man with his back to the wall

stood and removed his broad black hat. "Miss Fontenot, thank you for coming." Then he turned to the rest of the patrons who seemed in varying degrees of cleanliness and sobriety, sitting in stunned silence. "Boys, this is the photographer lady. Give her plenty of room to set up because the 'Prince of Second Street' is going to get his picture taken right here, right now."

"Is this the pose you want?" She motioned to the table.

"Yes." His easy smile concealed any real intent. "I want a photograph of me in my office."

At the word *office* the saloon patrons began to laugh.

Bishop stretched his arms out at both sides. "And I want the ladies at my side."

"What ladies?" Oliole glanced around at the smoky crowd of men.

The gambler waved his arm toward the long, rough pine bar. "Stella and Nancy Belle, come here!"

Oliole turned to see a red-haired woman, followed by one with short curly black hair, saunter through a thicket of men to the table. Both blurry-eyed, the women wore bright red lipstick and short-sleeved dresses with necklines scooped far below any sense of propriety.

"They promised they wouldn't sin," Bishop explained.

"We did?" the red-haired one protested.

"At least, not while the picture is being taken," he added.

The crowd roared.

"That's fine," Oliole commented. "You sit in the chair, but they have to stand straight up behind you. If they lean over the table, it would definitely be a sin."

Again hoots and hollers filled the crowded room.

Oliole turned to the saloon crowd gathered behind her like an audience at a fight. "I need two of you boys to go with Kaid and bring the rest of my equipment."

A dozen men volunteered. By the time Oliole had the gear set up, all activity in the saloon had ceased, and everyone huddled around to watch the proceedings.

Toothy smiles sparkled.

Flash powder exploded.

Smoke billowed.

There were shouts and applause.

"Now can we sin?" the one called Stella blustered.

The crowd roared and then filtered back to the bar and poker games, fights, lies, and the normal course of intoxicated activities. Oliole walked over to the table where the women still stood behind Conrad Bishop.

"Can we have one of them photographs, too?" Nancy Belle requested. She stood several inches shorter than Oliole and a good twenty-five pounds heavier.

"I'll tell you what, gals," Oliole suggested. "Why don't you come up to my studio sometime, and I'll take your photograph for free."

"Why would you do that?" Bishop shuffled the cards without taking his hands off the table.

Oliole ignored the gambler and looked straight into Stella's tired eyes. "I'm putting together a collection of women who live and work in the West. I'd like to include you two."

Bishop reached into the deck, pulled out a card, and turned it faceup on the table. It was the ace of spades. "You're photographing soiled doves?"

Oliole looked at the one with the short black hair. "I'm photographing women."

"I'd like that," Nancy Belle replied.

"Me, too," Stella nodded.

Oliole glanced down at the cards that were now spread out facedown in front of Bishop. "How about tomorrow?" She tapped her finger on the third card from the bottom. "I'd like to take the picture about three o'clock when the sun is bright enough to give us an outdoor scene." Bishop turned over the card she pointed to. "Maybe you'd like to come up for tea as well." The card was the queen of hearts.

"Tea? Are you joshin' with us?" Stella chuckled. "You want us for tea?"

Bishop gave Oliole a steely glance, then shook his head and picked up the deck. "Remind me never to play poker with you," he mumbled.

Oliole turned to the women. "I didn't mean to insult you."

"Insult us!" Nancy Belle exclaimed. "Nobody's ever asked us for tea."

"Especially a lady. A beautiful society lady," Stella added.

Society woman? Cantrell has society women? "Well, I don't know anything about beautiful or society . . . but we live and work in the same town, so I believe we can share some tea."

"We'll be there," Nancy Belle assured her.

"Good." Oliole looked at the gambler. "Mr. Bishop, your photograph will be ready by noon tomorrow. I'd better go take care of that negative. And remind me never to play poker . . . with anyone."

"Just send my photograph back with the ladies after they finish their tea," he hooted. "Say, did you ever work on a riverboat?"

"No," she replied and then strutted out of the saloon.

The house was lantern-lit when Oliole stared at the images in the albumen photograph. A mysterious gambler with hat pulled low across his eyes, framed by two pale, slightly puffy women who wore courageous smiles but whose eyes told stories of worn-out dreams and crushed spirits.

She recognized the ring of spurs jingling in her yard and looked up to see Kaid Darrant at the door. She motioned him to come in.

"How's your saloon picture?" he asked as he entered the parlor.

"I'm happy with it. It's not exactly a Napoleon Sarony, but —"

"Who?"

"He's New York's leading theatrical photographer."

"A friend of yours?"

"Not really. But I met him once. He even looked at several of my photographs," she reported.

"Did he like them?"

"I don't know."

"What did he say?"

"That I obviously had a lot of hidden talent."

"What did he mean, 'hidden talent'?" Kaid probed.

"That's what I've been pondering the last five years. Anyway, I do like this one. It turned out fine. I was afraid it would be too dark, but it came out. Of course, we left the saloon full of black powder smoke."

He continued to stand in the doorway. "I'm sure that's not the first time."

"Come over here." She motioned him closer. "What do you think?"

Kaid sauntered over and examined the photograph. She slipped her arm into his. "Give me your opinion."

"I think you're terrific."

"Thank you."

"And an excellent photographer, too."

She squeezed his arm. "Have I ever told you that you are an unashamed flatterer?"

"Many times. Do you want me to stop?"

"Never!" she laughed. Then she stared down at the photograph. "I hope Mr. Bishop likes it.

Personally, I think the girls' eyes steal the scene."

"Rather empty and haunting, aren't they?" Kaid's freshly shaven face and neatly trimmed mustache smelled of tonic water.

"Kaid, that life is such a trap. How can they ever get out? Sin is such a destructive habit. There's no pulling away. In the battle for souls, they are the prisoners of war."

"I reckon they have to want something different."

"I don't think they've taken time in years to even consider what they want. Every day is just a few drinks, a little morphine . . . and men."

"Do you think you can change them? Is that why you invited them to tea?"

She thought he was going to pull his arm away.

He didn't.

"No, I don't think I can change them. Only God can do that. But I can treat them better than they deserve. How can they understand God's love if no one shows them what it's like?"

He gently squeezed her arm. "Oliole Fontenot, you are one optimistic lady."

She let out a deep sigh. "There's got to be more to my life than just taking photographs."

He slipped his arm around her waist. "Now that's what I've been thinkin' myself."

Oliole spun slowly out of his grasp. "You've been thinking about what?" she teased.

He pulled off his wide-brimmed beaver felt

205

hat. "Actually I've been thinkin' about our life together."

"Oh? What have you decided?"

"I like it."

She fingered her braids securely fastened on the back of her head. "I like it, too, Kaid." Oliole swallowed hard and felt her heart beat in her throat. "And I especially like the fact that we're going out to supper. Let me get my hat."

"I take it that arm around your waist was a little too close for comfort?"

"Just the opposite. It was much too comfortable."

"You don't like getting too close to a man?"

"I don't know. I've never been 'too close' to a man."

"You're a very difficult gal to figure out, Miss Oliole Fontenot."

Oliole paused in the doorway to the back room. "I've lived with me for thirty years, and I still don't have me figured out."

"Well, that gives us something to talk about at supper. Grab your hat, Oliole. Let's stroll down to Quincys' Cafe and make ever' unmarried man in town jealous."

"You do know how to fawn over a girl, don't you?"

"Probably, but that was no exaggeration. When you walk down the street, every single man turns his head to watch you. And some of the married ones, too."

"That's because there are ten men in town for

every woman," Oliole said.

"I reckon it would be the same no matter what the numbers."

"Well, that's only because I have a reputation for strange behavior. They're just gawking to see what I'll do next."

Kaid laughed and jammed his hat back on his head. "There might be just a little truth in that, Miss Fontenot."

Quincys' Cafe was one of the oldest businesses in Cantrell, in existence for a little over eighteen months. In that time thousands upon thousands of hot, tasty, simple meals had been served by the large family of Drake Quincy.

Rough-cut wooden tables crowded the big room, chairs and benches so close together that the servers struggled to negotiate the floor space. When the room was filled, it seemed extremely crowded. When only a few diners were present, it was like floating on a raft in a sea of empty chairs.

By the time Kaid and Oliole made it down to Main Street, discussed hog prices with Mr. Chan at the laundry, listened to the latest news about Sam Black and his gang from Marshal Parks, visited with Mr. Ostine in front of the bank, and looked over the latest shipment of dried California fruit in front of the grocery store, they entered an almost deserted cafe. Supper hour was over.

"Molly Mae, are we too late for a meal?" Oliole

called out to the sixteen-year-old blonde clearing a table.

The young lady's voice danced across the room. "Oh, no, Miss Fontenot . . . provided you sit over in the corner at that clean table and want pork and cabbage. It's all we have left."

"Sounds fine. Are you sure we won't get in your way?" Oliole hesitated just inside the doorway.

"Miss Fontenot," Molly Mae scolded, "you know Mama and Daddy would feed you if you knocked at the door in the middle of the night."

Kaid led her to the corner round table large enough for eight people. "You have a lot of friends in this town." He grinned as he held a wooden chair out for her.

"I love it. Everyone allows you to go about your own business, but if you need anything, everyone's willing to help. I lived in New York City for ten years and never made as many friends as I made in Cantrell in a month." She sat down and scooted the squeaking chair closer to the table. "There are so few people out here, it develops an urgency in relationships. Everything is speeded up. Does that make sense?"

"Yep." He plopped down on her right with the wall at his back and leaned forward. "That's why I want to talk to you."

"About what?"

"About you and me. About a friendship developing fast. And urgency."

Oliole found it difficult to look him in the eyes.

Mr. Darrant, just what specifically are you urgent for?

"Miss Fontenot!" Molly Mae Quincy shouted from across the cafe.

Oliole found relief from Kaid's stare. "Yes?"

"Daddy said he has one more order of brick-oven-baked oriental spiced salmon and eggplant. Do you want that?"

Oliole glanced over at Kaid. His eyes were relaxed, almost laughing. "You take it," he urged. "I'm not much for fancy food. I'm going to stick with the pork and cabbage."

"Yes, salmon would be nice," Oliole called out as Kaid leaned back in the chair, his hands behind his neck.

"Now, Miss Fontenot, are you brave enough to resume our conversation about you and me?"

"I believe the subject was you, me, and urgency. It's that last topic that challenges me," she said.

He pushed his hat back and rubbed his square chin. "Oliole, you are without doubt the most magnetic woman I've ever met."

She massaged her hands as if rubbing in unseen cold cream. "I think that's a compliment."

He brushed the sleeve of his shirt as if something were on it and then tapped his fingers on the table. "The more I'm around you, the more I want to be around you. And the more difficult it becomes not to be around you. Does that make sense?"

"I believe so. You are certainly the most comfortable man I've ever known."

"Comfortable?" His easy smile reflected puzzlement.

"Easy to talk to. So peaceful to be around. You don't demand things from me." When she realized she was fiddling with the top button on her blouse, she put both hands in her lap. "I never feel like you're judging me. I treasure our friendship, Kaid. What I mean to say . . . now I'm the one stumbling around."

"Hello, Miss Fontenot! Howdy, Kaid! Surely is a lovely evenin', isn't it?" July Johnson waded through the empty chairs and tables toward them.

"Yes, it is, July," Oliole responded as she watched the sixteen-year-old pull back a chair and straddle it next to their table.

"Kaid, have you decided to take Milo Harrison up on that offer of his?" July quizzed.

Oliole peered into Darrant's blue eyes. "Offer?"

July leaned his narrow chin on the back of the chair facing the table. "You ain't told her yet?"

"We were just beginning to talk about it when you came in." Kaid unbuttoned the sleeves of his shirt and began to roll them up. "I haven't decided what to do."

July looked straight at Oliole. "Well, if you ask me, I say it's a chance of a lifetime. A man cain't turn it down."

Oliole glanced from July to Kaid, who now rolled his shirt sleeves back down and rebuttoned them. "Now I'm getting really intrigued," Oliole said slowly.

"Well, see," July began, "Mr. Harrison brought a herd up from Texas and —"

"July!" Molly Mae called out across the room. "Did you come in here to see me or to pester our customers?"

"Pester?" Wide, innocent brown eyes stared back at Oliole. "Was I a badgerin' you two?"

Oliole leaned forward and whispered, "Of course not, but I think Molly Mae wants your attention all for herself. That's her way of asking you to abandon us."

"Oh . . . yeah." He jumped to his feet almost knocking over the chair. He leaned over the table and whispered back, "Sometimes I ain't too good at this stuff, but I'm a quick learner."

And a willing one, no doubt. Oliole watched him retreat across the room to the young blonde server.

"Remind me to thank Molly Mae for rescuing us," Oliole said.

"Do you think she did that with us in mind?"

"Of course not. Now what is this big proposition with Texas cattle? Does it have anything to do with our 'urgent' relationship?"

Kaid sat up straight and leaned his elbows on the off-white oil cloth. "Yep. That's where this train is headed."

"Is the track straight, or does it wander all over the mountain?" she challenged.

"It meanders a bit," he explained. "But I need

to ask you a couple of things to help me cipher it out."

"Oh?"

"Tell me about the future of Miss Oliole Fontenot."

"The future?"

"Yes."

"Well, next week I go to Deadwood and perhaps down to Cheyenne or even Denver . . . to finish my series."

"And after that?" He never took his eyes off her face.

"I'll keep busy photographing prospectors, drovers, bummers, babies, families, weddings — things like that. Is that what you mean?"

Kaid cleared his throat and sat up. "What I want to know is, do you plan on living in Cantrell forever?"

"I plan on living in heaven forever," she said.

"You know what I meant."

"No one in this town knows if Cantrell will last forever. But as long as I can pay my way, be surrounded by good friends, and occasionally be involved in an artistic project or two, I do feel fairly settled. Now, Mr. Kaid Darrant, why the inquisition? What does this have to do with some Texican by the name of Harrison?"

"It looks like our supper is ready." Darrant pointed across the room. Molly Mae swirled through the empty tables, balancing a giant loaded platter. July Johnson trailed behind her like a pup.

"You will be eating alone, Kaid Darrant, if you think you're going to postpone this conversation. Is that quite clear?"

"Yes, ma'am. I have no intention of eating alone. Not tonight anyway."

"Good."

"Good, what?" Molly Mae asked as she slid steaming plates of food onto the big table.

"We were just saying how we were looking forward to eating supper," Kaid tried to explain.

"Yes, a quiet, peaceful supper," Oliole mused.

"Cantrell never was peaceful in the old days," July Johnson piped up.

"Old days?" Kaid smiled. "I thought the town was just founded two years ago."

"Yep, them was the old days. Why, one time me, Miss Carolina, Ranahan, and the Marquesa stopped none other than Cigar Dubois and his gang. Shoot, we had to stop them twice." July Johnson pulled up a chair and plopped down. Again. "Did I ever tell you about that?"

Before either Oliole or Kaid could say a word, a shout came from the door. "Miss Fontenot! Miss Fontenot! Come quick!"

Oliole scooted her chair around. Grant Mandara dodged empty chairs and trotted across the cafe.

"What's the matter, Grant?"

The young boy's round face reflected perfectly his every emotion. "Eh . . . it's an emergency. Sort of."

213

"What do you mean, sort of?" Oliole took his hand.

Grant scooted up close and whispered, "Georgia needs to talk to you."

Oliole surveyed the room. "Where is she?"

Grant's eyes dropped to his shoes. "Outside on the sidewalk."

"Why doesn't she come inside?" Oliole inquired.

He nodded his head toward Molly Mae.

Oliole glanced up at the young girl who stood behind July. "Oh, yes, well . . ."

"Listen." Kaid put his friendly arm on her shoulder. "If you need to go, I'll put your supper in a basket and tote it up to your house when I'm finished."

Oliole spun back toward him. "I do not intend to leave, Mr. Darrant. We are going to complete this conversation."

Darrant rubbed his chin. "Eh, yes, ma'am."

"Grant, tell Georgia I'm waltzing down the hill and can't possibly stop until I get to the river."

"You're doin' what?" Grant blurted out.

"She'll understand."

"Well, it's just that," Grant murmured, "if you don't, I'll have to . . ."

"You'll have to what?"

"We're going to practice our play that Georgia wrote. Saturday is the first performance. But Nellie came down with laryngitis and can't read her lines. And you always said that if there ever was an emergency, you would help out."

"I'm so sorry, Grant. Mr. Darrant and I have some important things to discuss. I just can't leave."

His chin dropped to his chest. "She said if you can't do Nellie's part, I'd have to wear a dress and do it myself."

"Really?" July gasped. "She'd make her own brother do that?"

"Why don't you have Molly Mae read the lines?" Oliole suggested.

"Oh, I don't . . . I don't reckon Georgia would . . ."

"Molly Mae, what do you think?" Oliole prodded. "Could you help out the Mandaras and read a part for them?"

"Me? On stage at the theater?" Molly Mae bubbled.

"But I don't think . . . oh, brother!" Grant moaned.

Molly Mae tugged off her apron and draped it across an empty chair. "I'd love to!"

"Can I come watch?" July asked.

"By all means," Oliole replied. "Perhaps they have a part for you."

"Really? That would be swell. Say, it ain't one of them English plays where ever'one talks funny, is it? I cain't talk funny."

"Georgia wrote the play," Grant informed them.

July jumped to his feet. "Sorry, I'll have to tell you that story later. Think I'll mosey over and watch the play practice."

"Not without me, you aren't," Molly Mae huffed. "I have lines to read."

Kaid and Oliole watched the trio parade out the front of the cafe. Then Kaid dug a fork into the steaming cabbage on his plate. "I suppose we ought to eat supper before it gets cold."

"Don't even think of eating, Kaid Darrant, until you tell me the story of Harrison from Texas!" she barked.

"Well, here goes." He plunked the fork down on his enameled tin plate. "Harrison is a friend of Ran Parks. They worked cattle together over in Oregon and a time or two out on the plains. Harrison has made a lot of money pushing cattle up from south Texas to the railroad in Kansas. But that trade is slowin' down now that they are building more lines. You know what I mean?"

"Mr. Darrant, is this conversation going anywhere?"

"Yes, ma'am. Now here's the deal. . . . Harrison believes the next real cattle boom will be up across the border in Canada. The Canadian Pacific Railroad is supposed to reach Ft. Calgary this year. Maybe it already has. Harrison believes there will be lots of people moving in, and they will all want to eat beefsteak. He leased some rangeland just north of Ft. Macleod, and now he's wantin' to hire —"

"Men to drive them north? Is that what this is all about? Are you merely trying to tell me you'll be gone on a cattle drive for a few weeks?"

"It's a little more complicated than that. Harrison is looking for a foreman to move up there and run the ranch. He asked the marshal, but Ran turned him down and recommended me."

"Oh, my!" Oliole raised her left hand to her mouth. "You're going to move to Alberta?"

"I didn't say that. I just said that Ranahan recommended me for the job. Harrison will be comin' through town in a week or two, and we'll sit down and see if it might work out. The promise of working for shares means I could build up a herd on my own. That part's mighty attractive. It's about the only way a man like me could get his own place now that this land is filling up."

She reached over and laid her hand on top of Kaid's. "If he makes you that kind of offer, you'll have to accept it, won't you?"

"Now, dadgumit, Oliole . . . just let me spit this out, or we're never goin' to have our supper. What I'm trying to say is, well . . . it's an opportunity for me to run a big outfit and build up a herd for myself on the side. That's been a dream of mine for as long as I can remember. But Alberta is even more lonely than Montana, if you catch my drift. It's still isolated and wild even with some folks movin' in. I don't really look forward to sittin' in some big old log house by myself night after night." He cleared his throat and took a deep breath. "So I was wonderin' . . . if you'd consider . . . you know . . . movin' up there with me."

"What?" she choked.

"Well, what I mean is . . ." He wiped the sweat off his forehead. "After we get married, of course."

Six

"Miss Fontenot! Miss Fontenot! I just heard the news. I can't believe everyone else knows!" Georgia Mandara clenched her yellow dress up to her knees as she sprinted up the hill. Her long white stockings flashed in the Montana sun.

Oliole sipped tea on the front porch, the sleeves of her brown cotton dress still pushed up above her elbows. She gazed across the stretch of mountainside that separated her from Miss Mandara. *One problem with this land is that there is not enough rain to grow a grass yard. I could do with a summer squall to settle the dust.* "Everyone knows what?" she called to the approaching fourteen-year-old.

Georgia raced to the edge of the yard and then stopped and put her hands on her hips, trying to catch her breath. Her chin sagged, but as always her small round nose kept its upward turn. "That you're going to marry Kaid Darrant — that's what!" she puffed.

Oliole set the flower-print china teacup beside her on the bench and stood. "Just who is saying I'm marrying Kaid?"

"Everybody!" Georgia waltzed to the porch.

"Who is everybody?" Oliole folded her arms across her stomach. "Did Kaid say that?"

Georgia strolled up the porch steps with an air of adolescent regality. "Eh, no. I haven't seen him. Nellie told me he rode down to Wyoming or somewhere to talk to that Texas cattleman."

Oliole plucked up her teacup and settled back on the bench, motioning for Georgia to join her. "So where exactly did you get this information?"

The young girl plopped down. "I heard it from Grant." She stretched her hand out next to Oliole's. "You have long fingers."

"And skinny ones," Oliole added. "Now where did Grant hear such important news?" She sipped the tepid tea.

"At the post office."

Oliole let the half-filled cup rest in her hands on her lap. "Oh?"

Georgia leaned against the wall of the house. "See, Mrs. Davenport was talking to Mrs. Rynalt. And Mrs. Davenport said that she overheard July Johnson tell Molly Mae that he had heard Carolina Parks tell the marshal that you and Kaid Darrant were getting married." She took a deep breath. "See? Everybody knows!"

"Well, everybody seems to be in a hurry to get Kaid and me married." She felt Georgia studying her expression.

"You mean, he didn't ask you to marry him?" Thin, almost coal-black eyebrows were raised.

Oliole inspected her short fingernails and tattered cuticles. "Oh, he asked me."

Georgia grabbed her arm. "You told him yes, didn't you?"

"Not yet." Oliole patted the young girl's soft, smooth hand.

"What do you mean, not yet?"

"I'm thinking about it."

"Thinking?" Georgia sprang to her feet and spun around. "What's there to think about? He's brave. He's strong and handsome, you know, for someone his age. And everyone knows he works hard. He doesn't get drunk or get in fights unless it's a good cause. He believes in the Lord. He told me that once. That's very important."

"Yes, it is."

"And Kaid's going to run a great big old ranch, building up a herd for himself. Why in the world wouldn't you want to marry him?"

"I didn't say I don't want to marry him." She held out her hands and took Georgia's into her own. "I've just got some concerns to think through."

"Like what? You love him, and he loves you. Don't you?"

"Miss Mandara," Oliole lectured, "just what exactly is love?"

Georgia wrinkled her round nose. "You're asking me?"

"This is a test of your maturity."

"I'm only fourteen," Georgia protested, rolling her eyes.

Oliole stretched her legs across the narrow wooden porch. "All right, to a fourte-year-old in the year of our Lord, 1885 — what is love?"

Georgia's face flushed red. "You mean, like loving a boy?"

"I mean, like loving a person you intend to marry."

Georgia licked her lips and chewed on her tongue. "Well, let's see . . . you like being with him . . . and he makes you laugh . . . and it feels good to, you know . . . all that stuff."

Oliole cocked her head, her blue eyes open wide. "Oh? Exactly what 'stuff' are you thinking of?"

Georgia took a deep breath and then let the words out all at once. "Holding hands, kissing, and all that! Didn't your parents explain that to you?" She took a gulp of air as if she had been submerged for some time.

"Oh, that stuff. Yes, well, is that all there is to love?"

Georgia rolled her eyes toward the sky. "Well, if you're really in love, you get a little tingle in your throat when he says sweet things to you, and your heart jumps a beat when he touches you, and sometimes when he smiles, you think you're just going to melt into a puddle." She turned and looked straight at Oliole. "I thought you knew all this."

Oliole put her hand over her lips to suppress a laugh. "Just where did you learn this?"

Georgia glanced back toward the two-story Marquesa Hotel down on Main Street. "From Nellie. She knows all about boys and girls."

"It's nice of her to tell you about it."

"She didn't exactly tell me. I read it in her diary."

"Well, that's nice of her to let you —"

"Don't tell her I read her diary. She'll kill me. She really will," Georgia said.

Oliole patted Georgia's dress-covered knee. "Your secret is safe. But you shouldn't read anyone's diary unless they give you permission."

"I know it's wrong. I try not to read it. I tell myself I'll never read it again. Then something gets into me, and I just can't keep myself from doing it. Do you know what I mean?"

"Yes, I do. Sin has a strong attraction. All of us have some things we struggle to overcome."

Georgia folded her arms across her narrow stomach and rested them on the bright yellow ribbon that served as a belt. "Well?"

"Well, what?" Oliole said.

"Are you in love with Kaid?"

Oliole leaned her back against the wall and closed her eyes for a moment. *Lord, did You send this girl up the hill to force me to make up my mind?* "I believe I do love Kaid Darrant . . . some."

"Some? What does that mean?"

"I believe if I let myself, I could love him a whole bunch."

"Enough to get married?" Georgia asked.

"Yes, I believe so."

"So why are you making him wait for an answer?"

"I'm not making Kaid wait. But there are some things I need time to think through. For in-

223

stance, if we were to marry, I'd have to leave Cantrell and move to Alberta."

Georgia studied her fingers and then hid them under the folds of her dress. "I've heard Alberta is very beautiful."

"I'm sure it is. But I've lived most of my life in big cities. Cantrell is more remote than anything I've ever experienced. I've never even imagined living on an isolated ranch."

"You mean, like Mrs. Andrews and Mrs. Odessa?"

"Even more secluded than that. At least they have each other, and Billings is only half a day away. Besides, in Alberta there wouldn't be as many opportunities to take photographs of people. You know how I believe that's part of my God-given responsibility."

"Well . . . well . . . maybe you and Kaid could start a town of your own or something. Mrs. Parks and July started this town just two years ago," Georgia said.

"Perhaps. But that's why I want to think about it for a while."

"How long are you going to ponder it?"

"Until I have an answer from the Lord."

"But — but how will you know that it's the Lord giving you an answer?"

"That's one of the many things I have to figure out."

"You sure do make it sound complicated. I thought all you had to do was find a cute boy who kisses good. Nellie says it's critical to find a boy who kisses good." Georgia puckered her lips and kissed the warm summer breeze.

"Well, I suppose that is important," Oliole said.

"Does Mr. Darrant kiss good?"

"Young lady, don't you think that's a rather personal question?"

Georgia's brown eyes looked as large as silver dollars. "I suppose. But how else am I going to learn anything?"

Oliole winked at Georgia. "As a matter of fact, Mr. Darrant has very sweet kisses."

Georgia leaped up and danced across the porch. "I knew it! I knew it!"

"You knew what?"

"I knew you kissed him. I just knew it!" She twirled around until her dress flared out. "I won!"

"You won what?"

"I bet Grant a nickel that you and Mr. Darrant have been kissing on purpose."

"How else do people kiss?"

"You said you got excited one time and accidentally kissed him — on the lips."

"Yes, well . . . we have kissed on purpose."

"Grant said Mr. Darrant is too tough and strong to kiss a woman, but I knew he had a tender side, too."

"Miss Mandara, I believe we should change the subject and talk about something else."

"Anything else would be boring."

"That might be, but my love life is not the only

subject that needs our attention." *Okay, it needs my attention. But this is getting much too personal.* "Did you hear that Samuel Black and his friends were arrested near the Idaho-Montana border?"

Georgia strolled back and sat down on the bench. "Really?"

"Marshal Parks said he got a telegram saying they tried to steal a gold shipment and got caught."

"So they won't be harassing you."

"Exactly."

Georgia grabbed Oliole's bare elbow. "Does that mean you'll be going to Deadwood to get those photographs?"

"Yes. I think I'll take the train to Miles City and then the Deadwood Stage down to the Black Hills," Oliole said.

"You aren't going to take your wagon and have Mr. Darrant drive it?"

"It would take too long. Besides, Kaid has to go up to Alberta with Mr. Milo Harrison and look at the ranch."

"He's going up there without you?"

Oliole rubbed her fingers across her lips and realized she hadn't put on any lipstick — again. "He's coming back."

"And then you're going to get married?"

"I already told you —"

"I'm just helping you ponder," Georgia scolded. "It's obvious you need help."

"What I need help with is my trip to Dead-wood. Do you think your father and the Marquesa would allow you to accompany me?"

Georgia's mouth dropped open. "Really? Deadwood is so wild. I mean, I don't think my father would ever let me go to a place like that."

"I don't think the entire town is wicked." Oliole stood, carrying her teacup. "Let's go heat up some more water."

"Nellie told me there are women in Deadwood that wear their dresses almost up to their knees!" Georgia followed Oliole through the studio into the back room.

"There are women on Second Street who do that." Oliole peered into the firebox of the cast-iron stove and shoved in two thin scraps of wood.

"Really? Right here in Cantrell?" Georgia examined a photograph hung to dry.

"That's Stella and Nancy Belle. They're down at the Aces & Eights."

"What do they do?"

"Eh, they . . . work there. Now I'd love for you to come with me to Deadwood. But your father and the Marquesa know what's best for you."

Georgia leaned her head on Oliole's shoulder. "Would you ask them for me?"

It's hard to imagine this girl not having her father wrapped around her finger. "Okay, I'll do the asking."

Georgia danced around the room. "Oh boy, I might get to go to Deadwood! I wonder if we'll see anyone get shot?"

"If I thought that a genuine possibility, I certainly wouldn't allow you to go with me."

"Oh, yeah . . . well, don't mention that part to my father. When are you going to ask him?" Georgia asked.

"Perhaps when I come down for supper tonight."

"Are you eating with us tonight?"

"I was invited."

"No one ever tells me anything! Oh, bother! Why am I always the last to know?"

Oliole adjusted her straw hat to block the bright sun as she stepped down off the Northern Pacific train at the Miles City depot. A cloud of red dust hovered just above the dirt streets in every direction.

"What do we do now?" Georgia asked, stepping off behind her. Her hat, held in place by a purple ribbon, rested on her back partially covering her long, thick dark hair.

"We'll wait at the freight office while they unload my gear. Then we'll find out when the stage heads south. We might have to wait awhile."

Everyone on the platform seemed to be in a hurry, leaving the two of them isolated in the midst of a crowd.

"Maybe we could go shopping," Georgia proposed.

"In Miles City? It's not much bigger than Cantrell. What do you need to buy?"

"A gun," Georgia announced with the authority of a judge delivering a popular verdict.

Oliole tugged off one of her white linen gloves.

"What on earth for?"

"I need to have my own revolver. I heard you can buy one for six dollars."

"Who told you that?" Oliole unsuccessfully brushed a lock of blonde hair behind her ear.

"Grant told me all about guns. He said if I'm going to Deadwood, I need some protection. Nellie said she wouldn't go to Deadwood even if escorted by a dozen handsome men."

The platform reeked of railroad steam and steer manure.

"A dozen?"

"She lied, of course. She'd go there with even one halfway handsome man," Georgia said.

"I don't think you should have a gun. It could accidentally hurt someone." Oliole pointed across the platform. "Let's go over there to that bench."

Georgia slipped her arm into Oliole's as they strolled away from the tracks. "Don't you carry a gun?"

"No, I don't."

"Did you know that when Carolina and the Marquesa first moved to Cantrell, they both carried guns around all the time?"

"Things are more peaceful now."

"In Cantrell perhaps but not Deadwood. Daddy wouldn't give me a gun, so I'm going to have to go buy one."

"If your father said no, then you can't do it."

"But he didn't say no exactly. He just said he wouldn't let me have one of his guns. What if we stumble into evil men who intend to cause us bodily harm?"

"We'll pray down the fire of heaven."

"We'll do what?"

"Look, there's the baggage car. Let's sit here and watch them unload," Oliole suggested.

They plopped down on a worn backless bench.

"Deadwood's more subdued since its early days. It's been almost ten years since Bill Hickok was shot in Deadwood. Those days are over. We'll just trust the Lord."

"You might be sorry you didn't let me buy a gun. I have six dollars of my own," Georgia said.

"There are our things. Let's make sure everything gets transferred to the stagecoach."

"Will it really take us two days on the stage to get there?"

"Two long days," Oliole reported.

"I prefer to take a train. Why didn't you want to go to a town on a train route?"

"Because any woman can travel by train. I wanted photographs of those that were hearty enough to take a stage. There's our stagecoach. It doesn't look too bad, does it?"

Two hundred two miles of dusty, rocky, rutted, winding road in a stagecoach with pipe-smoking and ever-changing unbathed passengers brought them to the Merchant's Hotel on Main Street, Deadwood, Dakota Territory. Oliole's blonde pigtails draped down her back. The straw hat pinned to the top of her head sported a layer of trail dust.

Georgia's face was streaked with sweat and dirt. Her high-necked blouse had the top four buttons unfastened. "I thought it would be bigger. It's mainly just one long street at the bottom of a gully," she observed.

Oliole surveyed the street. "I suppose there will be more to it once we look around."

A short man with dark suit, bow tie, bowler hat, and thick mustache greeted them at the boardwalk in front of the hotel. "Welcome to Deadwood, ladies. I'm Willard Parker. And I believe I have just what you want."

Oliole stood two or three inches taller than the man. "How can you have any idea what we want?"

He waved his arm toward the open front doors of the Merchant's Hotel. "A clean room, a hot bath, and a tour of the Deadwood area."

Oliole glanced down at his tattered brown boots. "Is this your hotel?"

"No." He bowed and pointed a thin finger toward a one-horse rig parked on the street. "But I can give you a jaunt in the finest of tour carriages for a very reasonable fee." He stepped over closer to Oliole and dramatically lowered his voice as if sharing a secret. "Plus I happen to have a few very fine mining certificates left at a discounted rate. Normally I don't —"

Oliole spoke more loudly than necessary. "Mr. Parker, if I need a hack, I'll keep you in mind.

But I do not now nor in the future want to talk about mining stock. Is that understood?"

"Yes, ma'am." He shrugged and stood straight, locking his thumbs in his woven leather belt. "Just what is your intention for you and your daughter here in the Black Hills? I do know the territory. Perhaps I can help you in some other way."

"Miss Mandara is not my daughter but my assistant. I'm a photographer. We'll be here about a week, and I plan to take a series of pictures of some of the interesting pioneer women in the Black Hills region."

"You're in luck." Again his shoulders slumped, and his voice lowered. "I know all the houses in the Territory."

"Mr. Parker, I do not need any more photographs of soiled doves. I'm interested in women who work, women who run businesses, women who have moved here to raise their families."

He scratched the back of his neck. "You mean respectable women?"

"Yes," she said.

"I know some of them, too." Parker rocked back on his heels.

"How fortunate." Oliole noticed the man sizing her up, trail dirt and all.

"Are you really a photographer?" he inquired.

"She's one of the best in the entire country." Georgia stepped between them. "Her photographs are on display in New York City."

"No foolin'?"

"Miss Mandara is enthusiastic." Oliole put her hands on Georgia's shoulders. "But it is true that I'm working on a series for a New York gallery."

"Maybe you could take my photograph. You know, by my carriage?"

Oliole glanced at the torn carriage seat and swayback piebald horse. "I think I can arrange that."

"When?" Parker pressed.

"You don't mean right now, do you?" She looked back to the west. The setting sun hovered just above the dark green treetops on Forest Hill.

Mr. Parker pointed to the stack of boxes and crates on the boardwalk. "That your gear?"

"Yes, but we've been on the stage for two long days."

"Well, it don't take very long, does it?" he inquired.

"Once I get set up, not more than fifteen minutes. But with the declining sun, I believe it would be better to wait until tomorrow."

Mr. Parker pulled off his round hat and held it in front of him. "What time?"

"My, you really want me to take your photograph, don't you? I'm not sure why. There must be several other photographers in Deadwood."

He pointed across the dusty street to a one-story red brick building. "Yep. There's one right over there. No offense, ma'am, but none of them photographers are purdy ladies with fancy yellow hair."

I don't believe anyone has ever called my hair

fancy. Perhaps the dust brings out a hidden quality.
"Why don't we meet right here at 9:00 A.M. to-morrow?"

He scratched his head and put his hat back on. "I reckon that will work. How much do you charge?"

"I will need a set-up fee of one —"

Georgia cut her off by pulling on her arm and pointing across the street. "Miss Fontenot! Do you know the photographer who has that shop?"

Startled by the tugging, Oliole glanced across the street. "What shop?" she snapped.

"The one that says Photographs $5.00 Each!"

Five dollars? They don't even charge that in New York. At least, I don't think they do. Miss Mandara, remind me to give you a raise. "Eh, no, I don't know him." She turned back to the waiting man. "Mr. Parker, I will need a one-time setup fee of, eh, say, three dollars. Then it will be three dollars per print."

"That's sure enough a bargain." Parker's wide grin revealed a shining gold tooth. "I want to send some photos to my kin back in the States."

Oliole strolled over to the crates and cases. "It might take awhile to carry down my gear from my hotel room in the morning and set up. But we will be ready by 9:00."

Willard Parker wiped some dust off a black leather case with the sleeve of his coat. "You ought to store it on the ground level."

"That would be nice, but I have to work with what I have, and I suppose most of the hotel rooms are upstairs," she said.

Parker banged his clenched fist on top of a wooden crate. "Wait a minute. . . . I've got an idea! Let me talk to Mr. Fortune."

"Who?" Georgia questioned.

"Not the old man. I mean Todd Fortune, one of the sons. You've heard about the Fortunes of the Black Hills, ain't ya?" He stepped out on the street and waited for a freight wagon pulled by four oxen.

"There's a family named Fortune?" Oliole quizzed.

"This is providence!" he exclaimed. "Here comes Mr. Todd Fortune and his wife right now."

"What does this have to do with my equipment?" Oliole's voice trailed off as the couple approached.

"Evenin', Mr. Fortune." Willard Parker tipped his hat. "Evenin', Mrs. Fortune!"

The tall, strong man with tanned face and wide, thick eyebrows, wearing suit, tie, and vest, escorted a plain-faced, elegantly dressed woman with rich brown hair stacked high under her straw hat. "Evening, Mr. Parker. Certainly is a fine summer night, isn't it? I trust you had good business today."

The man looked straight at Oliole. Her throat tingled, and her heart jumped. "Evenin', ma'am," said the man. His blue eyes danced. "Looks like you just got off the stage. Welcome to Deadwood. And this must be your sister." He tipped his hat to Georgia.

"Actually we're not . . . well . . . ," she mumbled.

Georgia scooted up and offered her hand to the man. "Miss Fontenot is a New York City photographer who has come to Deadwood for a week to take photographs of the women of the Black Hills."

"How fascinating," his wife remarked.

Oliole focused on Mrs. Fortune. "Actually I used to live in New York, but I have a studio in Cantrell up on the Yellowstone River east of Billings."

"But she is taking photographs for a New York gallery," Georgia insisted.

"Mrs. Fortune, may I be so bold as to ask you if I could take a photograph of you for that collection?"

Rebekah Fortune looked at her husband. He slipped his fingers into hers, and his eyes danced approval. She turned back to Oliole. "I'd be honored."

Willard Parker cleared his throat. "See, here's the thing, Mr. Fortune. Miss . . . eh . . . this lady —"

"Fontenot," she informed them. "Oliole Fontenot."

"O-l-i-o-l-e?" Mr. Fortune asked.

"You might be the first man who ever spelled it right at first guess."

"Are you Swedish?" Mrs. Fortune asked.

"No. My father was descended from French-

Canadians, my mother from Irish stock, but I'm mainly good old mixed American. Mama had a neighbor who had this name, and she borrowed it."

"You were saying, Willard?" Todd Fortune pressed.

"Miss Fontenot is going to have to store all this gear in her hotel room and then pack it down every time she wants to photograph someone, so I was thinking —"

"Why doesn't she use the hat shop?" Todd Fortune offered.

"That's exactly what I was goin' to ask," Parker concurred.

Oliole looked at Parker, then at Fortune. "Use the what?"

"I own that wood-frame building next to the hotel." Todd Fortune pointed up the street. "A hat shop just closed last week, and I haven't leased it out yet. You can use it this week for your studio. That way you don't have to tote that gear up and down the stairs."

"That's very considerate of you, Mr. Fortune, but rents must be high on Main Street. I'm not sure I could afford it." *Why does this man's voice make my throat tickle?*

"Rent? I meant you to use it for free," he said.

"But," she protested, "you don't know me and . . ." She put her hands to her side when she realized she was twisting her braids in her fingers.

"Are you a dishonest or evil person, Miss Fontenot?"

"No . . . no, of course not."

"Neither am I." He reached into his vest pocket, took out several keys, plucked out one, and handed it to her. "Here, help yourself. Willard, could you assist these ladies to carry their things inside? I'd help, but we're a little late to a church meeting."

Parker tipped his hat. "Be happy to, Mr. Fortune."

"But I have to pay you something," Oliole asserted.

"How about furnishing me with a print of my wife's photograph?" He leaned over and kissed his wife on the cheek, and she squeezed his arm.

The tingling in Oliole's throat died. "I'll be happy to take a complimentary photograph of your entire family."

"We just might take you up on that." Mr. Fortune took his wife's arm as they strolled along the boardwalk in front of the hotel.

"Mr. Parker, this is a real treat to have a studio for the week. Thank you for arranging it," Oliole chattered.

"Free of charge," Georgia added.

"That's the way them Fortunes are. You heard about his daddy, Brazos, haven't you?"

"No, sorry to say, I haven't."

"Sometime this week when you've got two hours, I'll have to tell you. Downright inspiring, it is."

"Maybe I should take a photograph of the senior Mr. Fortune's wife as well."

"Brazos? He's a widower. Lost the missus down in Texas years and years ago I heard. Still pinin' for her, I reckon. Now which of these crates do you want me to haul first?"

Oliole pointed to a large black leather case. "Let's take the camera and that green valise."

"Yes, ma'am."

"Mr. Parker, I want to give you your photograph — to thank you for helping me today. There won't be a setup fee either."

"That's mighty generous, ma'am. But a lady has to make her keep, just like the rest of us." They hiked toward the hat shop. "But there is one favor I'd like to ask."

Oliole fumbled with the key in the door of the small shop. "Certainly. What's that?"

"Well, now, don't take this wrong." Willard Parker backed into the dark, slightly musty room. "It's strictly an honorable request. Would you pose with me in my photograph?"

"Do what?" She motioned for him to set the case on the round oak table.

"Ya see, people back home pretty much figured I was dumb to move out here. And since I ain't got no gold mine, they think I'm stupid to stay. But if I sent a photograph of me and you, well, they'd say that old Willard Parker ain't so dumb after all." He turned toward the open door, and the ladies followed him out.

"You flatter me," Oliole responded.

He stopped in front of the hat shop and wiped his sweating forehead. "All I want is for you to stand next to me. That's all. Jist like we was friends."

"I'd like to oblige, Mr. Parker, but I'll need to operate the camera."

"I thought maybe your assistant could do that. This ain't got to be no award-winnin' photograph. They don't even have to see me too clear. Just you."

"You could set everything up, and I could click the shutter, Miss Fontenot. I've watched you do it dozens of times," Georgia offered. "I do believe I could do it. I've always wanted to try!"

"I don't know. I've never . . ." Oliole caught herself biting her fingernails. "Well, we can try it, but I can't guarantee the quality."

"Thank ya, ma'am. That kind of photograph would truly be worth five dollars."

"That would be normal, Mr. Parker. But I insist you get the discount rate of three dollars." *I can't believe anyone would pay extra to have me in the photograph.*

"Thank ya, Miss Fontenot. You just made my entire summer a success." He trotted up ahead to the dwindling stack of equipment.

Oliole leaned over to Georgia and whispered, "It doesn't take too much to please in a town with ten men for every woman, does it? Now let's go find a clean room and a hot bath."

It turned out to be a steaming hot bath.

Then a spicy supper at the China Dragon Cafe.

After that they collapsed into a soft bed with clean sheets.

Oliole figured she could sleep forever.

But she didn't.

By the breaking light of dawn, she sat by the hotel window reading in 1 Corinthians.

Lord, why did my heart jump like that when a happily married man spoke to me? I know he's handsome — and rich, I suppose — but such a reaction? Why such thoughts? I don't understand. Sometimes my heart is a deceiver and liar. I can't trust it. I feel ashamed to have those thoughts, especially with his wife standing right there. I'm even ashamed to tell You.

I do feel that way around Kaid, too. At least, sometimes. But if my heart's lying to me here on the streets of Deadwood, perhaps it's lying to me in Cantrell as well. How can I ever know? It's like a huge gamble.

I like sure things. Like taking a photograph of Mrs. Fortune. I know that it will be one of my best images.

I don't suppose You could just send a letter and tell me how to respond to Kaid's offer?

She stared out on Main Street. Freight wagons ruled the dirt street, and she could hear the constant thunder of a stamp mill somewhere to the west of town.

I didn't think so. I know I have to come to some decision by the time we go home. At least, I can put it off until then.

Neither Oliole or Georgia felt hungry enough for breakfast, so they lounged in the gaudily decorated room until almost 8:00 A.M. Finally they began to get ready.

"I don't want to ride on a stagecoach ever again," Georgia complained. "My back still hurts. And my dress still reeks of pipe smoke."

"The soles of my boots are sticky with tobacco juice," Oliole added. "And my ears still ring with foul language and lurid tales."

"What kind of tails?"

Oliole glanced briefly at Georgia's inquiring eyes. "Perhaps next week the stage won't be so crowded when we leave. I think more people are arriving than departing. I suppose I should wear my other dress today if I'm going to be in this photograph." She tugged on the bright blue silk dress with white lace collar and cuffs.

Georgia walked behind her, smoothing down the skirt. "The lace makes you look so elegant."

"Thank you, Miss Mandara. I don't believe I have ever been called elegant in my life."

"Really? My papa and the Marquesa call me that all the time."

Oliole sat on the edge of the unmade bed and pulled on her riding boots. "Your papa and the Marquesa are jewels, Miss Mandara. I trust you realize what quality parents you have."

Georgia began to comb out her long dark brown hair. "They are quite wonderful once you get past their obvious defects, aren't they?"

"That's not exactly the way I would have put it, but I understand what you mean."

Georgia set the engraved ivory comb down on the polished mahogany dresser. "Are you ready?"

"How do I look?" Oliole quizzed.

"Ravishing!"

"What a liar you are, Miss Mandara."

"No, I'm not. I see the way men gape at you when you stroll by."

"That's silly. I'm nothing but a thirty-year-old tomboy."

"Oh, sure," Georgia murmured. "It's going to be one of those days I hate walking next to you."

"Why's that?" Oliole said.

"Because compared to you, Miss Fontenot, I'm just a plain, dull, skinny little kid. If you don't stop every man's heart on Main Street, they're dead."

"Come on, you. We have work to do. I didn't invite you along just to say nice things about me. At least, that wasn't the main reason." Suddenly they both began to giggle. "You're going to take a photograph for me today," Oliole reminded her.

They breezed through the lobby and out the front door of the hotel, then turned east, and hiked along the boardwalk toward the little hat shop. Mr. Willard Parker's carriage was parked in front of the unpainted building. A group of thirty to fifty men huddled in front of a store on the other side of the hat shop.

"I wonder what's happening down there?" Georgia asked. "Maybe someone got shot. Did you hear a gunshot?"

"All I heard was freighters cursing oxen and that stamp mill crushing rock. They are probably just customers."

"At a clothing store?"

"Perhaps. Anyway, let's get this one done so we can get busy with the women's photographs."

As they approached the front of the closed hat shop, a scrubbed and shaved Willard Parker swooped his arm low toward the boardwalk and shouted to the crowd of men. "Here she comes, boys, and as you can plainly see, I didn't exaggerate one iota!"

The men burst into applause, followed by hoots, shouts, and whistles.

Georgia tugged at Oliole's sleeve. "I warned you this would happen."

"Thank you, boys." Oliole surveyed the several dozen uniquely individual, yet similarly grinning faces. "But I'm not sure I understand. Is this the way you greet all newcomers to Deadwood?"

"We ain't never had a newcomer as purdy as you, ma'am," one man shouted.

"You are very generous with your compliments. But we were wondering, just exactly what brings the bunch of you out this morning?"

"We're standing in line," one shouted.

"What for?" Oliole asked.

"To get our picture taken."

"You all want photographs?" Oliole gasped.

"Yes, ma'am."

"Well . . . well . . . I can only take and develop four photographs per hour. So you'll have to give your names to my assistant and take your turns," Oliole half mumbled.

"That sounds fair enough. Willard said ever'-

one of us could get his picture taken with the purdiest yellow-haired girl this side of St. Louis."

Oliole tried to swallow, but it caught in her throat. "You're all here to have your picture taken with me?"

"Yes, ma'am, and ever'one of us has our five cash dollars, too!" came a gravelly reply.

Oliole and Georgia ambled out on the platform of the Northern Pacific depot in Miles City, Montana, and tried to brush the road dust off their brand-new dresses. Above them the few clouds in the blue summer sky reflected a brownish tint.

"That is my last stagecoach ride ever!" Georgia groaned. "From now on I take the train . . . or ride a tall black horse. That's it."

Oliole hugged Georgia. "It's been a long trip, hasn't it?"

"Yes, and our time in Deadwood was the funnest time I ever had in my life. I can't believe we actually stayed two weeks."

"They didn't want us to leave even then. I felt blessed to have time for my images of the ladies. The men surely kept us busy. And you learned a lot about photography, young lady."

"Can you imagine how much money we would have made if we had stayed all summer?" Georgia tilted her head and flashed a toothy smile, imitating Oliole's standard pose. Both women started to laugh.

"Frankly, they wore me out," Oliole admitted. "I was exhausted before we got on the stage-coach. I never modeled a smile next to so many men in my life."

Georgia squinted her eyes in the bright setting sun. "All over the States, homes are going to have pictures of you on their mantels. It will be their son, brother, or father — and Miss Oliole Fontenot. Isn't that strange?"

"I might become a very well-known unnamed person. Let's sit over there in the shade. There's a hot breeze blowing." Oliole motioned away from the tracks. "The man at the ticket counter said the westbound can't leave until the east-bound arrives. It must have had a problem be-cause it's almost ten minutes late."

"I'm going to sleep all the way to Billings," Georgia said.

"It was a worthwhile trip," Oliole added. "I think I got eleven more of my series."

"I like the one of Mrs. Fortune and her chil-dren best of all. She reminds me of Carolina some . . . but, you know, not as glamorous."

"I think I'll call it 'Mrs. Fortune's Gold Mine,' " Oliole said.

"I like it." Georgia plopped down on the bench and smoothed out her skirt. "And I like my new dresses, and my new shoes, and my silver locket . . ."

"We did a lot of shopping, didn't we?"

"Yes, I can't believe we made so much money. You know what I like best? At first, everyone treated me like a little girl, like I was your daughter. But by the time we left, they were treating me like a lady. They asked me to the dance and talked to me about everything."

"Just what exactly do you mean, everything?" Oliole prodded.

"Oh, you know . . . that girl and boy stuff."

I believe I'm getting this girl back to her parents at just the right time. "Well, I appreciated your help. I certainly couldn't have survived without you." Oliole fought back the urge to yawn.

"Sometimes, I do good, don't I?"

"Yes, you do, Miss Mandara." *I think . . . I hope . . . I pray you behaved yourself.*

"I think I have more problems at home than when I travel. Why do you think that is?"

"Perhaps it's because you know others will keep you in line, so you don't worry about self-control."

"Yeah, I bet that's it. You've been out on your own so long that you've taught yourself how to do the right thing all the time. That's why you never give in to temptations."

"Where did you ever get that idea?" Oliole felt like stretching out on the hot, weathered wooden platform and going to sleep.

"Papa said that he hoped you would influence me. He said if his girls turned out to be like Miss Fontenot, he would be a happy man."

"He might want a better example. Sometimes I've been known to do strange things."

"Oh sure, but you always know what you're

247

doing, right?" Georgia asked.

"Not always."

"Really? When?"

Oliole stared down at her dusty brown boots. "Like finally deciding what to tell Kaid Darrant."

"You've made up your mind?" Georgia probed.

"I think so."

"What did you decide? You're going to marry him, aren't you? I know you are. I just knew from the first time I saw you two together." Georgia was bobbing up and down on the bench.

"I can't tell you."

"Why?" Georgia whined.

"Because it wouldn't be right to talk to anyone before I talk to him."

"Really?"

"Yes, and besides . . . maybe I'll change my mind tomorrow. But I do know what I'd tell him if he walked up right now," Oliole said.

Georgia surveyed the others on the train platform and those with their heads out the open windows on the side-railed westbound. "I don't think he's going to come."

"I don't think the eastbound is going to get here either. I don't know why they don't start this train and meet the other at another siding."

"Maybe that man knows. He seems to be talking to everyone else."

The uniformed train agent with round cheeks and thick sideburns huffed his way up to them.

"Ladies, if you're waiting for the eastbound, I have rather unpleasant news for you," he announced.

"Actually we're going west," Oliole informed him. "It's too hot in the Pullman, so we're waiting out here."

"Doesn't matter. Either way your trip's canceled."

"It's what?"

"It's terrible — that's what it is. This is 1885. We shouldn't have to put up with such lawlessness in this day and age." The man pulled out a white handkerchief and wiped off the back of his neck.

Oliole stood to face the short, heavy man. "What are you talking about?"

"The trestle at 44 Creek has been blown up and the eastbound robbed," he reported.

Georgia's chin dropped. "Blown up?"

"Train robbers. Maybe it was the James boys," the agent said.

"Jesse James died three years ago, and Frank is in prison. I read all about it last year in St. Louis," Georgia explained.

"Don't believe it, missy. I heard Frank James brought forty tons of Confederate gold up the Missouri River just last year and hid it in a cave near Gates of the Mountains."

Oliole clutched her stomach with folded arms. "What does it mean, the trestle is blown up?"

"It means the eastbound is stuck on the other side of 44 Creek, and the westbound is stuck right here until the tracks are rebuilt."

"How long will that take?" Oliole pressed.

"Can't be sure. They telegraphed me and said don't sell any tickets for a week."

"A week?" she moaned. "You aren't going to have train service for a whole week?"

"Apparently not. They could get the work done quicker, but at the moment, it doesn't look good."

Georgia grabbed her arm. "What are we going to do, Miss Fontenot?"

"Well, we aren't going to sit here a week. We'll have to take a stage."

"Oh, no," Georgia moaned, "I'm still eating dust from this morning! Please, please . . . I can't ride another stagecoach."

"Are there any carriages or wagons for rent?" Oliole asked. "We have to get home."

"I'd rent you my own personal carriage. It has a large cargo area behind the seat," the man offered. "But how would you get it back to me?"

"How about if I rent it to someone coming east? Those on that parked train are going to want to get this far. We're only a hundred miles from here. We can make that in a long, hard day."

"Not with only one team. You'll need at least two long days. Where is it you're headin'?" he asked.

"Cantrell," she said.

"Is that where Marshal Ranahan is?"

"Yes, do you know Ran? He's a very good friend of ours."

"In that case, I reckon it would be all right to rent it to you. It will be ten dollars each way."

"We'll take it. I'll give you twenty and then collect my other ten from whoever rents it coming back. That way you have your money guaranteed."

He shoved the handkerchief back into his pocket and tugged on the collar. "That's fair."

"Do you have someone who could load our equipment for us?" Oliole asked.

"I'll get one of the boys to do that as soon as I notify the rest about the delay."

"Good. We'll need to go into town for some trail provisions," Oliole reported.

"You two ladies really going to travel alone?"

"Yes, we are."

The ticket agent stared off at the setting sun. "It's almost dark. You ain't leaving tonight, are you?"

"No, we'll wait until daybreak. Could you direct us to an armory?" Oliole queried. "We'll need to purchase a couple of weapons. You know — for snakes along the trail."

"Do I get to carry a gun?" Georgia bubbled.

Oliole closed her eyes and then rubbed dust out of them. "Well, at least we should each have one within arm's reach."

With train traffic at a standstill, Miles City overflowed with hassled travelers. What few rooms were available soon filled up to twice their capacity. Some people chose to sleep on the

251

train. Others slept in bedrolls alongside the tracks.

Oliole rented a back room at the grocery store for five dollars. She and Georgia made makeshift beds out of wool blankets and 100-pound sacks of pinto beans. They slept with their clothes on and revolvers next to them.

By 6:30 A.M. they were on the trail driving west. The air was already hot, and the scattered clouds still carried a brown tint.

"I'm so tired I'm going to sleep for a week when we get home," Georgia announced.

"Why don't you crawl back there with the gear and see if you can nap?" Oliole motioned to the back.

"But I don't want to miss anything."

"Since we're on the well-traveled northern side of the river, I don't expect we'll see much other than the ordinary."

"If I get sleepier, maybe I will lie down." Georgia reached over to the carriage seat between them and fingered the polished walnut grip of the new revolver. "Do you think it was Frank James who blew up the railroad trestle?"

Oliole shook her head. "No. I'm sure you're right. He's in jail . . . or dead. But I suppose everything will get blamed on him until someone else that notorious comes along."

"Are we really going to get home by tomorrow night?"

"I think so. But we want to take it easy with this team."

"I wish Mr. Darrant were traveling with us," Georgia said.

"I was thinking the same thing."

Georgia reached over and poked Oliole in the ribs. "So you were thinking about Mr. Darrant?"

"Yes, I suppose I was."

"That means you decided to marry him, and you've been thinking about boy and girl stuff," Georgia triumphed.

"Not necessarily," Oliole cautioned. "It could be I've decided not to marry him and am just trying to think of how to tell him."

"Really?"

"Or . . . it could be I have decided to marry him, but I'm not thinking of girl and boy stuff. What if I'm thinking about sewing up a wedding dress or building a home in Canada?"

"Wow! Are you?"

"No . . . but I could have been."

"You were thinking about girl and boy stuff, weren't you?"

"Were you?" Oliole tossed the question back.

"Sort of," Georgia admitted.

"Oh?"

"Well, I don't know much. Nellie won't tell me any details. For instance, after you spend a lot of time kissing, what do you do next?"

I can't believe this. I don't have any kids. I don't have to face this problem. At least, not for fifteen years. "Georgia, let's change the subject."

"If you don't tell me about it, how will I ever know?"

"You'll know. Believe me, you'll know. But I can't go around your father's authority. It's up to him and the Marquesa to tell you things like that. I don't want to make them upset with me, so we're changing the subject."

Georgia rolled her eyes and groaned. "What are we going to talk about?"

"The wind," Oliole said.

"The wind? What is there to talk about?"

"It's been hot and blowing right into us. Now it's beginning to pick up sand and dirt and toss it in our faces. Do you think it will continue like this?"

"Are you really going to change the subject?"

"I predict we will have this same hot wind and sand in our faces all day long. I'm glad we're wearing our hats. Now it's your turn."

"To talk about the wind?"

"Yes."

"This is really dumb."

"The conversation or the wind?"

"Both. I'm going to take a nap," Georgia declared.

They didn't have the same hot wind in their faces all day.

It got worse.

And worse.

And worse!

At the crest of the hill before the road dropped down toward Whitetail Creek, a wave of dust and grit swept over the plodding team and carriage. The sky grew dark, as if in a storm, but the air was dry, hot, stinging to every exposed area of skin.

"I can't see anything!" Georgia called out from her seat next to Oliole. "My hat's about to blow off! Can you see anything?"

"Not very much," Oliole shouted. "Put our hats in that green valise." She let the reins drop to her lap and carefully untied her hat.

Georgia secured the hats and crawled back up to the carriage seat. "What are we going to do now?"

The roar of the wind was so loud Oliole had to lean into Georgia to hear anything at all. "If we find a grove of trees or a steep cliff, we'll park and try to wait it out."

"We haven't seen any trees since we left Miles City," Georgia hollered. "I couldn't see a tree right now if it were two feet in front of me. I've got sand in my eyes and everywhere else."

"Grab the lap blanket back there and pull it over your head."

"How about you?"

"Get my blue bandanna out of that black valise," Oliole bellowed.

Georgia climbed into the back of the carriage and sorted through a bag. She retrieved the scarf and hunched on her knees behind Oliole. "What now?" she asked.

"Pull my braids down."

"What?"

Oliole turned her head and shouted, "Pull my braids down."

She felt Georgia's hands fumble with the pins in her hair.

"I did it."

The braids blew straight behind her. "Now help me tie that bandanna over my nose and face." The folded cotton cloth prevented much of the dust from blasting into Oliole's nose and mouth.

"I think I'll stay back here. It's not as bad right behind you," Georgia called out.

"Why don't you lie down and pull that blanket over your head?"

"Are you sure you'll be all right?"

Oliole tried to read Georgia's lips even as she strained to hear each word. "Can you reach that cowboy hat with the stampede string you bought for Philip?"

"Yes. Do you want to wear it?"

"If it's all right with you. I can keep the brim turned down into the wind." Oliole could feel a pile of sand grind into her neck.

The brown beaver felt hat took the sting out of the sand, but much of it swirled into her eyes anyway. Oliole kept her eyes squinted, almost closed. "Hand me my heavy gloves, Georgia — the ones I use for loading my equipment."

With the worn deerhide gauntlets pulled over her hands and the leather reins laced between her fingers, she slapped the lead horse's rump and continued to plod into the dust storm.

The howl of the wind drowned out all other noise, even the squeak of dry axles. Oliole thought the wind had let up a bit as she allowed the horses to drink water from Whitetail Creek, but when she climbed the grade to the plateau to the west, the storm grew much darker. It was now like driving through a starless, moonless night. She heard Georgia shout something from the back.

Oliole turned and could barely see Georgia Mandara lying next to the crate and valises, a canvas tarp pulled up over her nose. Only her hand-protected, squinting brown eyes could be seen.

"Did you say something?" Oliole shouted.

"I said," Georgia hollered back, "you look like a bank robber! Cowboy hat, bandanna over your face, covered with dirt. All you need is a gun strapped to your waist."

"A what?" Oliole shouted.

"A gun!"

"Where are our guns?" Oliole said.

"I put them back in your black valise."

"Hand me one," Oliole called out.

"Really?"

"Yes. You never know when we'll run into a bank to rob!"

"Are you serious about the gun?" Georgia quizzed.

"Yes. I'll keep it under the folds of my skirt. In this storm trouble could pop up quickly. Makes me wish we'd stayed in Miles City."

Georgia handed her the gun. "I wish we'd stayed in Deadwood," she shouted.

With the .36 Colt tucked between the black leather carriage seat and her long brown skirt, Oliole squinted into the wind, hoping the horses could sense where the road was.

Lord, I'm not sure how this happened . . . or why. All we wanted to do was go home. The dangerous part of the trip was supposed to be over. Then a bridge is blown up, and a dust storm rolls in, and we're wandering out on the prairie. What's the lesson here? Stay home? Don't be so adventuresome? Don't leave home without a man to escort me?

What would Kaid do if he were here? I don't know, but I know what I'd do if he were here. I'd hide back there out of the sand and dirt with Georgia. If we had that old army ambulance, we could all three just stop and crawl in the back and wait out the storm.

If it were just me and Kaid, we could scrunch up in the back of the ambulance and . . .

Providing we were married.

And it wasn't so horribly dirty.

I might never in my life feel clean again.

Even though it's all packed up, I'll need to take my camera apart and completely clean it before I use it again.

Here I was planning on fretting all the way back to Cantrell about what to tell Kaid. Now I'll just be delighted to make it to Cantrell. I really don't know whether to stop or keep trudging. I really don't like being this isolated. I want to be back in my little studio — with a cup of tea and a good book and friends and a hot bath whenever I choose.

I wonder if it's windy in Alberta?

I don't know anyone who's lived there.
I don't know anyone who lives there now.

Oliole drudged on, straight into the dust storm. Hours and minutes blurred. She had no idea if it were nine or noon. When it got too hot under the canvas, Georgia popped out and huddled behind her. Oliole could feel sweat and dirt from head to toe. The constant sting of the sand made her eyelids and forehead seem sunburned.

Down in the coulees near the creeks, visibility improved slightly. She could feel the team want to turn toward what she hoped was the Yellowstone River. This time she allowed them to keep heading south.

"How come we're turning?" Georgia leaned so close her lips brushed against Oliole's ear.

"Maybe there are some trees near the Yellowstone. I don't think our horses want to go any farther into the wind."

"What if we can't find this road again?"

"Let's worry about that later." Oliole could feel the gritty bandanna rub against her chapped lips. "We've got to get out of this creek bed. I don't want to drive right out into the middle of the Yellowstone!"

She guided the team to what she thought was the west side of the creek and then lost sight of the ground when the coulee flattened out. She assumed she was near the mouth of the creek. After several more minutes, the horses quit plodding, and the wagon came to a halt.

Georgia was behind her, hugging her shoulders. "Why did we stop?"

"They won't go any farther."

"Did we reach the Yellowstone?"

"I have no idea," Oliole said.

"Are we standing in water?"

"I don't think so, but I'm not sure."

"You want me to get down and check?"

"You stay here. I'll get down," Oliole insisted.

"Don't let go of the reins," Georgia called out. "You'll never find your way back!"

Oliole stepped down off the carriage, her chin lowered into the wind. With the reins still in her right hand, she tugged off her left glove and squatted beside the carriage wheel. She dragged her bare hand along the rocks and dirt.

All right, we're not in water. But where are we? She felt her way along the rump of the lead horse. Its hair felt warm but not lathered.

You two must wonder what we're leading you into. The horse whipped its huge head around. Oliole gasped and jumped back. *Yeah . . . it's me. The one who brought you out here into this mess.*

Once she passed the horses, she held her hand out straight ahead of her and rammed it into something immovable.

A log? Several logs? Driftwood at the confluence of the creek and the river? She felt an opening between the logs and bent low to peer under them. *A windbreak! Thank You, Lord!*

Following the contour of the horse with her left hand, she hurried back to the carriage seat.

"What is it?" Georgia called out.

"A little driftwood windbreak."

"Are we going to stop?"

"Yes. Bring that canvas. I'll bring our canteen and that cotton sack with food," Oliole instructed.

"Shall I bring the guns?" Georgia hollered.

"The what?"

"Guns."

"All right." Still holding the reins, Oliole felt through the carriage and grabbed a cotton sack and a leather-wrapped canteen. "Hold on to my arm," she instructed Georgia. "And don't let go!"

They felt their way up to the pile of huge logs. Georgia scooted into the cavelike opening. Oliole tied off the horses and crawled in behind her.

"Can you see anything?" Georgia called out, now clutching Oliole's neck.

"Not any more than outside. But we're out of the wind, and the sand is not as bad. Where's the food sack?" Oliole pulled the bandanna off her face but left the cowboy hat on her head.

"I've got it over here," Georgia said.

"Let's sit on the tarp and try to find something to eat that's not full of dirt."

"There's a candle in the sack," Georgia reported. "And some stick matches. Do you think it would stay lit in here?"

"Maybe. It doesn't seem very windy back away from the opening."

"Here, you light it," Georgia hollered.

"Perhaps we can stop yelling now."

"I'm sorry." Georgia dropped her voice. "It seems like we've been screaming all day."

"We have. Well, I'm going to try to light the candle."

"Wait a minute," Georgia cautioned. "Let me get my gun."

"Why?"

"What if there's a bear or a cougar back in these logs?"

"They would have eaten us by now," Oliole said.

"Maybe not. Maybe they're full and just waiting for a snack."

"You can hold the gun, but don't point it at me or at the opening. You could shoot a horse."

"Do you want your gun?"

"No. If there's a bear in here, I'll die of fright anyway."

Light flared from the sulfur match drawn across the heel of a riding boot and flickered among the water-worn cottonwood logs. A small flame danced at the end of a fat white candle.

"It's staying lit!" Georgia squealed.

"See any bears or cougars?" Oliole questioned.

"Nope."

Oliole held the candle up between them so they could get a good look at each other. Georgia's dark hair was sand-streaked. Her face was packed with dirt. Small piles of grit caked the corners of her eyes. Her lips were swollen and chapped. Her pastel yellow dress was now brown, her neck ringed with dried sweat and layers of dirt. Her dark eyes stared back at Oliole, and then a white-toothed smile broke across her face.

"Am I as awful-looking as you?" Oliole grinned.

"You're the worst thing I've ever seen in my life," Georgia giggled. "Should we try to wash up?"

"I wouldn't know where to begin. And we need to drink the water in the canteen."

"Don't look at me!" Georgia protested.

"Perhaps we should blow out the candle."

"No . . . just set it down. I think we can eat this bread if we break it open and just eat out the soft part in the middle," Georgia said.

"Can you swallow bread?" Oliole asked.

"Eh, not really. Maybe we should just take a drink and wait. How long do dust storms last?"

"I have no idea. But it seems like in the summer the wind dies down about the time the sun sets." She took a swig out of the canteen and handed it to Georgia.

Georgia took a sip and replaced the cork. "Even the water tastes like dirt. What are we going to do now?"

"Let's try to get some rest. Perhaps we can fall asleep and dream of hot baths."

"I'm going to dream of a cold bath," Georgia said.

"It is warm in here, isn't it?"

"Miss Fontenot, do you think it would be acceptable if I unfastened the buttons on the collar of my dress?"

"Only if you let me do the same." Oliole fumbled under the bandanna and unfastened her four collar buttons. "Look at this." She held a handful of dirt. "This was on my neck. I've never been this dirty in my entire life. Compared to this, rolling down that mountain was like dipping in bath oils."

"Are you going to blow out the candle?" Georgia asked.

"If we've got our eyes closed, we might as well save the candle for tonight."

"You mean it's not night yet?"

"I don't think it's much past noon. But I'm not going out to my valise and try to find my watch."

"Oliole, can I sleep next to you?"

"Sure, come on." Oliole held out her arm. Georgia scooted next to her and slipped her arm around Oliole's waist. Oliole held up the candle and blew it out. *No matter how old or young, there are times you've just got to have a hug.*

Kaid Darrant, you get out of my thoughts. I have no intention of huddling in here and thinking about you.

In the pitch-black, she stroked Georgia's head, which now rested on her shoulder.

I wish I had a photograph of this scene. I'd call it "The Image of a Lady Photographer."

Lord, this is not a boring day. That's all I can say for it.

"Miss Fontenot, look! We're on an island!"

Georgia's excited words brought Oliole out of a deep sleep and to her hands and knees. A faint ray of setting sun reflected off the piles of smooth sand and rock just beyond the logs.

"The storm's gone, Miss Fontenot. Come look!"

Sharp pains shot up her legs, back, and shoulders as Oliole stood up beside the two brown horses and tried to stretch.

"You see, we came down that creek over there, but I guess we waded out to this island in the Yellowstone."

Oliole stared at the setting sun in the west.

"There aren't even any clouds in the sky," Georgia announced.

"There never were any clouds. Just dust and sand."

"Should we drive back over by the creek before it gets darker?"

Oliole examined the dirt piled in the carriage. "Perhaps. But this might not be too bad a place to camp. The river's been going down since the middle of June, so we'll be safe out here. I doubt if man or beast will hassle us."

"You mean, just camp in our little log shelter?"

"Is that all right with you?"

"Yes. Can we wash up in the river?" Georgia asked.

"Definitely."

"Don't you just wish we could pull off our

clothes and jump in?"

"Actually, no. I'm afraid if the cold water didn't put my body in shock, the embarrassment would."

"Really? Me and Nellie used to take baths together when we were little."

"You aren't little anymore, Miss Mandara, and I have not been little in twenty-five years."

"Yeah, you're right. Can I go over there and wash?" Georgia pointed toward the swiftly flowing Yellowstone.

"How about staying on the north side where the water isn't very deep? It looks like a dangerous current out there."

"Okay. Shall I fill the canteen with fresh water?"

"That would be nice," Oliole said.

Georgia hiked back to the logs, bent low, and reached inside.

As Oliole swept dirt and sand out of the carriage with her gloved hand, dust began to fog up in her face. "I'm going to try to clean out the carriage a little as long as I'm already dirty." She pulled the bandanna back up around her face and tugged her cowboy hat low.

Georgia hiked halfway to the water and then scampered back to the carriage. "Should I take a gun with me?"

Oliole shoved Philip's cowboy hat to the back of her head. "Look around. Do you see anything dangerous?"

"I don't see anything at all," Georgia reported.

Then she squinted and leaned forward. "Except . . . except those men!"

For the first time all day, a chill ran down Oliole's neck. "Where?"

"Over there by the mouth of the creek. There are some men on horseback," Georgia said.

Oliole could see the outline of four men astride dark-colored horses.

"Who do you think they are?" Georgia whispered.

"I have no idea," Oliole replied through the bandanna.

"Hey, mister!" a deep voice shouted from the shore. "Do you and the missus mind having a little company out there for the night?"

"He thinks you're a man," Georgia gasped, "and that I'm your wife."

"It's the hat and bandanna and dirt. And the carriage hides my dress. That voice sounds familiar."

The men on the horses began to cross the shallows to the sandbar without an invitation. "Looks like a good place to camp," the same man declared.

At the exact moment she recognized the voice, Oliole snatched up the .36 caliber revolver and cocked the hammer.

Seven

The bullet blasted water in front of the first rider. The big bay gelding reared straight up out of the river as if the submerged lead had ricocheted off his hoof. The rider, arms and legs flailing the air, somersaulted backwards with a splash into the shallow water at the river's edge. The other three men retreated to the bank of the river, guns drawn.

Georgia dropped the leather canteen and dove into the back of the dusty carriage. She hid behind the cases and crates.

Oliole cocked the hammer back again on the Colt and aimed it at the soaking-wet man struggling to his feet. He cursed.

The horse scampered for higher ground.

She shouted, "Sam Black, I've never shot a man before in my life, but I guarantee I would not hesitate to shoot you if you come any closer!" The cowboy hat dropped off the back of her head revealing the long blonde braids.

"There's a woman under that dirt, Blackie!" one of the riders called out.

"It's her!" Sam Black croaked as he fished his revolver out of the shallow water. "It's that Cantrell hellcat photographer and some other woman."

"You mean the one that bluffed you down and broke your nose?"

He spun around, waving his gun at the men on horseback. "Ain't nobody ever bluffed down Sam Black and lived to talk about it. Especially you three."

"You want us to charge her?" a gravelly voice shouted.

Oliole gripped the revolver with both hands and steadied them on the back of the carriage seat. She could feel her heart race. "I told you, Sam Black," she shouted, "you'll be the one I shoot."

"She's got position, boys. . . . Back on up."

"We aren't goin' to ride away, are we?"

"Boys, things are finally going our way. We got the train money, fresh horses, and now women. I ain't done with her — that's for sure. She ain't goin' nowhere. She's stuck out there. She'll have to come this way, and then we'll have position. Or . . ."

"Or what?"

"She'll have to negotiate — if you catch my drift."

"There's two of 'em out there," another man hollered.

"The other one's kind of puny."

"I like small fish. They fit better in the pan." The gravelly voice slid into a sickening laugh.

"We'll wait it out, ladies. In the meantime, you might want to wash the dirt off your faces. I don't aim to kiss no mud."

A dripping wet Sam Black mounted the bay horse, and all four men retreated.

Clutching the other pistol to her thin breast, Georgia peeked up over the edge of the carriage. "What are we going to do now?" Her voice, like her hands, quivered.

Her left hand still on the revolver, Oliole stretched her right hand behind the carriage seat and rubbed Georgia's back. "I don't know, Georgia. I think we'd better pray a lot."

Georgia Mandara's voice no longer sounded like a mature sixteen-year-old's, but more like a weak twelve-year-old's. "I don't want to be here," the girl whimpered.

"That makes two of us." Oliole continued to massage the back of Georgia's neck. "We'll figure something out."

The younger girl now strained to keep from sobbing. "I don't like the way they talked about me."

"Their intentions clearly are not honorable. Lord, deliver us from evil."

"I've prayed that prayer a lot of times, but this is the first time I really mean it," Georgia cried.

"One thing for sure, we can't just sit here and get more and more scared," Oliole said. "If they're the ones that blew up the trestle and robbed the Northern Pacific, they aren't going to let two .36 caliber pistols hold them back for long. Let's clean this carriage before dark, water the horses, and try to eat something."

Even though still in the back of the carriage,

Georgia sat up and scooted closer to Oliole. "We aren't going back over to the road, are we?"

"I don't know what we will do. But we aren't getting close to those men. I know that much." Oliole kept the gun pointed toward the cottonwoods but glanced back toward the middle of the river. "You go back out there and wash up. Be careful. The current looks really strong. And get us a canteen of fresh water."

Georgia clutched Oliole's arm. "Do you think they'll try to shoot me if I go out there?"

"No."

"How can you be sure?"

Oliole stood straight up on the carriage seat, revealing her profile against the darkening sky.

"Be careful!" Georgia tugged at Oliole's dusty skirt.

Oliole glanced down. "They aren't shooting at me, are they?"

"No. Why do you suppose? I thought they were mad enough to murder us."

"They don't plan on killing us. They want something else."

"Well, they aren't going to get it! I'd shoot them first," Georgia declared.

"That makes two of us."

"I'll go clean up and get water in the canteen. Why don't we lead the horses over to the water?"

"I think if we start to move the team, the men will think we are pulling out and come after us. If we leave it right here, they'll think we're staying the night. They'll wait us out."

"Are we staying for the night?"

"I don't know. I don't know what we are going to do, but the Lord will provide something. Maybe we need another dust storm. If it were blowing, we could ride out of here, and they wouldn't even know it."

"Yes, but we might accidentally drive straight into their camp," Georgia said.

"Let's not pray for a duststorm then."

By the time it finally got too dark to see anything but the men's campfire on the shore, Georgia and Oliole had cleaned the carriage, watered the horses, scrubbed their faces and necks, tried unsuccessfully to comb their hair, and eaten a little dusty-tasting food.

They huddled next to each other in the carriage seat, revolvers in hand, aimed at the light of the campfire.

"What do we do now?" Georgia whispered.

"I don't think they'll sneak over here in the dark. They know we're carrying pistols, and they surely believe that we're scared enough to shoot at anything that moves."

"You think they'll wait until morning?" Though soft, Georgia's voice no longer held an edge of panic.

"Perhaps." Oliole rubbed her cheek, which still felt dirty. "They'll certainly wait until the moon comes out and they figure we're asleep."

Georgia slipped her free arm into Oliole's and clutched it. "I'm not going to sleep, are you?"

"Not tonight."

Georgia leaned her head on Oliole's shoulder. "Maybe we ought to pray about it again."

"You're right. Would you like to begin?"

"I don't do very well praying out loud," Georgia admitted.

Oliole whispered in the girl's ear, "Lord, we sort of got ourselves in a bad situation. It's all my fault. I should have waited for the train. I was in too much of a hurry to get home. But here we are with a big river on one side and evil men on the other. We feel like the Israelites backed against the Red Sea by Pharaoh's army. Keep us safe in Your arms and give us peace and wisdom to do the right thing. In Jesus' name, amen."

"Amen."

For several minutes they hugged each other and stared across at the distant flickering flames of the campfire.

"Maybe we should just swim across the Yellowstone." Georgia pulled back and sat up straight.

"I've thought about it. But the current's swift . . . and that would put us on foot and soaking wet on the Crow Reservation. I'm not sure that we'd be any better off than out here."

"Yeah, and if we did leave, they'd steal or ruin all of your equipment."

"It can be replaced," Oliole said.

"Even your photographs?"

"Everything here can be replaced, Miss Mandara, except for our lives and our honor. Of course, if there is a way to save my images, I'd like to do that."

"Do you think there's any way of driving the rig right across the Yellowstone?"

"Not unless it's a dire emergency . . . which it is."

Oliole could sense confidence returning to Georgia's voice. "I heard Philip say a good place to ford a river is on the downstream side of where a creek enters, because over the years dirt and rocks pile up there."

Oliole turned to look at the pitch-darkness of the main channel of the Yellowstone. "Sounds like good advice. That's probably why this sandbar is where it is."

"Are we going to try it?"

"I have one other idea, Georgia. Have you ever swam a horse across a river bareback?"

"Yes! When Nellie and I rode out to visit Grandma, we'd swim our horses across Porcupine Creek."

"Good. But this might be a bit more of a challenge. We'll unhitch the smaller of the horses; outfit you with food, canteen, and a gun; and have you swim the horse across."

"What are you going to do?"

"I'm going to try to bring the carriage across with one horse. If I lose control, I'll cut the horse loose, and swim it to shore with you."

"What about the Crow Indians over on that side?" Georgia queried. "Do you think they'll be waiting for us?"

"I guess that's a chance we'll have to take. We know for sure what will happen if we try to go back to the north side of the river."

"Do you think this is the Lord's plan?" Georgia asked.

"I think it's our best alternative. I think He wants us to use our minds and make the best choice."

"When are we going to do it?"

"Right now. You stay here with your gun aimed at the campfire over there. If you see anything suspicious, shoot for the flames. You won't hit anything from this distance, but if they think we're jittery, they might wait a little longer."

"Are you scared, Miss Fontenot?"

"Not as much as I thought I would be," Oliole replied.

"Me either. Do you think the Lord's helping us?"

"Yes, I do." *And, Lord, we're going to need a lot more help in the next couple of hours.*

Oliole unhitched the small horse slowly. Every footstep or horse snort seemed to echo across the water. *Slowly and quietly, Fontenot. . . . We've got to just slip into the water, like skinny-dipping by myself down at the creek when I was twelve.*

She tied the unhitched horse off to the pile of logs and crept back to the wagon. "Georgia?" she whispered.

"Are you ready for me? I have the canteen and the food sack."

"Do you have your revolver?"

"Yes."

"Put it all in the sack and hold it above your

head if the water gets deep. Come with me, and I'll help you get started."

"Who's going to keep them from sneaking up while we're over there?"

"We'll have to leave that to the Lord."

When they got to the edge of the sandbar island, Oliole gave Georgia a hug and kissed her on a slightly grimy cheek. "Are you ready for this?"

"I can do it, Miss Fontenot," Georgia said.

"I hope we know what we're doing."

"I think the Lord will help us even if we don't."

"I believe you're right about that," Oliole said.

"How are we going to find each other on the other side?"

"Ride upstream for a mile or so, and then find yourself a safe place and wait," Oliole instructed. "If I don't find you in the dark, we'll spot each other at daybreak. We just don't want to be where those men can see us. Let me help you up."

"Do you think it would be proper to lift my dress to my waist so I can straddle the horse?"

"Miss Mandara, it is pitch-black, and we are trying to escape from evil men. I believe the Lord, who is the only one who can see in the dark, will not be offended in the least."

"Yeah. Well, here goes." Georgia jammed a shoe into Oliole's locked fingers and swung up onto the horse.

"Remember, take it real slow. Don't make any noise."

Georgia groped in the dark and patted Oliole's cheek. "I'll see you on the other side."

"Yes, you will." Oliole patted the girl's fingers and then slapped the horse's rump. It plodded into the main current of the Yellowstone River.

She will see me on the other side of what? Oliole waited until she could no longer hear Georgia's horse. Everything continued to be quiet at Sam Black's camp.

Now, Miss Oliole Fontenot, you have to bring a carriage across these rocks without making any noise.

It took almost half an hour to strap all the camera equipment, plates, prints, and cases into the carriage seat. *That's twenty inches higher out of the water . . . I hope!* Then she took a leather strap, made a necklace of the revolver, and hung it around her neck. Finally she tied her skirt high around her waist.

Lord, I'm glad it's dark because I not only don't want anyone to see me like this, but I don't even want to see me like this!

Gingerly she crawled up on the pile of drift-wood and swung her leg over the horse's back. Even in the dark the horsehair felt very warm against her legs as she plopped down on the animal's back. To her delight, the horse barely flinched. He seemed content just to stand and wait.

There is no way to move this rig without those bone-dry axles squeaking. And it's a cinch they have a lookout at the water's edge. Maybe they are all there, and the fire is a decoy.

Even though it was a moonless night, and she couldn't see anything above except for twinkling stars, she looked straight up when she heard a honking sound.

Geese? A flock of geese coming in this late at night? This isn't the time of year for them to migrate. Perhaps they were disoriented by the dust storm.

The sporadic honking came in waves of sound, followed by seconds of silence. Oliole immediately caught the pattern and slapped the horse forward for three steps during the honking, then reined him up during the silence.

Keep it up, geese. Don't land too soon. Keep circling. Maybe this was their sandbar. Perhaps they're waiting for us to leave!

Three steps.

Stop.

Three steps.

Stop.

Honk, honk, honk.

Silence.

Honk, honk, honk.

Silence.

The horse balked as it first felt the cold water but plodded ahead at Oliole's urging. When she gauged that the entire carriage was in the water, she lifted a leg across the horse's neck and tugged off her riding boots. She quickly tied them to the leather strap that carried the gun around her neck and eased the horse forward into the dark night.

Oliole felt a shock of cold water on her bare feet. As she inched the carriage forward, the water rushed under the horse's stomach. He whinnied, and she sensed him turn his head back toward her.

We're not stopping now, no matter what. No reason to look back at Sam Black and his gang. They're either coming after us, or they aren't.

How deep does this river get?

She leaned forward, resting her chest on the horse's neck and locking her bare feet on his rump. With her mouth close to the horse's ear, she urged softly, "Keep going, boy . . . keep going. . . . Your partner's already over there . . . I hope . . . I pray."

Lord, I've done a lot of dumb things in my life, but jeopardizing Georgia's safety might be the dumbest. If there are consequences for this foolishness, I need to pay them — not her. I'm glad I have a gun, because if something happens to Georgia, and I survive, I'll shoot myself. I couldn't take it. Is it possible to attempt one adventure too many?

Even with her legs stretched back along the horse's flanks, her knees started to dip in the water. She felt the carriage slide downstream and pull the horse back. She kicked his rump with her nearly frozen bare feet. "Come on, boy . . . come on . . . let's go!"

The whole carriage continued to slip toward the east. They seemed to be still going forward, but now she didn't know which direction they faced. Then they stopped moving completely.

We're stuck! Right out in the middle of the Yellow-stone River, we're stuck! Maybe I can wade back there and push. . . . No, I need to pull. That would work. But the current's too strong.

"Giddiup! Let's go! Come on, boy!" Her shout was still only a strong whisper.

Slipping down into the cold water took Oliole's breath away as she clutched the harness of the horse. The water swirled above her hips, and the long, wet dress hung heavy on her shoulders, but her footing was on solid river rock.

"Horse, there is . . ." She hesitated for a moment, trying to keep her teeth from chattering. Finally she took another gulp of summer evening air. ". . . no reason why you can't go farther," she scolded. Oliole waded past the horse's head and tugged on the halter. "Come on, don't you want to get out of this water? I want to get out of this water."

I'm freezing. . . . I can't breathe. . . . I can't get this horse to move. . . . I can't go back. . . . I can't see anything.

If I start to cry, Lord, I don't think I'll be able to stop.

Ever.

But it can only get better.

The horse took one step toward her.

"Good boy!" Her voice almost reached a normal level. Then Oliole waded back one more step. Her left foot rested on a mossy rock.

An extremely slippery mossy rock.

Her feet slid out from beneath her, and she

plunged under the water just as the horse bolted forward. The current washed her downstream enough for the horse's hooves to miss her, but when she bobbed back up for a gasp of air, the front of the carriage struck her forehead and sent her reeling back under the water.

Lord, I'm not through. I've got more photographs to take. The earthy has not been recorded. Not by me anyway.

I'm not dying here.

Not this way.

I refuse!

She could feel the carriage pass over her, and she flailed her way to the water's surface, gasping for breath and groping for the rig. Her hand caught a slowly turning spoke of the wheel, and she was lifted halfway out of the water.

She could feel the boots, now filled with water, pull her neck down like an anchor. Oliole clutched the back rail of the carriage and, still submerged up to her hips, let the rig drag her across the river.

Go on, boy ... go on! If I could speak, I'd holler and shout ... please go on.

She had given up trying to keep her chin from quivering but was determined not to let go. Her breathing was so labored she thought her chest would explode. Then her toes slammed into rock. Her feet began to drag.

We're at the other side ... or we reached some side.

Oliole struggled to put her weight on her feet

but found her legs wouldn't hold her. Then she tried to hold her feet straight back to keep them from dragging and allowed the carriage to pull her up on the rocky shore. She was out of the water, but the soaked dress encased the cold against her raw skin.

"St-st-stop! Wh-wh-whoa!"

Up an incline of packed sand the carriage rolled and then dropped into a dip. For a second Oliole found herself higher than the rig. With a panicked lunge, she threw herself into the back of the carriage. She crawled across the wet floorboard and reached up to the cases and crates lashed in the seat.

They're dry! At least, I think they're dry. I'm so wet anything would feel dry. She dumped the water out of her boots and tossed them and the gun to the floor of the carriage.

"Whoa!" she called out again, but the horse continued its methodical plodding.

Okay, so I haven't led you very wisely, but we're on land now. What's the hurry? I've got to go and find Georgia. I've got to get the reins, but I can't until I get into the seat, which is stacked with . . .

Oliole fumbled to untie the rope on the crates and began to stack them in the back until the seat was cleared. She climbed up front and groped for a lead line she knew wasn't there.

Well, at least the top of my dress is starting to dry in the summer air. . . . I will probably die of pneumonia, but that will take a week or two. I still don't have any feeling in my feet. If I could see dirt, I'd

*jump down and run ahead and grab that harness.
I've got to stop this rig somehow!*

She sucked wind and then shouted, "Whoa!"
She expected it to sound like nothing more than
a raspy whisper, but with her vocal cords
warmed, it came out a panicked scream. The
horse bolted straight into the night, causing
Oliole to tumble back on the cases behind her.

"No!" she hollered. "Stop! Stop it right now!"

Then, like an eerie voice from a forgotten
dream, other voices shouted, other horse hooves
thundered, and in the shadows there were riders.

*Sam Black? Did we drift to the wrong shore? Lord,
this is not what I asked for. Where's my gun?*

She thought she sensed a rider approach, and
abruptly the carriage stopped.

"Mister," she called out, "thanks for stopping
my rig." She fumbled along the floorboard
searching for the Colt. "But I have to warn you, I
have a gun in my hand and am prepared to use it
if you come any closer!"

"Don't fire, Miss Fontenot. We'll lead you to
our camp."

"You know me? Who are you? If you're one of
Black's men, I'll —"

"You're on the Crow Reservation now."

"Indians?"

"I'm Jim Crocker. Remember? We met up on
the Musselshell."

One time when she was only six, Oliole had
gone into Boston with her father but had
somehow managed to wander off and get lost.

For almost an hour she had sat on a wooden bench and cried. When her father finally found her, she had felt such a sweep of peace that she never forgot that experience. This very moment was almost but not quite the same.

"Crocker! Oh, I'm glad it's you! You can't believe what I just . . . but how could you tell it's me in the dark?"

"Miss Mandara told us to wait for you, and this is the only trail wide enough for a carriage."

"Georgia? Where is she? Is she all right?"

"She's teaching the others a new dance she learned in Deadwood."

"What?" Oliole said.

"She's at our camp. I'll lead you there."

Oliole dug out a blanket from the top of a leather case and wrapped it around her feet. Just over a draw she could see a campfire and at least a dozen faces huddled around.

"Mr. Crocker, I'm afraid I look a terrible sight."

"That's all right, Miss Fontenot. We've seen you look bad before."

"But you did see me after I cleaned up."

"Yes, I think I like that better."

As they got closer, the firelight reflected on several Crow men, most dressed in regular army trousers and buckskin shirts. A young lady with a damp, dirty yellow dress was dancing barefoot by herself.

"Miss Fontenot," Georgia yelled, "what took you so long?"

The next morning Oliole and Georgia huddled near the crates and cases, letting the carriage serve as a screen between them and the Crow encampment.

"You look like you were tied behind a plow and dragged across Kansas," Georgia declared.

"Thank you, Miss Mandara. You look like you were abandoned as an orphan and raised by mudhens."

"Thank you," Georgia giggled. "I bet you say that to all the beautiful women."

"Well, at least the dip in the river took a little of the dust off."

"I may not look as bad as yesterday, but I feel so dirty I hate to walk," Georgia admitted. "It's like the dirt was baked on all over my entire body — and I do mean all over!"

"It's going to take hot water and soap. And we aren't going to get that until we get home," Oliole said.

"Crocker said if we made good time and didn't fall in the river again, we could be there before dark," Georgia answered.

"I don't think we should even change dresses this morning. This one is ruined. I'm going to burn it when I get home. It's not only dirty, but it's starting to smell like mildew. Why ruin another?"

"One time the Mississippi flooded my grandma's house, and her clothes got ruined. They smelled just like this."

"We have been through a flood, and the Lord delivered us."

"But He didn't part the waters, did He?" Georgia said.

"We might not have passed over on dry land, but we made it. None of my gear, my plates, or prints were ruined. That's a miracle."

"Jim Crocker said we must have stumbled onto Little Bear Crossing. He said his father used to talk about a place where the Yellowstone was shallow, and they crossed to hunt in the north. But after a big flood, the crossing was lost, and they couldn't find it again."

"Let's wash our feet, put on some clean stockings and boots, and then drive straight home. I don't want to stop until I'm in my front yard."

"We don't have to drive down Main Street, do we?" Georgia asked.

"Definitely not. No one is going to see me until I'm clean and wearing fresh clothes."

"I'll go tell Crocker and the others," Georgia offered. "Would you like me to ask one of them to hitch our team?"

"That would be nice."

Both women, crumpled and smudged, sat in the carriage as Crocker handed Oliole the reins.

"Just follow this river trail. It will lead you into Cantrell. Anytime there is a fork, take the branch to the right."

Oliole knew that her shoulders slumped, but she didn't bother sitting up straight. "Thank you for providing us with a camp for the night."

"I like to think we would have done it for any ladies, but for Captain Mandara's daughter, we would have fought the Sioux."

"I'll tell Daddy all about it," Georgia promised.

"Tell him he should join the army again."

"I'll tell him. But I don't think he ever wants to leave Cantrell."

"Mr. Crocker, I still want to come out and take photographs of your family," Oliole insisted.

"You are always invited. But I am not always home."

"I will send a message before I come out."

"I will return the message if I can."

Oliole glanced back toward the river. "I told you last night that Sam Black and the other three might try to follow us. Although I doubt it. They robbed a train and have money. I presume they are going to Deadwood or even Texas to spend it. It would not be very wise to swim the Yellowstone and enter Crow country over a couple of women."

"Two very pretty women."

"Not today," she said.

"Yes, but I have seen you both in fancy dresses. And on that day you had only one feature missing to be extremely beautiful."

"What did we lack?"

"Brown skin, of course. I'm not even sure skin that pale is healthy," he teased.

"We can't all be fortunate enough to be born with beautiful skin."

"Yes, that is true." He nodded with a wide smile and bright white teeth.

"If Sam Black and the others come across the river, be careful. They are violent and stupid men."

"We have dealt with violent and stupid men before. Most, but not all, have been white. We will be following you later and then turn south about midday," he said.

The horses tugged at the harness and almost pranced as they rolled west of the Indian encampment. The wind was in their faces but carried only a little dust. Oliole couldn't see a cloud in the blue Montana sky.

"Was it just yesterday that we started off from Miles City?" Georgia asked.

"It seems much longer, doesn't it?"

"I think I grew up some last night," Georgia said.

"Oh . . . what makes you say that?"

"I found out I'm tougher than I thought. We faced down those evil men. I swam a horse across a big river. I rode up to an Indian camp to get help, and I prayed almost all night long. Doesn't that sound mature?"

"Yes, it does." Oliole reached out and patted Georgia's knee. "But I'm quite sure your father will never let you even come over to my house, let alone travel with me again."

"Really?"

"I'd probably feel the same way if you were my daughter."

"Would you like to have a daughter? You and Kaid are planning to have children, aren't you?"

Oliole didn't look over at Georgia, nor did she answer.

"Did you hear me?" Georgia prodded.

"I heard you."

"Well?"

"I have a lot on my mind right now. I guess I don't feel like talking."

"Boy, you're grouchy this morning."

Oliole hugged Georgia's shoulder. "I'm sorry, my sweet Miss Mandara. I just need a little quiet time this morning. You are a delightful traveling companion. As far as I'm concerned, you can travel with me anytime."

"Even to New York City?" Georgia pressed.

"If I ever go back, I would be happy to take you. But . . . there is not much chance your father would allow that."

"Or Kaid."

"What?"

"He isn't going to want his new wife going off to New York, let alone with some teenage girl to look after."

Oliole stared out between the lead horse's ears and into a lifetime.

The sun was straight up when the rough, rutted roadway climbed up into boulders and scrub cypress. A deep depression in the granite carved by ancient glaciers held a pool of water, and Oliole parked the horses where they could drink from the stagnant but clear water.

She climbed down and stretched her legs. "Shall we rest over there in the shade of that small grove of trees?"

"Are you hot?" Georgia asked.

"No. It's quite pleasant."

"Then let's hike up to that big boulder." Georgia pointed to the highest elevation in the foothills. "Maybe we could see all the way to Cantrell from there."

"I think the summer air is too breezy and dusty to see that far."

"It's better than yesterday."

"It's absolutely wonderful compared to yesterday. Get the canteen, and I'll grab the food sack. A little hike would probably do my legs good."

"Shall we bring our guns?" Georgia asked.

"Why?"

"Snakes."

Oliole instantly examined the rocks around her. "You're right. Let's bring the guns, but be careful. Your father is really going to pitch a fit when he finds out I let you tote a pistol."

"I haven't used it, but you got to shoot yours last night."

"I thought I might actually have to shoot at someone. I don't ever want to have to fire it again. It wasn't fun."

The top of the hill proved to be a granite slab at least the size of Oliole's cabin. On a stretched-out canvas they sat, legs folded beneath them, eating apples and dry, sharp white cheese.

"I can't see any towns at all," Georgia sighed. "Cantrell is off that way, isn't it?" She pointed to the west.

"Yes, it is. But there are several ridges of hills between us."

"Isn't it something to sit and look in every direction and not see anything or anyone?"

"Quite different from the East, isn't it?"

"I know. The land is so big out here . . . and so empty."

"I love it," Oliole added. "It makes me seem so tiny and God so big."

"I hear Alberta is big . . . and open," Georgia said. "Or am I not supposed to talk about that?"

Oliole pointed to the east. "What's making that dust back there?"

"You're changing the subject, aren't you?"

"Yes. Now what do you suppose that is?"

Georgia pulled her straw hat back on her head to block the sun's bright glare. "It must be Crocker and the Crows."

"Why would he run the horses so fast? They're stirring up a lot of dust."

"Maybe they are having a race or something. Isn't that another horse back there?" Georgia motioned.

"It's another cloud of dust, but I can't see how many horses."

"It looks like they're turning south!" Georgia exclaimed.

"Crocker said his village was south of here. Maybe they are racing home."

"But if they were that close to home, would we see their village from here?"

"I would think so."

Like distant, muffled firecrackers, muted rifle reports drifted up to the rocks where they perched.

"That's gunfire, Miss Fontenot. Crocker was just kidding about fighting the Sioux, wasn't he?"

"I think so."

Georgia plucked up the revolver that lay beside her. "Do you think we ought to go back and help them?"

"With a gunfight? I don't think we'd be much help. I'm not sure I could tell a Crow from a Sioux . . . could you?"

"No." Georgia wiped her forehead and left a smear of sweat and dirt.

"Let's go get the carriage and head down the trail. We'll give a full report to Marshal Parks. He'll know what to do."

"After we clean up," Georgia reminded her.

"What?"

"We'll give a full report after we clean up."

"Definitely. Now grab our things. Let's get on that trail home."

The two scurried back to the carriage. Oliole waved her arm toward the pass. "Georgia, go stand on that rock and watch the road. I'll pack things up."

"What am I watching for?"

"I want to know if any of those involved in that

fracas decide to ride this way," Oliole said.

"I think they are all going south."

"I'm glad for that."

With everything in place, Oliole inspected the rigging and then climbed into the carriage. She drove up to where Georgia stood sentinel on a granite boulder the size of a bull. "What's happening now?"

"I don't know," Georgia reported. "The dust has died down, and I can't hear any more gunshots."

"Maybe they were chasing deer or antelope. Come on, let's go."

"Wow, if they are chasing pronghorns, one of them's running up here."

"What?"

"Look! There are two dust clouds headed this way." Georgia waved both arms toward the east.

Distant gun reports drifted up to them.

"And the pronghorn is shooting back!" Oliole shouted. "Come on, girl. One of them's breaking for these rocks, and I don't know if it's a friend or foe. Let's get down out of these hills."

Georgia crawled into the carriage, and Oliole turned it around to the west.

"Are we going down there next to the river?" Georgia pointed.

"I think we should get far away from the conflict as quickly as we can."

"That's not what Stuart Brannon would do."

"Brannon?" Oliole questioned.

"I read in Grant's book *Stuart Brannon and the*

Apache Kid that Brannon said never to get caught in a gunfight out in the open. It's always better to hide in the rocks or trees."

Oliole brought the carriage to a halt near the pool in the granite. "Well, we aren't some famous fictitious gunfighter who wins every fight."

"Stuart Brannon is a real person!"

"But the story is made up by some guy named Hawthorne Miller."

"Even so, wouldn't it be better for us to hide back in the rocks and wait for this to get over with? If we're hidden, they don't know we're here. If we ride west, they'll spy us when they get up to these rocks."

Oliole looked down at Georgia, then back down the road, then straight west. "All right, Miss Brannon, perhaps you're right."

"We can park the carriage behind the cedars over there and then hide in that lookout."

"What lookout?"

"Remember, when we were up there having a picnic, there was a little cluster of boulders closer to the trail," Georgia explained.

"No, but you can show me."

Oliole secured the team behind the cedars. The women held their long dresses halfway up to their knees, toted their revolvers, and scampered to a cluster of rocks and boulders that allowed plenty of room for them to hide out of sight.

"Are they still headed this way?" Georgia asked.

Oliole peeked around the rock and then jerked her head back.

"I can't see anything, but there's sort of a dip in this trail down near the base of these hills. I hope we're doing the right thing, Miss Mandara."

"It worked for Stuart Brannon."

"You mean the bad guys rode on by and didn't know he was there?"

"Oh, no. There was this big gunfight, and he was surrounded by thirty men, but he chased them off, killing six. And not only that, his bullet wounds were not serious," Georgia said.

"How many times did he get shot?"

"Three," Georgia recounted.

"I don't like this plan. Let's see if we can get by without firing our guns at all. I don't think they're coming this far any . . ." Her voice faded as a galloping horse came into view. "Get down!"

"Who is it?"

"I don't have any idea."

"Maybe it's Jimmy Crocker coming to warn us," Georgia suggested.

"Then he'll have to find us, because we aren't going out there." Oliole squatted and could feel caked dirt in the crevice behind her knees. She held the revolver in her right hand. Georgia clutched her pistol with both hands. "I wish we were home, Miss Mandara."

"At least, we're not bored," Georgia added.

Oliole peeked around the boulder toward the road.

Georgia was at her shoulder. "What's happening?"

Several shots were fired. The gunfire sounded closer.

"I wish Kaid were here," Georgia whispered.

"I wish Stuart Brannon were here," Oliole whispered back. "Keep down. There are two of them. . . . They jumped off their horses and are running up through the rocks." Several more shots rang out. "Shooting at each other . . ."

"That much I can tell," Georgia replied.

Then the gunfire stopped. There was silence. No birds sang. No wind whistled. No distant rifle reports. Nothing.

Oliole held her finger to her lips.

Lord, I'm sure You have better things to do than to keep delivering us, but all we're trying to do is run away from trouble. Whoever wants to kill whom is their business . . . and Yours. We don't want to be a part of it. We don't want to see it. We just want to go home.

"Now ain't that a purdy sight!"

The voice came down from the rock behind them. It was a winded, menacing, familiar voice. Both women looked up at the same time to see a gun-wielding man standing on top of the huge boulder.

"Sam Black?" Oliole gasped.

"This is my lucky day," he growled, waving his gun at them. "I get to kill Injuns and ravish women!"

A bullet blasted off the granite near his feet.

Black leaped down into the safety of the boulders where they were crouched. His boot caught loose gravel as he landed. He stumbled to his knees between the women, his dirty brown hat tumbling to the rocks. As his gun hand dropped to the dirt to balance himself, Oliole glanced into Georgia's startled eyes. Then, as if on cue, they both raised their revolvers and slammed the barrels into his matted dark brown hair.

The crack of the steel on the back of his head was followed by a loud smack as Black's forehead crashed into the granite floor. He didn't move.

"Do we shoot him now?" Georgia asked.

"No! I mean . . . he's unconscious, isn't he?"

"I think so." Georgia reached down and picked up Black's pistol. "The barrel's hot. Did you know guns get hot when you shoot them?"

"I never thought about it much."

"What are we going to do now?"

"It depends on who's shooting at him," Oliole said.

"Maybe it was Crocker."

"Shh . . . maybe it's a Sioux warrior."

"This is Crow country." Georgia stood straight up. "Hey, Crocker!" she shouted.

"No!" Oliole yelled.

A familiar voice rang out from the rocks below. "Is that you, Miss Georgia?"

"Yes!"

"Is Miss Fontenot with you?"

"Yes!"

"Keep down. That man Sam Black is prowling around in the rocks behind you."

"Not anymore."

"What happened?"

"We busted his head," Georgia announced.

"Where are you?"

Georgia crawled up on top of one of the rocks and waved. "Over here!" Then she looked back down at Oliole. "See, I was right. It was Crocker."

"There it is, Miss Fontenot! There it is!" Georgia shouted as they crested the limestone cliffs east of town.

Oliole had been privileged to see some beautiful cities in her time. She loved rebuilt Richmond in the springtime, San Francisco in the winter, Montreal in the fall, and Boston any time of the year. But the sight of the scraggly, ill-planned wood-frame buildings of Cantrell, Montana Territory, was the most beautiful sight she had ever seen.

Her heart leaped.

Her eyes watered.

There was a lump in her throat.

"Did you ever see a town so wonderful?" Georgia bubbled.

"Never in my life, Miss Mandara. It just dawned on me that for the first time since I left Maine, there is a place where I truly belong."

"You mean a place where you know almost everyone, and everyone knows you?"

"That's part of it, isn't it? But it's the land . . .

my house . . . my business . . . the Yellowstone down there and the bluffs to the south . . . I love it. Especially since there have been a few times in the past couple of days I thought I might not see it again."

"I wonder if Mr. Black still has a headache?" Georgia pondered.

Oliole stopped the carriage and looked back. Stretched out in a row behind the carriage were four horses tied in a string to the back of the rig. Into each saddle a man had been flung, stomach-down like a sack of potatoes, hand and feet lashed together under the belly of the horse, each with his own dirty bandanna tied in his mouth, and each with his hat looped to the saddle horn.

Two were wounded.

One had a good-sized lump on his forehead and a huge one on the back of his head.

"Are we going to ride up Main Street?" Georgia asked.

"We have to now. We have to take these men to Marshal Parks."

"It's a good thing the jail is on this side of town. Maybe no one will see us."

"Young lady, we are so dirty no one would recognize us."

"We aren't as dirty as we were," Georgia said.

"True. But I'm thinking we could give them something to talk about in Cantrell for years to come."

Georgia rubbed the sleeve of her dress across her mouth. "What are you talking about?"

"Give me Philip's cowboy hat. I want to wear it." Oliole motioned to the bags in the back of the rig. "And my dirty bandanna. Hand me Sam Black's holster and pistol. I'm going to strap them on."

"Over your dress?"

"Yes. This town has never seen what two tough bounty-hunter women look like. Well, they're going to see it now!"

"What are we going to do?" Georgia crawled into the back.

"I'm going to swing down to Second Street and drive slowly past the saloons. Then we'll circle in front of the hotel and back this way to the jail."

"Everyone in town will see us! I look horrible."

"So do I. That's the point. We look like we've been in a terrible fight."

Georgia handed Philip's wide-brimmed cowboy hat up to Oliole. "We have . . . sort of."

"Exactly. By the time we reach the jail, most of the town will have spied us out. Let's show them what Western women are really like."

"I guess we are Western women, aren't we?"

Oliole laughed. "We're carrying more Western soil on our bodies than Eastern women ever see in their lifetime."

"Can I wear one of these guns in a holster?" Georgia pointed to the pile of confiscated weapons.

"Yes, and carry a carbine in your lap. But don't cock it or point it at anyone."

When they were outfitted, Oliole swung the carriage around to the north on the river road and then back through the trees toward Second Street.

"If anyone calls out to us, don't say a word," Oliole cautioned.

"Why?"

"No smiles. No words. Have you ever seen bounty hunters ride in? They act like it's against the rules to look cordial. That's what we'll do."

"You want me to look tough and mean?"

"Eh . . . I don't think either of us could look very mean, but give it a try. Not one word until we reach the marshal's, all right?"

"This is like being in one of the Marquesa's plays!" Georgia said.

"Only those are real train robbers back there — not actors."

"And this is real dirt." Georgia grinned.

"No smiling."

"Yes, ma'am."

By the time the carriage and parade of bound men had circled by The Marquesa Hotel, the entire town of Cantrell was on the boardwalk and in the street. When Oliole and Georgia reached the marshal's office and jail, the crowd packed so close to the carriage that neither Oliole nor Georgia could get down. Marshal Ranahan Parks quieted the crowd.

"Oliole? Is that you?" he quizzed.

Oliole stood up. She towered above the crowd. She pushed her hat to the back of her head and spoke with a deep, phony voice. "We're Fontenot and Mandara, bounty hunters. We got Sam Black and gang here. A couple of them didn't want to come along peaceful and are carrying some lead. Black has a couple of blue lumps on his head where we had to teach him the error of his ways. I believe they're responsible for the train holdup and blowing up the Northern Pacific trestle at 44 Crick. I'm sure there's a reeward out for them, and we came to collect."

The whole crowd stood still in stunned silence.

Oliole looked over at Georgia, who glanced back. Both women surveyed the immobile crowd.

"Really," Georgia blurted out, unable to hold back a grin. "That's Black and his gang."

Captain Mandara pushed his way through the crowd. "Georgia? My word, you look so . . . so . . ."

"Dirty, Papa? I know, it's just —"

"You look so grown up!" the captain said.

"Really?" she beamed.

"What happened?" Carolina Parks questioned as she swooshed through the crowd that instinctively parted for her and young Davy riding her hip.

"It's a long story." Oliole let her shoulders relax for the first time in a long while. "And we'll tell you all the details later. When we found out the bridge was out, we rented this carriage in Miles City, but we hit a dust storm that would make the plagues of Egypt seem minor. Then we were chased across the Yellowstone by Black and gang."

"You forded the Yellowstone in that rig?" Captain Mandara probed.

"With the Lord's help. But Black followed us into the Crow reservation."

"Your friend Jimmy Crocker helped us capture them," Georgia announced. "The only one we actually collared on our own was Black."

Grant scooted up next to the captain. His eyes were as big as conchos on a saddle. "Really?"

"Yes," Oliole confirmed. "We did knock him out." She pulled off the holster and handed it down to the marshal. "Now, Ran, if you'd take these prisoners, Georgia and I have a date with a hot bath."

"You're right," Ranahan concurred. "There is a good-sized reward on these men. I'll take them into Billings and check with the agent at the Northern Pacific station."

"If there's a reward, split it between the Crows and the fund for a new schoolhouse. Right, Georgia?"

"Oh, yes," she replied.

Oliole looked at the crowd in front of the pair of horses. "Now, boys, if you'd clear us out a path, we're going to swing this rig around and let Miss Mandara off at the hotel. Then I'm going up to my place and clean up. If any one of you says one single word about how dirty and awful we look, it will be the last words you speak on the face of this earth. Is that understood?"

"Yes, ma'am," one of the saloon patrons shouted. "You two are surely the most beautiful women I ever saw in my life!"

"Thank you. There is a man of discriminating vision," she laughed. "May he never sober up!"

The crowd roared with laughter and gave her room to turn the rig.

July Johnson grabbed the harness on the lead horse as the carriage circled through the crowd. Then he walked back to the carriage seat where they sat. "Don't worry, Miss Oliole, Kaid didn't see you. He's building a temporary rope corral in the brush between here and the river."

"He's back from Alberta?"

"Oh, yes, ma'am. They drove down fifty head of big old Canadian horses. Goin' to use 'em to drive the herd north, I hear. He, Mr. Milo Harrison, and crew are building corrals. Shall I tell him you're home?"

"Tell him he'll be shot if he comes up to see me before I'm clean," she said.

July scratched the back of his neck. "How long will that take?"

"Years," she chuckled.

"What?"

"Tell him . . ." She looked over at Georgia and took a deep breath. "Tell him I'll visit with him first thing in the morning."

"You're that dirty?"

"Yes. July, would you come up to my place and

help me unload and then bring this rig back to the livery?"

"Yes, ma'am."

The crowd, still buzzing about the scene, began to filter back into the buildings of Cantrell.

Oliole drove Georgia to the hotel. *Lord, this is one image of the earthy that I am glad is not recorded. How can I ever be pretentious in a town that has seen me look like this? For every newcomer that looks at my long blonde braids, there will be some ol' boy who steps up and says, "Yeah, but you should have seen her when . . ." But that's okay, Lord. I'd rather be here dirty than almost any other place clean.*

The entire house was steaming hot from a woodstove kept busy boiling water and an enameled cast-iron tub that stood full for almost two hours. Wrapped in a thick cotton robe and wearing white socks, Oliole circled her small house, trying to straighten things up. Her long yellow hair hung damp down her back almost to her waist. A smile accompanied the song she was humming. Her eyes danced around the two rooms.

I love this place, Lord. I know it's not much, but it's mine. And the view is wonderful! Not at the moment, of course, since it's dark outside.

She opened the one window in the back room and shoved the curtains aside. The summer evening air drifted in and felt cool against her hair, yet warm to her face. In the front room, she closed the bottom half of the Dutch door and left the top open.

A comfortable home with no neighbors to peer in. Thank You, Lord.

Oliole sorted clothing between those to be taken to the laundry and those to be burned.

Lord, thank You for delivering Georgia and me from our enemies. I'll try to be wiser next time I travel. But I can't promise to be real smart. I'm impulsive, Lord. You know that. Headstrong and impulsive. It's the part of me that I like best . . . and least.

Oliole gazed at the photographs that lined her studio/front room parlor.

Lord, if I weren't so stubborn, I'd never have had the nerve to get these wonderful images. Counting those of Carolina and the Marquesa, I have twenty-three totally different women who are of strong enough spirit to make the West their home.

She held her palms against her cheeks. They felt clean but scrubbed raw. *One more photograph. I only need one more image. Perhaps Crocker's wife . . . but that should be a whole new series. Maybe I'll call that set "Native Born."*

Oliole meandered to the back room, poured herself a cup of tea, and glanced at her bed still piled with dusty cases and satchels. *Maybe I'll just pile all of that on the floor and go to bed. I could sleep for days.*

She plucked up the small revolver whose walnut grip protruded from the green valise.

Lord, I'm glad that Marshal Parks and the posse took Sam Black and gang to Billings tonight. You know I want them to hang . . . but I — I mean, You have to decide that. Keep them someplace where they will not bring evil into other people's lives.

"And thanks for this revolver. I hope I don't need it again." She addressed the gun, "But, Mr. Colt, I'll keep you in a parlor drawer just in case . . ."

The shadowy image on the darkened porch staring in through the half-open door sent a shiver down her back. She immediately raised the gun.

"Don't shoot, ma'am!" a laughing voice called out in the night.

"Kaid?"

"Welcome home, darlin'," he said.

She scampered toward the doorway. "What are you doing out there?"

"Listening to you talk to your pistol."

She immediately slammed the top half of the Dutch door between them. "How long have you been spying on me?" she called out, leaning against the closed door as if ensuring that it stayed closed.

"I wasn't spying on you," he hollered.

"How long, Mr. Darrant?"

"Just a minute or two."

"I don't want you to see me like this! I'm in my robe. You shouldn't have —"

"You are a beautiful woman, Miss Fontenot. Even when you are wet," he reported.

"Wet?" Oliole suddenly felt very exposed. She wished the windows were shut and the curtains drawn. "Did you see me wet? I'm not wet now!"

"I meant, when your hair is wet."

"I'm not properly attired for visitors, Kaid."

"I'll wait out here on the porch until you get yourself fixed up."

"It will take awhile."

"I'll wait."

Even though the door was closed between them, Oliole clutched the robe tight to her neck. "Why don't we talk in the morning?"

" 'Cause I'm bursting with things to tell you about the RX Ranch up in Alberta."

"And I have things to tell you about our trip."

"I heard you brought in Sam Black and gang," he called out.

"We had help from that Crow Indian named Crocker and his friends. But we can talk about that tomorrow."

"Oliole, listen. I want to know what you've decided. I don't aim to wait until morning," he insisted.

"Decided about what?"

"About what?" he exploded. "I laid my heart on the line and asked you to marry me and move to Alberta. I've been lyin' awake nights for over two weeks wonderin' how you'll answer, and you can't even remember?"

"Kaid, I'm sorry." She heard her voice rise in pitch and volume. "It's been on my mind almost every moment since I've seen you last, really. I'm just tired and disoriented tonight."

He was silent for a minute.

"You promise we'll have a lot of time to talk tomorrow?"

"I promise." She felt her neck muscles relax.

"That's fair enough," he said. "All I need tonight is to set the time of the wedding service and show you the ring."

"What ring?"

"I stopped off in Helena on our way back and bought you a wedding ring. Just on speculation."

"But I haven't agreed to —"

"Well, you can agree right now."

"I told you, I'm not dressed," she protested.

"I don't have to see you to hear you." His voice reflected anxious persistence, almost a demand.

"But . . . I . . ." Oliole felt her whole body grow tense under her robe. "I really need more time to think about it."

"More time?" he shouted. "You've had weeks! What in the world have you been doing? This is not like you. You are a very decisive person. So why the delay? You love me, don't you?"

"Do not yell at me, Kaid Darrant!"

His voice lowered only slightly. "You do love me?"

"Yes, however, I —"

"And you know I love you," he hollered.

"I told you not to yell, Kaid. I don't want anyone to hear us."

"Anyone!" he shouted. "There's no one to hear, and so far you've said absolutely nothing worth hearing!"

"I can't answer you now," she called out. "That's all there is to it."

"This is ridiculous," he bellowed. "I'm locked out of a lady's house — the lady I'm begging to marry me. I'm spillin' my heart, and she won't even talk to me!"

Oliole felt tears trickle down her cheeks. "I'm tired, Kaid." Her voice was soft, almost a quiver. "I'm just not thinking straight. Please, let's talk about it tomorrow."

"I want to know one thing," he hollered. "Right now, at this very moment, do you love me enough to move off to Alberta and spend the rest of your life with me?"

Oliole slumped to the floor, her back against the door. The tears now flowed freely. She gulped for breath but didn't respond.

"Well?" he demanded. "That's a straightforward question. All you have to say is yes or no. Which is it?"

She tried to say something, but it came out a mumble.

"What?"

"Kaid, don't do this," she wept. "Don't make me answer tonight. I don't feel good."

"Yes or no?" he demanded.

"I don't know," she murmured.

"What?"

"I don't know," she cried. "I just don't know."

"You don't know what?" His words sprayed like bullets.

"I don't know if I love you enough to move away from Cantrell and give up everything and everyone the Lord has led me to! I just don't know . . ." She covered her mouth with her hand to keep the sobs from growing uncontrollable.

"Oh, that's great," he groaned. "I can't figure you out, Miss Fontenot."

"Kaid . . . I don't want to talk anymore now. I want to talk tomorrow . . . please!"

"And tomorrow you'll say one more week and then next month."

"Kaid, please don't . . ."

"Oliole, I'm pushing that herd north come day after tomorrow, and I'm not coming back. Not for a long, long time. I've got to know!"

Oliole wrapped her arms around her chest and clutched herself, rocking back and forth. She couldn't stop crying. And she couldn't answer.

"Is that it? You're not going to say anything?" he shouted.

Lord, am I going to spend my life wondering if I did the right thing? Am I going to spend my life hugging myself because there's no one else around to hug me? Oh, Lord, I'm so tired.

"There's only so much fool a man can play, Oliole Fontenot," Kaid yelled. "I'll be going now. Maybe I'll see you tomorrow . . . maybe not."

Oliole lay on her side on the hard wood floor of the parlor and continued to sob. *I can't decide,*

Lord. I hurt so bad I wish I could die. I can't decide. Kaid's right. I'm treating him horribly. He's a good guy, Lord. A really good guy. Why am I this way? I hate myself. I feel so alone. I just want to sleep and wake up and have everything settled.

The taste of the summer morning breeze drifted through the open window across her bed, coming with life, adventure, and excitement. Still wearing her cotton robe, Oliole pulled the flannel sheet up to her neck and rested her head on the fluffy down pillow.

Sometime during the night she had dragged herself to bed.

Sometime during the night she had kicked the comforter to the floor.

And sometime during the night she had made the decision she was prepared to live with.

Lord, it's like the dust storm in my mind has finally blown over. Everything is still like it was, but now it's clear. Now I can see it.

Once she had the fire started in the woodstove and water warming, she lit a lantern and surveyed her room. She unboxed the green satin dress she had impulsively purchased in Deadwood.

It's a bit wrinkled, but it's beautiful. She carried it out to the parlor and looked out her window toward Main Street. With the sun not yet up, town seemed to hover between darkness and dawn.

Cantrell, you saw me at my worst yesterday. But

today I will dazzle you with my fancy green dress. Papa said I might look New England simple, but I could always look New England proud. Well, today, dear Daddy . . . I will look Montana proud . . . and Montana pretty. This is the day my life takes an extremely important turn.

For almost an hour Oliole fussed with her hair, her dress, her makeup, her stockings, and her hat. Then she held her hands out to her side and waltzed around the room.

I really do feel wonderful, Lord. I was right last night. I needed some rest. Sleep is wonderful, Lord. Bed is wonderful! She strolled to the front door and flung it open wide and shouted, "It's a beautiful day, Lord! A wonderful day!"

Cantrell lay silent down the hill below her.

It's too early to go to breakfast. I believe I will just sit on the porch and watch the town wake up.

She unpinned her hat, laid it on the table, and retreated to the back room for a cup of tea. Finally she dragged the wooden rocking chair out of the parlor onto the front porch and sat down.

This feels so good, Lord. Really good. Of course, I'm a little overdressed. Actually I'm a lot overdressed. You don't mind, do You? You're a friend who doesn't care what I wear. Do You like the way You made me, Lord? I like the way You made me!

In the distant east, the sun broke slowly above the hills that signaled the start of the Crow Reservation. It was a golden glow of a sunrise.

There's probably still some dust over there. . . . It

313

gives the whole town a rich tint.

The bobbing head of a dark-haired girl rounding the Chinese laundry and scampering up the hill caught her attention.

Oliole stood and watched the girl approach. *The captain is right. She does look older.*

"Georgia? What in the world are you doing up and out at this hour?"

"What are you doing dressed like that? Are you waiting for Kaid?"

"Perhaps. But you didn't answer my question," Oliole said.

"I went right to bed after my bath yesterday evening and woke up early this morning. So I was walking along the veranda when I spotted you up here on your porch. Isn't this a marvelous morning?"

"One of the most beautiful I've ever seen in my life."

"I call it an Oliole morning," Georgia said.

"Why on earth . . ."

"Because it's a golden one, just like you."

"You flatter me."

Georgia wrinkled her nose. "You know what would be a wonderful photograph?"

"What's that?"

"A picture taken right out your front door, with you in the rocker on your porch and golden Cantrell in the background. It could be your twenty-fourth photograph."

Oliole stared at her friend.

"What's the matter?" Georgia chewed on her

tongue. "Wouldn't it work? Is it a bad idea?"

"It's a wonderful idea."

"Really?"

"Let's do it!" Oliole said.

"You mean it?"

"Yes, but we'll have to hurry before the sun gets any higher and the shadowy effect disappears."

For the next twelve minutes they both scampered to set up the camera and prepare the glass plates. Then with Georgia back in the parlor next to the camera and Oliole in the rocking chair on the porch, teacup in hand, they waited.

"Now, Miss Fontenot?" Georgia called.

"Just a few more minutes. I want the cupola on the hotel to catch the sun's light. There is just a moment every morning when it's the only thing in town that has direct sunlight. I want that exact moment."

Still in the front room, Georgia pointed past Oliole toward town. "Who's that?"

"Where?"

"Riding up here. Isn't that Mr. Darrant? Has he seen you since we got back?"

"We talked briefly last night." Oliole's voice faded with each word.

"I'll hide in the back room so you two can talk," Georgia offered.

"You stay right by that camera so we can get the photograph."

"But I'll keep out of sight and won't tell anyone what you two say, no matter how personal it might be," Georgia promised.

Oliole continued to rock, watching the man on the gray roan ride up the trail that led to her place, across her dirt yard, right up to her front steps.

He tipped his hat. "Mornin', Miss Fontenot."

"Good morning, Mr. Darrant."

"If you don't mind me sayin' so, you look absolutely resplendent this mornin'."

"Thank you, sir. I don't always go around grouchy in a robe. I must apologize for my behavior last night," she said. "I was horrible, and I am embarrassed that I caused you such grief."

"No, it wasn't you; it was me, and you know it," Kaid insisted. "I've spent too much of my life bossin' cows around. I guess it's the only style I know. I had no business pushin' you like that. There are some things I want so bad, I can't stand the thought of not havin' them."

"I had no excuse for treating you so badly. You deserved an answer."

"I reckon that sort of takes care of the apologies." He took off his hat and ran his finger through his dark brown hair. His square jaw was set, but his blue eyes softened. "I, eh, did a lot of thinkin' last night after I left here."

"As did I."

"I'm going to start those cows north tomorrow. So I'll be gathering the remuda this morning and heading out of Cantrell by noon," he informed her.

"I did come to an answer to your proposal finally," she announced.

"I know." He nodded and looked back over his shoulder to the north.

"You know?"

He kept staring into the distance. "I knew last night, but my heart just wouldn't let me accept it. Does that seem strange?"

"No. I believe I felt the same way. I do love you, Kaid Darrant, and I am not at all sure I will ever feel so deeply about another man."

"But you just don't love me enough to give this up and move to some remote ranch for the rest of your life."

She looked down at Cantrell. "This is where I'm supposed to be, Kaid. The Lord has led me here but no further."

"And the Lord's leadin' me to Alberta. Funny how a clear fall mornin' helps a person see better. This mornin' it all makes sense," he added.

"It does?"

"Sometime during the night, it dawned on me that I love you very much, Miss Fontenot. Certainly more than anyone before and maybe more than anyone I ever will."

She squinted her eyes and looked into his. "But you do not love me enough to give up that big ranch in Alberta and hang around Cantrell doing odd jobs while I take photographs."

"That's about it. It's like the Lord's driving me north. If I didn't do this, Oliole, I'd spend the rest of my life depressed for passin' it by. Do you understand what I mean?"

"Actually I understand perfectly."

Kaid pushed his hat back on his head. "We're a pair to draw to, Miss Fontenot. Too much the same, I reckon."

"You might be right."

"I wish you happiness, Oliole Fontenot."

"And you as well, Mr. Kaid Darrant."

He brushed back a tear from the corner of his leather-tough cheek and stared off at the sunrise. "You know, ever' once in a while a man sees a sight that he can never forget. I forget who I had supper with last night, but I can remember the first time I saw the Tetons rising jagged and snowcapped out of Jackson Hole. I can remember like it was yesterday my first horse. I was seven, and I paid three cash dollars for that old swayback. It was the most beautiful horse I ever saw in my life. I remember the day my daddy died. He was only fifty-one, but he had looked so old and so tired for so long. Then suddenly there he was, all peaceful-like. And I'm never, ever, going to forget the way you look this morning. With golden hair and beautiful smile. Satin dress and silver earrings. I'll carry that image of Oliole Fontenot to my grave."

She tried to wipe back a tear from each eye.

"I didn't mean to make you cry," he apologized.

"It's all right, Mr. Darrant. Like a summer rain that washes the dust out of the sky, sometimes I need to cry. I know what you are saying. Our memories do seem to be selective. I can still feel the salt air hit my face the first time I sailed out around Cape Cod with my father. I can see that silly little grin on my sister's face in the very first photograph I ever developed. And I can close my eyes and feel your strong arms around my shoulders and waist as we waltzed down that mountain near Roundup. It was and always will be the waltz of my life."

He tried to speak and then turned his head away. She knew tears streamed down his face, too.

"Thanks for the dance, Mr. Darrant." Her voice was almost a sob.

He took a deep breath, managed to nod, and tipped his hat. Then he turned his horse back to town.

"It's time, Miss Fontenot!" Georgia shouted from the parlor. Startled, Oliole swung back toward the camera, tears still streaming down her face.

Then she heard the shutter click.